THE SHŌWA ANTHOLOGY 1

THE
SHŌWA
ANTHOLOGY
Modern Japanese Short Stories

1

1929–1961

Edited by
Van C. Gessel
Tomone Matsumoto

KODANSHA INTERNATIONAL LTD.
Tokyo, New York, and San Francisco

ACKNOWLEDGMENTS

The editors wish to thank the following authors for graciously allow-ing the translation and publication of their stories: Ibuse Masuji, Ishikawa Jun, Abe Kōbō, Yasuoka Shōtarō, Kojima Nobuo, Yoshiyuki Junnosuke, Shōno Junzō, Shimao Toshio, Kurahashi Yumiko, Inoue Yasushi, Minakami Tsutomu, Endō Shūsaku, Abe Akira, Shibaki Yoshiko, Ōba Minako, Kōno Taeko, Kanai Mieko, Kaikō Takeshi, Ōe Kenzaburō, Tsushima Yūko, and Nakagami Kenji.

In addition, the estates of the following have granted permission for the use of the included works: Hori Tatsuo, Dazai Osamu, and Kawabata Yasunari.

Concerning works previously published elsewhere, the editors gratefully acknowledge the following:

International Creative Management, for permission to use a slight-ly revised version of the translation of Abe Kōbō's "The Magic Chalk," which appeared in Asia Magazine, translated by Alison Kibrick. © 1982

Peter Owen, Ltd., for permission to reprint "The Day Before" by Endō Shūsaku, from Stained Glass Elegies, translated by Van C. Gessel. © 1984

Columbia University Press, for permission to reprint a slightly revised version of "Bad Company" by Yasuoka Shōtarō, from A View by the Sea, translated by Kären Wigen Lewis. © 1984

Japan P.E.N. Club, for permission to reprint "The Silent Traders" by Tsushima Yūko, from Japanese Literature Today (no. 9, March 1984), translated by Geraldine Harcourt. © 1984

Publication of this anthology was assisted by a grant from the Japan Foundation. The in-house editing was done by Stephen Shaw.

LCC 85-40070
ISBN 0-87011-739-4
ISBN 4-7700-1239-x (in Japan)

First edition, 1985

CONTENTS

I

II

INTRODUCTION

Van C. Gessel

The reticent marine biologist who currently sits upon the Japanese throne has occupied that position for sixty years now. It is sobering to ponder the scope of the changes he has seen take place in the lives of his subjects. When he gave his reign the name of S<u>hōwa</u>, "enlightenment and peace," in December of 1926, he could have had little inkling how painfully ironic that title would prove to be. It has been a period that has seen much ignorance pass for enlightenment and a peace that has often been sanguinary. From his perch "amid the clouds," Emperor H<u>irohito</u> has witnessed a fourteen-year war that engulfed the entire world, fire bombings that ravaged the landscape of Japan, the visitation of two atomic bombs, the first foreign occupation in the long history of his independent, isolationist country, and a contemporary reputation that remains murky in some parts of the world, due both to Japan's past misdeeds and her present technological virtuosity.

The literature of the Shōwa era is as varied and accurate a portrait of the Japanese nation's meandering, tortuous progress through the past six decades as we can hope to find. The present collection was conceived with the intent of bringing together stories by the finest authors who have produced short fiction during this period, primarily those who have not been adequately represented in English translation. As the anthology took shape, it became evident that the stories were remarkably varied in the experiences they describe as well as in the techniques they employ. This suggested that stories by several familiar writers should also be included, particularly works that display sides of their creators not generally recognized overseas.

It would be foolhardy to suggest that the present collection is in any way a "panorama" of Japanese life in the Shōwa era; Japanese artists are seldom at home in the painting of vast landscape murals. They prefer instead the creation of genre-style vignettes rich in detail and in brief flashes of inspiration. But when these small scenes are placed one beside another and the entire scroll is rolled out before the viewer's eyes, the subtle and complex portrait of human life presented there is truly impressive.

Some critics argue that the modern period has finally severed Japan's literary ties with its traditional roots; that the Shōwa author has once and for all become as artistically deracinated as all his international contemporaries. I for one don't believe that for a moment. It may be possible to cite authors such as Abe Kōbō as evidence of such a phenomenon, but the substance of this anthology strongly suggests that much continuity remains, both in form and in content. The stubborn persistence of that uniquely Japanese literary form known as the "I-novel" (*watakushi-shōsetsu*) is one testimony to the tenacity of literary tradition. These egocentric quasi-novels emerged as a distinct form early in the twentieth century, but they in fact have subterranean links with the literature of the tenth century in Japan. The I-novel has been criticized for being overly precious, too narrowly concerned with the private agonies of its authors, and too little aware of the feelings of surrounding individuals and ideas. While all of these criticisms are justified, Japanese writers have been reluctant to jettison the form altogether, finding it a congenial and fluid means to examine and define themselves and their surroundings. But in the Shōwa period, particularly in the postwar years, authors have been willing to stretch the confines of the I-novel to determine whether it can be employed for a more objective study of human relationships, and for such purposes as satire and religious contemplation. In this attempt, they have poured a new distillation of wine into the old bottles left by their literary predecessors; the present anthology provides several examples of the form for readers to relish, including "Bad Company," "Stars," "The Day Before," and "With Maya."

A further argument for continuity may be found by comparing the anthology's first story, "Kuchisuke's Valley," written in 1929, with such later works as "Mulberry Child" (1963) or "The Immortal" (1984). While even the traditionally pastoral setting of "Kuchisuke's Valley" is shaken by the suggestion that modern technological progress may eventually obliterate every trace of the past, the two more recent stories forcefully reaffirm the presence of an unsevered conduit that allows the contemporary Japanese author to remain in communication with his classical predecessors.

Amid the continuity there is also change; the stories presented here range from the discursive ("Moon Gems" and "Under the Shadow of Mt. Bandai") to the experimental ("Mating," "One Arm," "The Monastery"); some, like "Les Joues en Feu," approach sheer poetry. "The Magic Chalk" is perhaps best described as "scientific surrealism," while "The Pale Fox" is more along the lines of fantasy. Shōwa literature has seen a wealth of trends swell and fade, and has ridden the tides of proletarian fiction, wartime propaganda, Occupation censorship and a myriad of modernist influences. One of the healthiest and most welcome aspects of the postwar scene has been the appearance of many truly talented women writers—six of them are represented in these pages.

In short, there may well be something that will appeal to every literary taste in this compilation of twentieth-century stories. The works in this collection clearly demonstrate that literature in Japan over the past six decades has been a living, changing entity, responding to and commenting upon the many vicissitudes of the society. And since twenty-one of the authors represented here continue to be active on the Japanese literary scene as this collection goes to press, it seems safe to say that the interplay between continuity and diversity will remain strong hereafter. Mirroring the fortunes of the Japanese nation over the past sixty years, the Japanese short story has survived wars and defeats and high-tech and evolved into a durable and universal form of literary expression during the age of Shōwa.

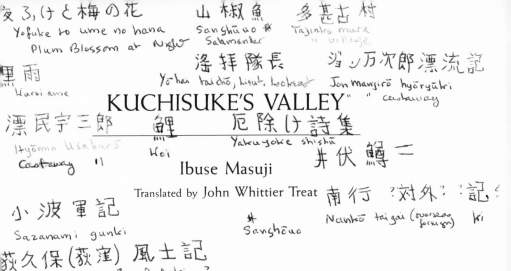

KUCHISUKE'S VALLEY

Ibuse Masuji

Translated by John Whittier Treat

Ibuse Masuji's long career in literature spans most of the twentieth century and many of its genres and themes. After making a precocious debut in the 1920s with such stories as "Koi" (Carp, 1926; tr. 1971), Ibuse went on to build a diversified yet solid reputation with novellas (Kawa [The River, 1932]), modern poetry (Yaku yoke shishū [Talisman Poems, 1937]), historical tales (Sazanami gunki [A Chronicle of Ripples, 1938]), wartime diaries (Nankō taigai ki [Sailing South, 1943]), accounts of shipwrecked sailors (Hyōmin Usaburō [Castaway Usaburō, 1956]), and most notably his novel of the Hiroshima atomic bombing, Kuroi ame (Black Rain, 1966; tr. 1969). Ibuse's latest work, Ogikubo fudoki (An Ogikubo History, 1982), is a memoir surveying the more than fifty years in which he has observed, and participated in, the world of Tokyo writers and their public.

Born in 1898 in a small village near the eastern extreme of Hiroshima Prefecture, Ibuse grew up in comfortable surroundings with an older brother and sister, parents and maternal grandparents. He left for Tokyo in 1917 to pursue studies in literature at Waseda University, but dropped out in 1922 to devote himself full-time to his own writing. His first efforts at fiction reflected not so much the literary trends of the time as his tentative and plaintive search as a young man new to the city seeking both a voice as a writer and an identity as a person. With style, humor, and sensitivity, the Ibuse Masuji of the 1920s explored with words the uneasy relations between town and country, friend and stranger, self and other. By 1929, the year he published "Kuchisuke's Valley" in the magazine Sōsaku gekkan,

1

Ibuse had begun to understand much of what he sought to say and how to say it; consequently this story is perhaps the best of his early career. Its assured use of language and secure point of view combine to create a distinct and independent narrator and a finely, believably drawn central character, both of whom resurface regularly as the disinterested first-person observers and willful old men that populate Ibuse's later work. Kuchisuke's old-fashioned ways and his young friend's perspective on them, together with the story's wit, shy eroticism, and even its intimations of violence, make "Kuchisuke's Valley" a veritable catalog of what has earned Ibuse his place as one of Japan's most acclaimed modern authors.

*   *   *

Seventy-seven-year-old Taniki Kuchisuke is especially fond of me. Each year when fall arrives and one's breath turns white in the air, he sends me a gift of rare pine mushrooms even if I am far from home on a trip. He lines an old noodle box with moss, fills it with the dried morsels, and addresses its cover with the salutation "Happy Autumn."

Kuchisuke is the caretaker of the mountain where these mushrooms grow. Although we sold this mountain to another family back in my grandfather's time, Kuchisuke stubbornly continues to do things as he did in the old days.

Before I forget to mention it, I would like to explain how Kuchisuke and I came to be friends.

My older brother, myself, and a younger sister were each in turn reared in the same baby carriage. It was a present to my family from Kuchisuke when he returned from working in Hawaii. It was also Kuchisuke who, as part of his job, would watch over us whenever we were in the carriage.

On its hood was embroidered a four-line poem in a foreign language. It translated to mean "Sleep, sleep, little child, sleep. The evening sun has begun to set yonder." Since I never felt in the least inclined to nap in the carriage, I did not care much for this alien verse.

Kuchisuke would load me in the buggy and spend all day strolling back and forth through the grove of trees in the garden. He consequently wore

2

a path around the pond under the sweet osmanthus trees that even rain failed to efface. Besides a sty in his eye that slowed him down to a snail's pace, Kuchisuke had the annoying habit of frequently stopping altogether to retie his sash. Not wishing the progress of my buggy ever to be interrupted, I remonstrated with him each time this happened.

"Kuchisuke! Hurry up and get going!"

"I'm adjusting my sash just now. Don't speak to me like that."

"Don't talk so big. Who cares about your sash?"

No doubt because I was trying to rush him, Kuchisuke kept redoing his sash even though he ordinarily wore it loosely anyway.

Beneath the sheets in the carriage was a cushion printed with a pattern of black bats. I was convinced that these bats were escaping from the cushion to fly up into the sky after dark.

"Kuchisuke! The bats are taking off again! Hurry up and catch them!"

"If you'll just be quiet, they'll come back in the morning. Don't worry."

"Really? They'll come back?"

"Yes. All right, let's go around one more time."

"When I close my eyes it feels as if we're moving backward. Shall I let you in with me to try it?"

"Of course not. I'll get in alone later."

As he pushed the carriage Kuchisuke would sometimes attempt to teach me foreign words.

"Things like the osmanthus and pines are called 'tree.'"

I always forgot this word "tree" very quickly, and each time Kuchisuke would scold me for it.

"A child who can't remember anything is 'aizuru.'"

"Aizuru" is how he pronounced the English word "idle."

Eventually I passed the carriage down to my little sister. I was in the first grade at the time, and it was decided that I should continue to see Kuchisuke at his home on Sundays to be tutored in English. His house stood alone in the valley. Apparently he had not learned any farming in Hawaii, and for lack of any other skill he served here as caretaker of the mountain. Still, as a teacher he was extremely strict with me. He always wore the formal *hakama* skirt that my grandfather had given him, even though it was so long that it dragged on the floor whenever he rose from his side of the desk. He sat quite stiffly and read to me from the third volume of an English primer. He never, not even once, allowed me a glimpse of the text. Instead I kept my hands folded on the lap of my formal kimono and struggled to memorize the sentences as he recited them.

"'The night was very dark. The general, leading his desperate men, boarded the boat. The willow branches on the shore brushed against the general's shoulders and wet them with dew. The sound of the oars was very faint. The general surveyed the dark river and began quietly humming to himself. He hardly looked like a man who was going off to battle.'"

When Kuchisuke was done with the recitation, I repeated it.

"The night was very dark. The general boarded the boat. . ."

"The general, leading his desperate. . ."

"The general, leading his desperate. . . ?"

"Leading his desperate men, right?"

"Leading his desperate men. . ."

In this way Kuchisuke eventually corrected all my mistakes.

When each lesson was over and it was time for me to walk home, Kuchisuke always repeated the same warning. "When you cross the bridge, don't stop to look down into the river."

He was warning me about a section of the valley stream where its clear waters collected to form a swirling whirlpool. Overhead huge silk trees reached out with their branches and liberally scattered their peach-colored blossoms in the current below. Floating round and round in the whirlpool, these colorful flowers drew circles, as if with red crayon, only to vanish beneath the surface.

These memories of mine are now more than twenty years old. Today I live in Tokyo where I am trying to become a writer. I have yet to respond candidly to Kuchisuke's inquiries about my choice of career, since I am sure literature would please him the least.

Every time I visit my family in the country, he comes over and immediately interrogates me about my work. I avoid a direct reply and have allowed him to form the false impression that I am a dentist, or at other times, an engineer. On his way home he stops in at the neighbors' and boasts that I am a Tokyo dentist, or engineer, as if it were all his own doing.

I do not mean to ridicule Kuchisuke's great interest in me. After all, I am the only student that he ever had. Twenty years ago, when he finally finished reading all of the English primer to me, he looked up and said, "If you don't succeed in life, it will be harder on me than you. Should you fail, I will be the one who feels badly."

I did not know what to say. Deciding that it was time to leave, I stepped outside only to notice that snow, blanketing both the valley and the mountain peaks, had fallen while I was indoors.

I knew only too well that were I to correct Kuchisuke's latest supposition and tell him that I was not a lawyer in Tokyo, his reaction would be one of disappointment and dismay.

". . . I will be the one who feels badly." It wouldn't surprise me if he placed his hand over his heart and expired from grief on the spot. I had no choice but to continue the charade that I was a young attorney.

I have neglected to say anything about a girl called Taeto. There was not much, in fact, I knew about her until later, when we met. But you can learn something of her past from a letter she sent me, and from which I must quote:

> I hope you are in good health. My grandfather Kuchisuke is doing fine. Since the year before last, construction has continued every day here. Soon the dam will be completed. It is an immense wall that will seal off the valley from one mountain to the other, creating a lake more than five miles around. We will have to vacate our home to make room for it. This is a project authorized by the national government, and we cannot refuse to move out, yet Grandfather still refuses to cooperate no matter what. When the lake is ready and it fills with water, our home will lie submerged in the deepest part. Grandfather tells me that you are a lawyer, and I thought that if I asked you to intercede then perhaps he could be persuaded to leave. Please write Grandfather and talk some sense into him. The other day our local Diet member came by and told Grandfather to clear out and stop being a nuisance. It is a question of his prestige in the upcoming election, he said. Grandfather retorted that the representative had planned this lake in order to buy the voters with it in the first place. The last time we had an election, this same politi-

cian dispatched surveyors with red and white striped poles to take measurements, proclaiming in his speeches that he was having a railroad built, but so far we have seen no signs of it. Even now, Grandfather bothers people by complaining about this. I worry that people will look down on us if he is speaking out for no particular reason.

I must tell you something about myself. My name is Taeto, and I came to my grandfather's place from Hawaii two years ago. My grandparents were both Japanese, but my mother married an American. Some years ago Father left Mother and me without warning and returned to the mainland. I may look like an American, but in fact I am Japanese. My mother brought me here in December of the year before last. At the time, the valley and its trees were barren in the winter and I suffered from the cold and loneliness. Mother, who passed as a Japanese, managed to save a little money and soon found herself a new husband. Only two months later, however, she died. Perhaps the change in climate was too much for her. But she raised me as a Japanese, and I came here with her willingly. Japan is a better place than Hawaii. Japan is the land of my ancestors. I act and feel like a Japanese, and am very content now to live in this valley.

This letter gave me pause for thought. So, Kuchisuke has the unexpected responsibility for a foreign, and loquacious, granddaughter. I imagined him driven by all her chatter into the woods, and sitting there with arms folded, doing nothing. Why had he never mentioned a word about either Taeto or the lake to me? I had to go to him immediately, I had to act in defense of his rights. And if the situation warranted, I would go all the way to the provincial government with his case.

I departed for Kuchisuke's valley.

Walking through a deep valley on a moonlit night can be a very pleasant thing. The road had been widened for construction and was etched with deep ruts made by the trucks. The thick branches of the pine trees cast their speckled shadows onto the illuminated road. I stopped several times to gaze at the distorted reflection of the moon in the waters of a deep pool and to knock the flowers off a vine with my walking stick. However, my pleasant stroll was unexpectedly short, abruptly ended by a stone wall as big as that around a castle. It had been erected to bridge the gap between the two mountains forming the valley. This was the dam.

I calculated the distance from the base of the dam to where I was standing, estimated the angle of my line of vision to its top, and thus determined its height to be more than three hundred feet. The lake this wall would create would certainly leave Kuchisuke's home deep underwater. I walked along its base looking for an opening where I might pass through. I did find a sluice gate, but the river was rushing out of it and plunging in a waterfall with a terrible roar. Beneath was a deep pool. This was obviously the gate that would be closed as soon as construction was complete. Still, there had to be another opening for drainage purposes. I searched for it. Finally, not in the stone wall itself but in a hill of rock I discovered a large tunnel. Using my matches for light, I entered. A cool breeze swept through the tunnel, which was about as high and wide as a railway underpass. Water dripped from the ceiling, carved out in an arch through the thickest section of the hill. Bats dwelled in the crevices.

As I emerged from the tunnel I could see the windows of Kuchisuke's house. His lanterns were lit, and illuminated an apricot tree in silhouette. Wishing to avoid a dramatic reunion, I called out to him still some distance away.

"Kuchisuke! Are you still up?"

The next morning I was woken by the sounds of a cow mooing and a sickle being sharpened. I opened my eyes and saw a small crucifix hanging on the wall to one side of my pillow. I shut my eyes again.

Kuchisuke began to chop firewood outside my window. He opened the screen a crack and asked, "With all this racket out here, you haven't been able to catch a wink, have you?"

I replied that it wasn't loud, and that it wouldn't bother me even if it were.

The sound of logs splitting stopped, and then branches were being violently shaken. It was like leaves rustling in the wind. Soon I heard great numbers of apricots tumbling to the ground. I got out of bed and shouted, "Kuchisuke! All the unripe fruit will fall, too!"

"I don't care. I'm going to try and drop a few more."

He began shaking the branches again. When I looked out the window I saw that he had climbed the apricot tree and, striding a limb, was shifting his own weight to and fro. He rocked the tree so much that it looked as if it were in pain. The ground below showed signs of having been swept clean with a broom, but all the fruit and leaves that came hailing down now covered the area with a layer of fresh litter. The scent wafting from split apricots added a tart accent to the morning air.

I sat by the window and smoked a cigarette. All the construction in that part of the valley which would become the bottom of the lake was finished, the land reduced to a gentle slope of red clay.

Kuchisuke continued rocking the branches energetically in quest of one apricot that remained at the top of the tree. The morning sun shone through the leaves to bathe his face in a rich green light, and drops of dew from the branches clung to his skin. I told him to stop handling the apricot tree so roughly, but he only shook it more violently and said, "You're telling me I should leave, right? So I've got to get out, do I? Well, I've taken the advice you gave me last night. I've given up the idea of fighting it further."

He climbed higher into the tree and shook a smaller branch. "But I still want to hear you talk in front of everyone and defend my right to stay. I doubt I'll ever have another chance to see you give one of your fancy speeches."

I told him that if he had indeed decided to relocate, then there was no longer any need for me to speak on his behalf. Kuchisuke had told me that the construction people would build him a small house, and even try to have him appointed as the caretaker of the dam's sluice gate. He could expect to receive a monthly salary for his services. I had come from Tokyo to change his mind for naught.

When the sun's rays reached the mountaintops, Taeto came home leading a big black cow. She wore canvas shoes and a loose, green, high-collared jacket. She was an attractive foreign girl. Her cow carried four bundles of long green grass, two slung on each side. The beast was six times Taeto's size, but it obeyed her signal and went into its pen after she had unloaded its burden. The cue had been three quick clicks of her tongue. As I put trousers on over the long underwear that doubled as my pajamas, I studied her from behind with interest.

When I arrived the night before she had already gone to bed and I did not meet her. Wearing a thin cotton nightgown, she quickly turned her face away and pretended to be asleep when I came in. This allowed me to stare openly at her sleeping figure while I spoke in a low voice with Kuchisuke. Her short hair owed little to the efforts of a beauty parlor, but revealed instead the simple layered lines of a scissor cut. Her nightgown exposed the roundness of her young shoulders, and in the light of a lamp set on a high footstool I could even see the fullness of her breasts. A paperback book she had cast aside lay near her blue checkered pillow. On the wall was the crucifix which would be beside my own bed when I opened my eyes the next morning. Perhaps it was Kuchisuke, with the unsolicited idea of decorating my room, who moved it sometime during the night.

Taeto was picking up the fruit on the ground. Unable to grasp more than four at a time with one hand, she lifted the front of her blouse to make an apron and placed them in it. Then, laden with apricots, she came up to me and announced in perfect Japanese that last year she had eaten the apricots without washing them first. I did not want her to leave, and so I took one of the apricots from her apron and bit into it, slowly, one mouthful at a time. Kuchisuke had already left for the mountain with the cow.

Taeto stood silently beside me. If I were the romantic type, I would have been more interested in her rolled-up blouse, but I am not. I feigned a total preoccupation with eating the apricot. Yet, in a voice no less intense than that of a seducer, I said to her, "You have one, too. The ripe ones are delicious. A bit sour, but delicious."

Attempting to whet her appetite I deliberately bit into one of the greener apricots and, sucking in my cheeks, let the juices drool from my mouth as if it were indeed that tart. She was unable to resist the temptation.

"Thank you," she said as she took the smallest, greenest fruit and bit into it rather bashfully.

"Good?" I asked. She replied that it was.

It was then that we both noticed a group of six or seven men gathered at the top of the highest mountain. They were shouting something in the direction of an immense boulder that towered over the red clay of the summit like a black cancer.

"I bet they're going to break up that rock."

My guess was correct. Another man appeared out of the boulder's shadow and ran as fast as he could to his associates.

Just as he reported that the charges were lit, a series of explosions went off. The blasts were unbelievably loud and seemed to physically dislocate the entire atmosphere of the valley by several inches. My cheeks were struck by the forceful change in air pressure. I was further surprised to see the boulder split into two equal halves, which soon lost their balance and came tumbling down into the valley. The one in the rear rolled to the front as both increased their velocity.

"Look, the one that's behind now seems to be moving ahead again," exclaimed Taeto. The pursuing fragment crashed into the other with an ominous boom as it launched a wild leap-frogging bound and rolled at full speed into first place. The bypassed boulder now pursued a separate course. Both mowed down the dense mountain forest with cracking and thumping sounds. The two rocks reached the red clay of the valley bottom at the same moment, one teetering onto its side after a waltz-like spin, the other plunging halfway into the dirt.

The roll of the rocks had cut two swaths through the woods. Clouds of dust rose in their wake and a total hush spread over the valley.

"I hear the sound of water," said Taeto.

Later I realized she was listening to the rush of the river.

I know. We see a lot of it. It seems that those girls in the big city dance halls, the ones who are always ahead of fashion, find a look like Taeto's interesting. They apparently think it sophisticated to sport a jacket both one size too big and a bit too worn. But none of the green, high-collared jackets you might see at the dance halls would ever be as grimy or ill-fitting as Taeto's.

Taeto, squinting in the bright sun, was cutting and gathering indigo plants. The plants grew behind the house in the terraced rows alongside the millet and cotton. From the ends of the millet stems peeked budding flowers, and the cotton bloomed with deep yellow petals. Most bore no seed yet, but those that did displayed pure white cotton tufts atop their brown outer coverings. Occasionally Taeto would pause in her labors to wipe the sweat from her cheeks with her sleeve and open her blouse to let the breeze cool her chest. I opened my window a crack and watched how she worked in the fields.

Apparently she did not realize that I was observing her. She began to sing her own little song. It made me smile. The words were in a foreign language, but easy to translate. It went something like this: "I am hungry, I am sweating. My back is all wet, and even the soles of my feet are soaked."

She continued with her little song, repeating the lyrics over and over. Finally the sheer repetition made reading impossible, and I went outdoors to help Kuchisuke heat the bath water.

The tub was located under the eaves by the back door. It was surrounded by thick shrubs and a cherry tree that provided a canopy of branches overhead. The wooden tub was preposterously big.

Kuchisuke and I got in together. We fell into small talk as we sat up to our necks in the hot water.

"When you don't have your glasses on you're even more 'ugly' than usual. Hurry up and put them back on. Wait, let me have them first."

Kuchisuke reached for my eyeglasses from the shelf and tried them on. I took them off him and put them on myself. Now I could see the valley clearly. It looked just like those landscape murals done on the walls of Tokyo bathhouses.

"Somehow you've gotten skinny. You're really 'ugly' these days."

"It must be poverty."

"Come on. You mean women, don't you?"

"If I'm so 'ugly,' my problem can hardly be women."

"Anything's possible."

Kuchisuke lifted the upper half of his body out of the water and slapped his wrinkled chest with the palm of his hands. Then he stepped completely out of the tub.

I got out as well and walked through the thicket of shrubs. As I let the breeze dry my naked body, the afternoon sun shone through the leaves of the trees in the garden and playfully painted my skin shades of green.

Taeto finished her harvesting and now took her turn in the bath. Amid the sounds of water spilling and splashing there was suddenly a shrill scream from a terror-stricken voice. What could have happened? Taeto, without a stitch on, came flying from the bath toward me.

"Caterpillars!"

She pointed to the rim of the tub where one fat caterpillar was crawling in a desperate rush to find somewhere to hide. I brushed it off with a bamboo broom and went back to the far side of the shrubs to watch the green light again filter through the trees onto my body. Taeto, however, let out yet another high-pitched scream and came running to me.

"What *are* all these caterpillars? The branches of the cherry tree are crawling with them!"

The limbs of the tree that extended over the tub were indeed infested with hundreds of big black caterpillars. They wriggled all over each other to form a single massive clump.

Taeto slipped on her pants and went to get Kuchisuke. He took one look at the caterpillars and said with a sneer, "In four or five days we'll be out of here. That's not enough time for them to turn into butterflies."

That evening rain began to fall and the wind rose. Both grew worse as the night wore on.

Taeto knelt toward the wall where her crucifix hung and recited her bedtime prayers. She seemed to be in total earnest as she made her supplications in some foreign language. She got into bed afterward, but turned to Kuchisuke and complained that the wind was keeping her awake. The entire valley seemed to be groaning under the fury of the storm; one might have thought the very earth was howling. Kuchisuke and I played game after game of checkers.

"If you can't sleep, try eating these," suggested Kuchisuke as he handed Taeto some of the apricots. She opened her eyes wide and took two in each hand.

"Close your eyes. Then maybe you'll fall asleep."

She replied that she did feel sleepy, and shut her eyes only to open them a moment later.

12

It was very easy to beat Kuchisuke at checkers. "Don't be such a show-off," he would say each time he lost. "One more game." This is how we countered the nighttime cacophony of wind and rain.

Taeto, deciding that she must have been negligent in her prayers, slipped out from the covers to say them over again. She wore only her thin cotton nightgown. After making the sign of the cross with an arm bare beneath its short sleeve, she began to mumble once more in a foreign tongue. As Kuchisuke agonized over his next move, I took the opportunity to steal a glance at Taeto in prayer. Her naked legs trembled on the straw mat where she knelt. On her feet were short handwoven stockings the length of traditional Japanese ankle socks.

When these second prayers were done she took four apricots and returned to bed. As soon as she fell asleep and the apricots rolled from her loosened grasp, the wind and rain came to a stop.

Kuchisuke and I concluded our game and retired. All three of us slept in beds side by side. I fell straight asleep even though Kuchisuke continued to speak to me. When I woke a little while later, he was still talking aloud.

"Consider which is tastier, thrushes or shrikes. Shrikes are better, I'd say. But pheasant is better still. What I mean is, a pheasant has some meat on its bones. After pheasants come shrikes, then thrushes, in that order I suppose. Oh well, this rainy valley is about to become a rainy lake. They say it's going to be more than five miles around, but if a mallard or a heron were to fly high enough overhead, it might go right by and never realize there was a lake directly below. They say you'll be able to fish for carp in it. Twenty years from now the carp'll be two feet long. If I live till then, I'll go looking for them. What a sight it would be to see two-foot-long carp leaping up out of the lake in the evenings just before it rains. The water, as it follows the curves of the mountains, will make nine little inlets. I'm saying that if this big rainy valley is going to become a big rainy lake with nine little rainy ravines, well, then, that's what's going to happen. Don't blame me, but as a rule any one lake with eight or more little valleys to it is bound to contain a monster. I don't know, maybe the monster will look like a nine-foot-long carp, and if it does, it will come in all sorts of colors."

I pretended to snore. Kuchisuke gave up trying to talk to me any further and lay down, only to make snoring sounds even louder than my own. As soon as he noticed that I had ceased my performance, however, he stopped too and picked up where he had left off.

"I think that once the lake is full I'll buy hundreds of baby carp and release them in the water. I'm fonder of mountain birds, like pheasants, but human beings can't raise them. It was about ten years ago when I came across a pheasant's nest in the mountains with eggs in it, and made a chicken try to hatch them. Only one of the eggs made it. I put a big chicken coop over the hen sitting on the eggs, and when the mother pheasant came home it cried all night outside the gate before it gave up and went away. Oh, it was pitiful. I brought home the one chick that hatched and tried to feed it, but it died only ten days later. Baby pheasants don't know how to eat without getting excited. It would eat a little bit, then run all around, eat a little more, and run around some more. They don't eat right like chickens. It must have been famished. All that running around probably helped kill it, too. No, now I remember. It died from a bite on its head. I suspect that its mother followed it here and pecked it to death. Could there ever be anything worse than a mother like that? To peck your own child to death, even if it has been stolen out from under you, that's really something. I've seen it lots of times. The mother bird flies right into your house looking for its young. And it doesn't stop there. The cock pheasant then tricks the hen that's been taking care of the chick, and has its dirty way with it. I've even thought of letting the hen's eggs hatch, but I stop myself when I think I might be responsible for creating some kind of half-breed. It would be my fault, all my fault."

Kuchisuke stopped his rambling and heaved a deep, sad sigh. Perhaps the thought of Taeto made him grieve. A little later he spoke again.

"It's all my fault."

Suddenly he was trembling with tears. Anyone listening to an old man sobbing late at night would be moved, and a few tears rolled from my own eyes. I couldn't imagine how I might help him in his sorrow, however, and so I simply began to snore again. Kuchisuke soon ceased his crying and fell asleep with some very noisy snores of his own.

We finished moving. The three of us carried all the small things ourselves and had the cow transport the bedding and the tub on its back.

We went back and forth again and again across open fields of red clay in a caravan of man and beast.

The new house consisted of a six-mat room, a four-and-a-half-mat room, and one large area with only a dirt floor. The design and the materials were no different from where Kuchisuke had lived until now. An apricot tree was planted outside the window of the six-mat room, and a cow stall and latrine had been erected on the east side of the house. The only difference was that everything was new. The six-mat room served as a combination dining room, bedroom, family room and parlor; the four-and-a-half-mat room could be a storage area for the bedding and trunks as well as a hiding place for scolded children to run to and cry.

Once we finished moving we began to clean. We found loquats and apricots strewn on the floor and cigarette butts snuffed out on scraps of tin. Someone had written graffiti on the walls with charcoal, under which others had added their own comments. The workmen had probably done it.

Even after we had cleaned everywhere Kuchisuke found reason to criticize his new house. "I don't feel at home here," he said. "It may be all right now, but there's no cross-ventilation for when it's hot and humid. And this is the sort of worthless house that'll be freezing in winter."

He spat out the window several times and continued his diatribe.

"I feel as if I'm in someone else's home. I never dreamed this would happen to me. My other place was so much better! I'm going to spend one more night there."

After he finished dinner that evening, Kuchisuke did indeed grab his bedding and walk off into the darkening valley. Taeto tied the cow to a stake and plucked the ticks that had burrowed into the animal's brow and sides. She did not reproach Kuchisuke for leaving. Instead, she concentrated on her work, crushing all the mites that she found on the beast under the heel of her shoe. The ticks died smeared in the dirt and their own blood.

I had just finished repapering the sliding screen and was gluing a maple leaf onto its handle when I thought to myself that Kuchisuke, for all of his seventy-seven years, still had his childish moments. Sooner or later he was bound to return.

15

But I was wrong. Night fell, Taeto was done twisting more than half the rope that she was working on, and still Kuchisuke did not reappear. I went out to bring him home. A fog had completely filled the valley and looked like gray smoke under the glow of the moon.

Kuchisuke was not in bed. He had opened a window halfway and sat by it deep in thought, his elbows on the sill and his chin resting on his arms. The sound of my approaching footsteps broke his concentration.

"It's bad for your health to doze off in a place like that."

"I don't feel like sleeping. I'm just worried and upset about things."

"It's late. Let's go home."

"I like this house so much more. It should be up to me what roof I want to live under."

"Stop being such a 'bad boy.' Let's go."

"I'm going to wage a new fight against this. Don't you worry about me."

There was nothing I could do to dissuade him. I started home but then stopped to glance back. Assuming I was gone, Kuchisuke had put his chin back on his arms and resumed his thoughts. That is how I left him.

Taeto was still busy at work. She was braiding dozens of thin, six-foot-long strands of rope. Seated on a straw mat that she had spread over the earthen floor, she anchored the strands between her knees as she twisted. When she had as much as she could hold in her outstretched arms, she reached behind with one hand and pulled the twisted part through her legs. As she did this over and over, rain began to fall again.

The next morning Kuchisuke came home through the rain with his bedding.

The sound of trees being felled could now be heard in the valley. At first, the echo of two axes suggested that there were only two lumbermen, but gradually their number multiplied. It was obvious they were planning, rain or no rain, to clear in short order all the trees from the land that would soon be underwater. There seemed to be dozens of lumbermen at work, and that evening the sound of the rain was joined by a hail of falling axes.

Kuchisuke stood in one corner of the house and listened to the clamor with close attention. He remarked that the highest-pitched sounds came from three axes chopping away at one huge, dead oak tree. Then there was one sound that reverberated more solidly than the others: this was undoubtedly from the single tree that stood off by itself. It had the measured tone of a cello at the heart of a symphony. Kuchisuke recognized this muted sound as that of cherry wood being chopped.

The downpour did not let up, but Kuchisuke, bored with nothing to do, led the cow out. He wore a raincoat of woven straw similar to the sort that he placed over the back of the animal. I remained under the thatched eaves of the cow stall to avoid the rain as I watched the water rush out of the dam's sluice gate. The river had swollen tremendously and shot out through the gate with full force like a solid column of water. Within this column could be seen a great many logs. The lumbermen were apparently trimming the trees they had felled and floating the trunks downstream through the valley that still resounded with the crack of their axes. Logs flowed out of the sluice gate with no respite.

The water fell in a great cascade that created a pool at its bottom and raised clouds of mist. The plummeting waters generated a driving wind that blew the spray high into the sky. The logs in the pool were standing on end or revolving in perfect circles; one of them slipped in between two others to form a slender raft of three which raced headlong down the river. Another log surprised its companions by throwing itself atop them only to slide back, out of control, into the deep waters.

The rain lasted a full four days. The following morning the skies cleared and the valley shone a brilliant green.

The lumbermen had finished the job by the fourth day, and the sound of their axes did not echo under the blue skies of the fifth. They had carried out their mission in a very short period of time. The mountainsides had been cleared up to the exact height of the dam without a single tree left behind. The denuded area depicted a lake utterly drained of its water; this was how we would last see the valley, and I stood on the grass atop the dam astonished at the transformation.

"Now this is something. It's sure going to be big," Kuchisuke commented.

"From here I can see only five little valleys."

The timberline cut by the lumbermen made five nooks carved into the curve of the mountainsides. Kuchisuke disagreed with my count, however, and pointed out that there were four more small valleys under the shadow of the peak that jutted out to our left.

"So a monster lives here, heh?" I said to Kuchisuke.

"Sooner or later one will, yes."

The steep deforested hillsides were ashen in contrast to the red clay of the gentle incline that would become the bottom of the lake. Through the center flowed the river. At this point the land possessed almost none of the charm associated with a lake. It seemed more like someone's eye wide open in anger. At the waterless bottom of this menacing lake Kuchisuke's house still stood intact. Together we walked down from the dam and toured the area that would be deepest underwater. Kuchisuke stopped on a particular patch of ground and sighed as he stared at it. "Maybe this is where the monster will rise up," he murmured.

Two officials were present. Both had their suit coats off and were directing the workmen. They ordered the gates of the sluice closed. As the iron handles turned, three cogwheels of various sizes spun to lower doors as big as stage curtains to seal off the opening.

The waters flowing through the valley had lost none of their volume. Within moments the river was drowning in its own flood.

Kuchisuke and I, together with Taeto, went down below a grove of trees to watch. A turbid pond began to take shape in the red clay slopes at the bottom of the valley. Its surface was smooth and calm, apparently indifferent to the speed with which it was growing, but the scene at the very edge of the water was one of waves rolling to shore at high tide.

Kuchisuke's old home was increasingly isolated below the terraced fields. The cow stall and the trees around it had been cleared away, but for some reason the workmen had stopped before putting their destructive hands on the house itself. That made it all the worse for Kuchisuke now. The encroaching waters were beginning to trespass on his empty house.

Kuchisuke suddenly became as upset as if he were in the house himself. "No, it's a tidal wave! It's all over!"

I grabbed his arms flailing in desperation and warned that people would sneer at his angry shouting. He broke loose from my hold and cursed out loud what everyone had done, claiming that people had it in for him and planned all along to sink his house at the bottom of a lake.

The water pressed its unsparing attack and poured into the home

18

through its battered door. Walls were uprooted and eaves inundated; soon the entire structure was trapped in a whirlpool and disappeared beneath the surface.

"Sunk," said Taeto with a nervous sigh. A number of wooden beams forced their way to the surface above where the house had stood. They shot up two-thirds out of the water before they began to sink once more, falling onto their sides only to become pieces of driftwood that floated helter-skelter to shore.

The water began to seep into the fields. There, millet not yet ready for harvest was taken in the effortless sweep of a single wave and reduced to clumps of seedlings in the current. Similarly, the cotton plants with their deep yellow flowers and tufts of pure white vanished with the terraces beneath the deluge. The water started to create two bays. According to Kuchisuke it would be several days before it flooded all the nine inlets. Yet one could see that it was one single lake that was filling the valley. Its surface, dark as mud, reflected the surrounding mountains and blue sky in an effort to mollify the changes it had wrought.

When the sounds of the river flowing downstream died away for good, Kuchisuke tugged at his ears and complained of a ringing in them. The two officials went home with the workers in tow. Kuchisuke and I left for the top of the dam. A small sign there announced that a dedication ceremony for the lake would be held on the first of the month.

We sat down beside the sign and gazed at the lake in common silence. A small bird skimmed the surface of the water and flew about in confusion: the lake was a sudden apparition which had invaded its home. Spying its own reflection in the water, the bird let out a shrill cry and beat its wings excitedly. It soared high into the air, drew its wings in, and swooped down close to the surface again. Taeto had been watching the water too and commented that the creature would soon tire. What sort of bird was it anyway? I replied that it looked like a warbler to me.

It grew dark, yet the bird did not stop its wild flight. As the surface of the water turned the color of tarnished silver, the bird's path seemed to etch a black line across it. Perhaps it was the sound of its own flapping wings that kept it in such a state of agitation.

Kuchisuke spoke. "Just how cruel can this lake be."

Taeto picked up some pebbles and called out to the bird as she took aim and threw them. One stone grazed the top of its head. Surprised, the bird beat its wings desperately as it flew in a parabola and disappeared amid the mountain trees.

Kuchisuke rested his chin upon his knees and began to sigh as though something had just occurred to him. Each sigh was a deep breath followed by a forceful exhalation from the shoulders, as if it were meant to dispel the troubled thoughts from his system once and for all. The tail end of each breath that he inhaled and let out quivered slightly with the emotions inside him. Gradually, the old man's sighs turned into sobs.

I felt tired and did not want to get up just yet.

Taeto patiently waited for us to rise. There was a look in her auburn eyes that told me she would never, ever, leave Kuchisuke behind on the dam.

MATING

Kajii Motojirō
Translated by Robert Ulmer

Kajii Motojirō was born in Osaka in 1901 to a merchant family. Although he originally planned a career as an engineer, Kajii became interested in literature during his studies at the Third Higher School in Kyoto. In 1924 he entered the English literature department of Tokyo University but withdrew two years later due to illness. After spending a year and a half in the hot spring resort of Yugashima (the setting for the second part of "Mating"), Kajii returned to Osaka and lived there with his mother until his death from tuberculosis in 1932. Due to his untimely death, and perhaps to the temper of the times—the proletarian literature movement on the one hand and increasing militarism and government control on the other—Kajii's works were denied serious consideration during his lifetime. After World War II, and especially in the late 1950s, many more writers in Japan came to regard Kajii's writings as an important link between the prewar and postwar periods of Japanese literature.

Kajii's first, and possibly best-known story, "Remon" (Lemon, 1925), describes the ennui of its young hero and how the purchase of a single lemon from a fruit stand rejuvenates and purifies him. Almost all Kajii's stories are brief, prose-poetry pieces, and feature a hero who is a solitary figure or, as Kajii describes him in "Mating," "a lone traveler in the universe."

As in several of Kajii's stories, "Kōbi (Mating, 1931) presents an affirmation of the poet as outsider. His description of the cats and frogs suggests an awareness of the transience of life, the elements of death within life which create a balance that the hero of the story draws from to establish a stability within himself. There is also a total involvement in nature, which does not consume the writer's being but instead enlightens and enriches that inner, private world.

*   *   *

As I look up at the starry sky, bats are flying silently about. Though I cannot make out their shape, when they momentarily block the glimmer of the stars I can sense the presence of some kind of eerie creature.

People are fast asleep. I am standing on the rotting clothes-drying platform of a house. From here I can look out over the back alley. Like countless ships moored in a port, the houses in this neighborhood are built close together, and many other platforms are rotting like this one. I once saw a reproduction of the German artist Pechstein's *Christ Lamenting in the City*. It depicted Christ kneeling in prayer in the back streets of an enormous factory area. Associating with this image, I feel that where I'm standing now is somehow like Gethsemane. I do not feel like Christ, however. When the dead of night comes, my sickly body begins to burn and I am wide awake. But it is only to escape that monster, fantasy, that I come out here and let the poisonous night dew attack my body.

In every house people are fast asleep. From time to time I hear the sound of a weak cough breaking the silence. Because I have heard it in the afternoon, I know it as the cough of the fishmonger who lives in this back alley. His illness is making it difficult for him to carry on his business. The man who rents the second floor flat from him told him to see a doctor, but he would not listen to this advice. Insisting that it isn't that kind of cough, he tries to conceal the truth. The man who lives upstairs, however, goes around the neighborhood telling everybody about the fellow's illness. In a town like this, where only the rare lodger can pay the rent regularly every month, people can't afford a doctor's bills. Tuberculosis is a war of endurance. All of a sudden the hearse arrives. The memory of the deceased is still fresh in everyone's mind, but it is of him working as usual. It seems he was just in bed for a matter of

22

days, and then died. Truly, in this life everyone brings despair, everyone brings death upon himself.

The fishmonger is coughing. Poor fellow. I listen to his cough, wondering if mine too sounds like that.

For a short while now, the alley has been astir with the activity of white animals. As night deepens they emerge, not just in this alley but in other back streets too. Cats. I've thought about why it is that in this neighborhood cats stroll about as if they owned the streets. First, it's because there are hardly any dogs around here. Keeping dogs is somewhat of a luxury. Instead, merchants keep cats so that their goods won't be destroyed by rats. Without dogs there are many cats, and they prowl the streets at will. Still, it is curious to see so many cats monopolizing the late night streets. Leisurely, they walk like ladies on the boulevard. They move casually from corner to corner like a surveying crew.

From a dark corner of the drying platform next door comes a rustling sound. A parakeet. When it was popular in the neighborhood to have birds as pets, some people even got hurt trying to retrieve these birds. Then, when people began to ask themselves, "Who started this crazy idea?" swarms of these scruffy abandoned birds came flocking with the sparrows in search of scraps to eat. But they no longer come. A few sooty parakeets next door are all that remain. During the day no one pays them any attention. But when night falls they become living things that give out this sound.

Then, to my surprise, two white cats that have been chasing each other in the alley stop near me and begin to grapple and moan. But it is not fighting in earnest. They are grappling on their sides. I have seen cats copulating but it was not like this. I've also seen kittens playing, but it wasn't like this either. I don't know what they are doing, but it is captivating and I watch them closely. From far away comes the tapping of the night watchman's stick. Except for that, there is no sound from the neighborhood; all is silent. Though they are absorbed in their grappling, the cats are quiet.

They embrace each other. They bite each other gently. They thrust their forepaws against each other. As I watch, gradually I become fascinated by their actions. Looking at the nasty way they nip at each other and seeing them thrust their forepaws out, I'm reminded of the sweet way they put their paws on people's chests and the thick warm fur of their bellies which is soft to the touch. Now one of them is pawing at this fur with its hind legs. I have never seen cats appear so lovely, so mysterious, so enthralling. After a while, still embracing tightly, they cease their movement. As I watch I feel a choking sensation. Just then the sound of the night watchman's stick echoes in the alley.

Whenever this man comes I duck into the house, not wanting to be seen prowling around clothes-drying platforms late at night. Of course, if I move close to one side of the platform it's hard to see me. But the shutters are open, and if he did happen to see me and call out, it would be most embarrassing. So when the watchman approaches I usually hurry into the house. But tonight, wanting to see for myself what will happen to the cats, I decide to stay where I am on the platform. The watchman draws slowly nearer. The cats remain embracing each other as before, not seeming to make any effort at all to move. The sight of these two white cats entwined gives me the illusion of watching a man and a woman absurdly doing as they please. I derive an immense enjoyment from this scene.

The watchman has gradually drawn nearer. He runs a funeral parlor during the day, and has an aura of unspeakable gloom about him. As he comes closer I wonder how he will react when he sees the cats. Now only a few yards away he seems to notice them for the first time and stops. He is watching them. I watch him looking at the cats, and somehow have the feeling that I am there with him, observing this midnight scene. But the cats have not moved at all. Have they not noticed him? Perhaps. Yet they do not care, for they are finishing their business. This is one aspect of these brazen animals. If they sense that you won't harm them, they have no fear and remain perfectly calm when you try to drive them off. But in fact they watch you keenly, and as soon as it appears that someone means them harm, they instantly take flight.

Seeing they have still not moved, the watchman comes a few steps closer. Then, without breaking their embrace, the cats turn their heads around. From my point of view the watchman is now the more interesting. Suddenly, he strikes his nightstick sharply on the ground. The cats dart off into the alley, two streaks of light. Watching them run off, the man regains his usual bored expression and, rapping his stick, walks off. He has not noticed me.

I once went to observe some singing frogs.

To see them, one first has to venture resolutely to the edge of the shallows where they sing. Since they will hide no matter how cautiously one approaches, it is just as well to move quickly. One then hides by the shallows and remains perfectly still. Imagine you are a rock. Nothing moves but your eyes. If you are not careful it is difficult to distinguish the frogs from the stones in the shallows and you won't see anything. After a while, from the water and the shadows of the rocks, the frogs slowly show their heads. As I looked on they seemed to emerge from almost everywhere. All at once, as if by previous arrangement, they timidly appeared.

I remained still as a rock. Letting their fear pass, they all climbed out to where they were before. In front of me they took up their interrupted courtship song again.

I was overcome at intervals by an odd feeling, watching from this proximity. Akutagawa Ryūnosuke wrote a novel about men going to the land of the mythical *kappa*, but in fact the land of the frogs is much more accessible. Through observing just one frog I suddenly entered their world. This frog sat by the small current that ran between the rocks in the stream and, with something uncanny in its look, stared at the rushing water. Its appearance was exactly like the human figures in classical literati paintings: something between a fisherman and a *kappa*. As I thought about this, the small current suddenly widened and became an inlet. And, in that instant, I had a sense of being a lone traveler in the universe.

That is all there is to the story. And yet, it may be said that I observed the frogs in the most natural of conditions. Once before, though, I had the following experience.

I went to the shallows and caught a frog, planning to study it carefully. I placed it in a bucket from the bathhouse and filled the pail with water. I put in some stones from the stream and, using a piece of glass as a cover, carried it back to my room. The frog, however, would not act naturally at all. I caught some flies and put them in the pail, but the frog just ignored them. Bored with this, I went for a bath. I had forgotten about the frog and was returning to my room, when all of a sudden the sound of a splash came from the bucket. Thinking to myself, "At last," I hurried over and looked. But just as before, the frog remained hidden and would not come out. Next I went for a walk. When I returned I again heard the sound of a splash. Looking in, it was just like the time before. That night, placing the bucket at my side, I sat down to do some reading. I forgot all about the frog, but when I moved it jumped with a splash. It had been observing *me* in my natural condition. The next day, because all I had finally learned from the frog was that it jumped from fear, I uncovered the bucket. It leaped toward the sound of the rapids outside my window, to cleanse itself of the dust in my room. I never tried this experiment again. In order to observe them naturally, I had to go to the shallows.

The day I went the frogs were singing loudly. Their voices could be heard clearly from the main road of the village. From this road I walked through the cedar grove to the shallows where I always went. In the thicket opposite the stream, a flycatcher was chirping prettily. The flycatcher was a bird that, like the frogs in this valley, always gave me a pleasant feeling. The villagers said there was only one of these birds in the whole valley, where the woods were thickest. If another flycatcher went there, the two fought and one would be chased away. Whenever I listened to its song I was reminded of the villagers' story and felt it must be true, for this was the song of one that rejoiced in hearing its own voice. The bird's voice carried far, echoing in the valley as the sunlight changed. Idling my time away in the valley, I would hum this ditty to myself:

If you go to the bridge of Nishibira
You'll hear the Nishibira flycatcher;
And if you go to Seko Falls
You'll hear the Seko flycatcher.

One of these birds was near the shallows. Just as I expected, the frogs were wailing. Quickly I walked over to the edge of the shallows. At that, their music ceased. Following the plan I had formed, I crouched and waited. In a while they began to sing as before. Their many voices resounded in the shallows, reverberating like a wind coming from afar. From among the small ripples of the current nearby it grew louder, and moved en masse to reach a tide. This diffusion of sound moved delicately, steadily swelling and rolling phantomlike before me.

Scientists say that the first living things with a "voice" were amphibious creatures that appeared during the Carboniferous Period. Thinking of their voices now as the first living sound to chorus forth on the face of the earth gave me a sense of the sublime. It was the kind of music that touches the listener's heart, makes it throb, and finally moves him to tears.

In front of me was a male frog. Obviously drifting with the waves of the chorus, his throat trembled intermittently. I looked around, thinking that his mate must be nearby. A foot or two away in the stream, in the shadow of a rock, another frog was sitting with quiet reserve in the background. I thought it must be the mate. Whenever the male croaked, I noticed that the female answered "geh! geh!" in a contented voice. As this went on, the male's voice grew clearer. My heart responded to his earnest cries. Then he suddenly broke from the rhythm of the chorus. The intervals between his cries grew shorter and shorter. The female continued to reply. And yet, perhaps because her voice did not carry, she sounded a bit nonchalant in comparison to that other passionate call.

But now something had to happen. Impatiently, I waited for the moment. As I expected, the male frog abruptly stopped his ardent croaking, smoothly slipped off the rock, and began to cross the water. Nothing has ever moved me so much as the tenderness of that moment. Swimming across the water toward the female, he was like a child who has found its mother, crying appealingly as it runs to her. As he swam he cried out, "geeyo! geeyo! geeyo! geeyo!" Could any other courtship be so tender and devoted? I watched, feeling an awkward envy.

He arrived happily at the feet of his mate, and there they copulated in the fresh limpid stream. Yet the sight of their desperate mating came nowhere near the tenderness of his crossing the water. Feeling I had seen something in the world that was beautiful, for a while I submerged myself in the cadence of the frogs' voices vibrating in the shallows.

LES JOUES EN FEU

Hori Tatsuo
Translated by Jack Rucinski

The fragile, poetic writings of Hori Tatsuo (1904–53) are unique in the annals of Shōwa literature. In an age fraught with war, extremes of experimentation, and despair, Hori wrote poems and stories for that minority of the human race for whom wild roses and dreams are the vital concerns of life. He stood for artistic conscientiousness and propriety, and his finely wrought prose remains a model of a chaste, poetic style.

As a sensitive, lonely young man, Hori enjoyed the association and tutelage of such important literary figures as Murō Saisei, an important avant-garde poet, and Akutagawa Ryūnosuke. It was Murō who first took Hori to the locale with which his name will always be associated, the fashionable summer resort town of Karuizawa. At Tokyo University, Hori read French literature voraciously: Stendhal, Anatole France, Gide, and Mérimée. His own poetry was highly influenced by Cocteau and Rilke, while in prose his models ranged from Proust to the Heian court ladies who penned personal diaries.

In the 1930s, when other writers turned either to the new revolutionary literature of the proletarian movement or to the opposing forces of pure aestheticism, Hori was left to the pursuit of the introspective, the refined, and the delicate in literature. His first prominent story, "Seikazoku" (The Holy Family, 1930), derived from his personal reactions to Akutagawa's suicide three years earlier, but it is noteworthy for its attempt to achieve objectivity and consciously battle the tendency toward autobiography that was overwhelming the literature of the period. Hori carried this attempt even further in Utsukushii mura *(Beautiful Village, 1933; tr. 1967), set in Karuizawa, and* Kaze tachinu *(The Wind Rises, 1936–37; tr. 1958), an attempt to objectify the days Hori spent caring for his fiancée as she slowly succumbed to tuberculosis, a disease that constantly plagued and finally killed Hori also.*

In the late thirties, drawn to the portraits of docile women resigned to their fates that he found in Heian court diaries, Hori began writing works in the classical mode, adapting Kagero no nikki *(The Gossamer Years, 1937) and the eleventh-century* Sarashina nikki. *His final works were poetic evocations of the beauty of the Japanese natural landscape in the environs of Nara and Kyoto.*

"Moyuru hoho" (Les Joues en Feu, 1932) was intended, like Mori Ōgai's famous Vita Sexualis, *to be a frank account of sexual attitudes and experiences. Hori's title is taken from an expression much used by Cocteau and Radiguet; the image of "flaming cheeks" aptly captures the mood of the story, a shy and hesitant awakening to sexuality. To reveal the universality of the emotions of young love, Hori draws upon his own experience, but avoids pure autobiography again by the use of other sources. Various scenes and characters are borrowed from Cocteau's* Le Grand Ecart *and Proust's* A la recherche du temps perdu. *As in Proust, women in Hori's literature are the personification of the ideal, almost more divine than mortal. Saigusa here is a near forerunner of the pure heroines of* Beautiful Village *and* The Wind Rises. *Kawabata Yasunari noted the absence of carnality in Hori's treatment of sex, and remarked of "Les Joues en Feu," "What a wonder it is that the author should have such purity of perception, like the innocence of a naked child!"*

*   *   *

I turned seventeen. I had just gone from middle to preparatory school. My parents were afraid that life under their roof might be bad for my nerves and had me board at the school. This change of environment could not but have had a great impact upon me. Because of it, the shedding of my childhood was to be curiously hastened.

29

The dormitory was divided up for all the world like a honeycomb into many small studies, each one kept in a perpetual state of turmoil by the ten or so boys occupying it. These "studies" were furnished with nothing more than a few huge, scarred tables, each heaped high with school caps, dictionaries, tablets, ink bottles, and packs of cigarettes and such, all languishing for want of an owner. Among all this might be found a boy doing his German, or another precariously straddling the old chair with the broken leg, idly puffing away at a cigarette. Of all the boys I was the smallest. To be one of them, I tortured myself trying to smoke and timidly took a razor to my still beardless cheeks.

The bedroom on the second floor had a strange smell of soiled linen that made me queasy. The smell even found its way into my dreams while I slept and imbued them with sensations unknown as yet to my waking hours. But gradually I grew accustomed even to that.

And so my innocence was tottering. It needed only the final blow.

One afternoon recess, I was wandering alone in the deserted flower garden to the south of the botany laboratory. I halted all of a sudden. A honeybee, dusty with pollen, flew up from a great riot of pure white flowers I did not know, blooming in a corner of the garden. I thought I would watch and see to which flower the honeybee carried the pollen clustered on his legs, but he appeared indecisive and not about to settle on any of them. At that moment, I sensed that every one of the flowers was coquettishly arching her styles in a stratagem to entice the bee to herself. He finally chose one and alighted upon her. He fastened his dusty legs around the tiny tips of her styles and presently flew up again. As I watched, I suddenly felt that cruelty only children are capable of and yanked at the fertilized flower. I scrutinized her styles flecked with the pollen of the male, crushed her in my palm, and wandered on again through the garden blossoming in flaming reds and purples. Just then someone called my name through the glass doors of the botany laboratory. It was Uozumi, an upperclassman.

"Come and have a look. I'll let you see the microscope."

Uozumi was on the discus-throwing team and seemed about twice my size. When he was on the field, he bore a slight resemblance to *The Discus Thrower*, one of the Greek statues on the German picture postcards that we circulated among ourselves. Consequently, the lowerclassmen idolized him in spite of his perpetual look of disdain for everyone. I wanted him to like me. I went into the laboratory.

Uozumi was the only one there. His hairy hands were fumbling with a specimen. Every now and then he peered at it through the microscope. Then he let me have a look. I had to hunch over, shrimplike, in order to make anything out.

"Can you see?"

"Yes."

Awkward as my position was, I still was able to keep a secret watch on him out of my other eye. I had already noticed a peculiar transformation in his face. Whether it was due to the bright light of the laboratory or to his having removed his mask for once, the flesh of his cheeks was oddly slack and his eyes were deeply bloodshot. A faint smile, like a girl's, kept flickering on his lips. For some reason, I thought of the honeybee and the strange white flowers of the garden. His warm breath grazed my cheek.

I abruptly raised my head from the microscope and, with a look at my wristwatch, stammered, "Well, I . . . I've got to get to class."

"Oh?"

His mask was already deftly back in place. He stood looking down at my face drained of color, with his customary expression of disdain.

In May, Saigusa, who was in the same class as myself though a year older, was transferred to our study. He was known for being a pet of the upperclassmen. He was a slender boy and made me envious of his fragile beauty, for his skin was translucent, blue-veined, and fair, while his cheeks still retained the tint of roses. In the lecture hall, I went so far as to steal occasional glances from behind my textbook at the back of his slender neck.

At night he would go up to the second-floor bedroom before anyone else. This was about nine o'clock even though there was a regulation that lights could not be turned on in the bedrooms until ten. After he went up, my mind would evoke a phantasmagoria of his faces, all asleep in darkness.

I had acquired the habit of not going to bed until midnight, but one evening I had a sore throat and I seemed to be running a slight fever. Soon after Saigusa went up, I took a candle and climbed the stairs. I opened the bedroom door without a forethought. It was pitch-black inside, but suddenly a strange shadow in the form of a large bird was thrown on the ceiling by the light of my candle. It flapped about eerily, as if in a fierce struggle. My heart skipped a beat. Then it was gone. My only thought was that the phantom on the ceiling was created by a caprice of the flickering light of the candle, for when the flame stopped its wavering, except for Saigusa in his bedding against the wall, I saw nothing more than a dark, sullen form in a hooded cape, sitting beside him.

"Who's there?" the huge boy in the cape asked, looking around.

When I realized it had to be Uozumi, I became flustered and put out the candle. Ever since that time in the botany laboratory, I was sure he hated me. I didn't say a thing and crawled under my shabby quilt next to Saigusa's. Saigusa too was silent all this time.

I lay there choking for several minutes. The man I took to be Uozumi eventually got up. Without a word he stomped through the dark and left the room. When his footsteps grew fainter, I told Saigusa in a suffering tone that I had a sore throat.

"You must have a fever, too."

"Maybe just a little."

"Here, let me see." He stretched over and laid a cold hand on my throbbing forehead. I held my breath. Then he grasped my wrist. If he intended taking my pulse, it was a strange way of doing it. But all that worried me was that he might find the beat had suddenly quickened.

All the next day I stayed buried under the covers and even wished my sore throat might never get better so that I could go up to bed early every night. Several days later, my throat started hurting again in the evening. Deliberately coughing, I went up to the bedroom soon after Saigusa, but his bed was empty. Wherever he had gone, he was a long time coming back. A whole hour went by as I suffered in solitude. It seemed to me my throat had taken a turn for the worse and might well be the end of me.

He finally reappeared. I had left a candle burning beside my pillow. Its light traced a weird, writhing form on the ceiling as he undressed, and the memory of the phantom of the other night came back to me.

32

I asked him where he had been. He hadn't felt sleepy, he said, and had gone for a walk alone around the playing fields. Something in his tone made me think he was lying, but I didn't question him any further.

"Going to leave the candle burning?" he asked.

"As you like."

"I'll put it out then." To blow out the flame, he drew his face close to mine. I kept my eyes raised to his cheeks where the shadows of his long lashes fell and flickered in the candlelight. Compared to mine, flaming as they were, his cheeks seemed celestially cool.

At some point, my relationship with Saigusa passed beyond ordinary friendship. If he grew closer to me, Uozumi, on the other hand, became all the more overbearing to everyone in the dormitory, and from time to time was to be found alone on the field, practicing discus throwing like a demon. He disappeared altogether while we were in the midst of preparations for the half-year examinations. The entire dormitory knew he had gone, but not one of us said a word about it.

Summer vacation came. Saigusa and I planned an excursion of a week or so to the seacoast. We felt somewhat heavy-hearted, like children sneaking off from their parents, as we set out one leaden gray morning.

By leaving the railway at a seaside station and then walking a mile on a road that followed the shore, we came to a small fishing village cradled in the jagged hills. Our inn had a woebegone look about it, and the smell of seaweed came drifting in with the night. A maid brought in a lantern. Saigusa took off his shirt to go to bed, and in the dim lantern light his bare back showed a peculiar ridge on his spine. An unaccountable urge to touch it came over me.

"What's this?" I asked, putting my finger to the spot.

"That?" He reddened a little. "That's a scar from tuberculosis of the spine."

"Let me feel it, will you?"

I stroked the curious ridge on his spine as I might a piece of ivory, not allowing him to dress. His eyes were closed and he shuddered slightly.

The weather had not cleared by the next day, but nonetheless we set out once more over the pebbles of the road that led us through the little villages along the sea. Around noon, we were coming upon yet another village when the sky grew ominous and rain threatened to fall at any moment. Furthermore, both of us were tired of walking and somewhat cross with each other, so we decided that when we got to the village we would ask when the bus passed through.

On our way was a small wooden bridge where five or six village girls, each with a fish basket on her arm, had stopped to talk. When they saw us coming they fell silent and watched us with curiosity. I discovered among them a girl with particularly beautiful eyes and kept looking just at her. The girl, evidently the oldest, gave no sign of annoyance at my stare. In order to make the best possible impression on her in the shortest possible time, I attempted that swagger boys affect in these situations. I wanted to say something, anything at all, but my wits completely failed me, and I was just about to pass by without a word when Saigusa suddenly slackened his pace and, to my surprise, went boldly up to her. He was asking her about the coach—quite a shrewd maneuver. Now this tactic of his was likely, I thought, to give her a better impression of him than of myself. Not to be outdone, I went up to her and, while they were talking, took a look in her basket.

She was answering him without the least trace of shyness. Her voice was unexpectedly rasping and failing in its duty to the beauty of her eyes; yet, the very harshness of it added mysteriously to her charm.

I decided to speak up. I pointed at the basket and faintheartedly asked what the little fish inside were called. There must have been something odd about the way I asked, for she seemed to find it unduly funny. The other girls followed her lead and burst out laughing. The blood rushed to my cheeks and, with a glance at Saigusa, I caught the flash of a malicious smile. A sudden hostility toward him came over me.

We headed for the end of the village where the bus was to stop, neither of us saying a word. We had a long wait and it had already begun raining. Once aboard, we were left largely to ourselves and hardly spoke; I was depressing him as much as he was me. We finally arrived in a misty rain at a town by the sea, where we might find lodgings for the night. The inn was just as gloomy as that of the night before. There was the same faint smell of seaweed and the same light from the flame of a lantern, conjuring up hazy ghosts of ourselves as we were twenty-four hours ago. The restraint between us eventually melted. We blamed our low spirits on having had such bad weather for traveling. My proposal was that the next day we go directly by bus to a town where we could get a train and return to Tokyo for the time being. He agreed, evidently not knowing what else to do. In our exhaustion both of us soon fell sound asleep.

Some time close to dawn, I happened to wake. Saigusa was sleeping with his back to me. I noticed the small ridge on his spine under his bedclothes and gently stroked it as I had done the previous night. When I did so, I found myself thinking of the beautiful eyes of the girl on the bridge. That strange voice of hers still echoed in my ears. I heard Saigusa lightly grind his teeth as I drifted back to sleep.

The next day as well brought rain, or rather a dense mist. We no longer had a choice; the trip had to be given up. In the bus rattling on through the rain, and later in the crush of the third-class carriage of the train, both of us did all we could—and it is this that marks a full stop to love—to spare the other pain. Something made me feel that hereafter we were never to meet again. A number of times he seized my hand. If I did not give it to him, neither did I withdraw it from him. All the same, when fragments of a strange rasping voice came drifting to me from time to time, I was deaf to all else. We were all the sadder when we said good-bye.

The most convenient way for me to get home was to get off the train at a station along the way and change to a branch line. While I made my way through the crowd on the platform, I kept looking back at him in the railway carriage. To see me better, he pressed his face to the window beaded with rain but succeeded only in clouding the glass with his white breath, and hid me all the more from sight.

August came and I went with my father to a lakeshore in Shinshū. I hadn't seen any more of Saigusa but he sometimes wrote what might be called love letters to me at the lake. In time I gradually stopped answering. Echoes of strange voices had effected a change in my love. From one of his last letters, I learned he was ill. I gathered he was suffering again from his spinal tuberculosis. Regardless, I wrote no more.

The autumn half began. On my return from the lake, I once again moved into the dormitory. Everything was different now. Saigusa had gone somewhere by the sea for a change of climate; Uozumi took no more notice of my existence now than he did of the air around him.

With winter, there came a morning all encrusted in a thin shell of ice, when I discovered Saigusa had died. The announcement was on the school bulletin board. I read it through vacantly, as if it concerned someone I had never known.

Several years went by. Every now and then I would recall all that had happened in the dormitory and could not help feeling that I had ruthlessly stripped away the beautiful skin of childhood and left it to lie like an opalescent snakeskin entangled among the brambles. In the course of those years, how many were the strange voices I heard! There was not one among them that did not lead me to grief; and I was all too fond of grieving over them, until one day I was finally dealt a wound to the heart from which there was no recovering.

In the uplands near the lake I had once visited with my father was a sanatorium, and here I was sent after a serious hemorrhage of the lungs. The doctor's diagnosis of tuberculosis has no particular importance to this story save to demonstrate that the petals of the rose must fall and that I, too, had now lost the bloom from my cheeks for all time.

There was, besides myself, only a single patient in what was known as the White Birch Ward of the sanatorium. He was a boy of fifteen or sixteen and had been treated for tuberculosis of the spine but was simply convalescing then, and for several hours a day he would conscientiously sunbathe on the veranda. When he learned I was confined to bed, he took to paying me calls occasionally. On one of his visits, it struck me that his lean face, although darkened by the sun until the only trace of red was in the lips, bore the stamp of the dead Saigusa. From that time on, I did my best not to look directly at him.

One morning was so fine I had a sudden desire to get up from bed and ventured cautiously over to the window. There, on the opposite veranda, was the boy, totally naked, sunning himself. He was leaning slightly forward, intent on a part of his body. He could not have known he was being watched. My heart was pounding. I am nearsighted, and squinted for a better look. When I made out on his dark back what seemed to be that distinctive ridge of Saigusa's, a sudden dizziness came over me. I managed my way back to the bed and collapsed.

The boy left the sanatorium several days later, without the slightest notion of the great shock he had given me.

MAGIC LANTERN

Dazai Osamu

Translated by Tomone Matsumoto

Dazai Osamu (1909–48) was born in Aomori Prefecture, the tenth of eleven children of a grand landowner. Raised by his aunt and servants, Dazai, precocious and sensitive, never had the feeling that he belonged to his own family. He excelled in composition, and his interest in literature led him to organize a literary group at Hirosaki Higher School. With his sponsorship this group published periodicals to which he contributed short stories. Dazai entered Tokyo University in the French Department in 1930. He was involved as a student with the then ebbing Marxist movement, but withdrew from it after two years.

After he made his literary debut in 1933, he published short stories such as "Romanesuku" (Romanesque, 1934; tr. 1965) and "Dōke no hana" (Flowers of Buffoonery, 1935). He was nominated for the Akutagawa Prize in 1935, but was never able to obtain it. Despite his literary success his personal life was chaotic: he was disowned by his family because of a continuing relationship with a geisha; one of the women who participated with him in his four suicide attempts died by drowning; an operation left him addicted to drugs, and he had to be committed to an asylum for treatment.

Dazai's marriage in 1939 to Ishihara Michiko, a secondary school teacher, changed his personal life as well as his writings. The structure and style of his work became much clearer, more natural and simple. This happy period lasted until the end of the Second World War.

His third and final literary peak came in the post-1945 era, but lasted only a year and a half. He produced Shayō (The Setting Sun, 1947; tr.

1956), Ningen shikkaku *(No Longer Human, 1948; tr. 1958), and "Viyon no tsuma" (Villon's Wife, 1947; tr. 1956), the works regarded as his masterpieces. His fifth suicide attempt was successful: he drowned himself with a lover in 1948. As one of the most controversial writers in modern Japan, Dazai's popularity has increased after his death, and a gathering on the anniversary of his suicide has become a yearly event.*

*   *   *

The more I talk about it, the more suspicious people become. Everyone I meet is wary of me. Even when I go to see them for the simple pleasure of their company, they greet me with the strangest of looks, as if wondering why I've come. I find it unbearable.

I no longer want to go anywhere. Today I went to a public bathhouse near my home, but I waited till early evening so that no one would see me. Back in the middle of summer, my cotton kimono still shone white at dusk, and I was worried how conspicuous I must be. But it has turned noticeably cooler since yesterday. It won't be long before we're using our fall wardrobe, and I'll be changing to an unlined kimono with a black background. I can't stand the thought of having to spend another whole year with things the way they are—to have people staring at me in that white cotton kimono again next summer. . . No, it's unthinkable! By next summer I must attain a social position that will allow me to go out in public dressed even in that eye-catching kimono with the morning-glory pattern. And I want to wear a little makeup as I walk among the crowds at the festivals in the temples and shrines. My heart throbs with emotion when I think how wonderful that would be.

Yes, I committed a theft. I won't deny it. I'm certainly not proud of what I did, but, well . . . let me tell you how it all began. Not that I care what people think. Their opinions don't matter to me. Still, if you can believe my story . . . well, so much the better.

I'm the daughter of a poor Japanese clog-maker—his only daughter. As I sat in the kitchen last night cutting up a spring onion, I heard one of the neighborhood kids out back call, half in tears, "Hey, Sis!" I stopped cutting for a moment and sat motionless. I realized that my life might not have turned out quite so miserably if I'd had a younger brother or sister who needed me from time to time, who called out to me like this child. Hot tears welled up in my eyes, already smarting from the onions, and when I tried to wipe them away with the back of my hand, the stinging worsened. The tears streamed down endlessly, and I felt helpless.

It was last spring, when the cherry trees were past their prime and pink and blue-fringed flag irises were beginning to appear at the flower stands, that the gossip started down at the hairdresser's: That spoiled girl has finally started chasing men.

I was still happy then. Mr. Mizuno would come to see me each day at dusk. Before nightfall I would change my kimono, put on some makeup, and wait for him, stepping in and out of the house to see if he'd arrived. I was told, later, that the people in the neighborhood were well aware of all this, and would secretly point at me and whisper among themselves, "Look! Sakiko from the clog shop is in heat," and laugh at me. I think both my parents were vaguely aware of what was going on, but they couldn't bring themselves to speak to me about it.

I'm twenty-four years old this year but still unmarried. The reason I haven't yet married is, of course—other than being poor—very largely Mother. When she was still the mistress of an important landowner from the neighborhood, she had an affair with my father. She ran off with him, forgetting everything she owed her former patron, and soon gave birth to me. The problem was, however, that I didn't look like either the landowner or my father. Mother became more and more isolated, and for a time she was a social outcast. Being the daughter of such a woman, I naturally had little chance of marriage. But, with my looks, my fate would have been the same even if I'd been born to a wealthy aristocrat.

I don't bear a grudge against my father, though, or against my mother. I am most decidedly my father's child. I firmly believe that, no matter what anyone else may say. Both my parents look after me well, and I take good care of them. They are vulnerable people. Even toward me, their own child, they behave with a certain restraint. I believe that we should be kind to weak and timid people. I thought I was prepared to endure any pain and loneliness for my parents. Until I met Mr. Mizuno, I never neglected my obligations to them.

Though it's embarrassing, I should explain that he is five years younger than I am, and that he's a student at a commercial school. But you must understand that I had no alternative. I met him in spring, in the waiting room of an eye specialist, when I was having trouble with my left eye. I'm the sort of woman who falls in love at first sight. He had a white bandage on his left eye, just like mine. He was leafing through a small dictionary, frowning and looking uncomfortable. I felt sorry for him. I too was depressed because of my bandaged eye. The young pasania leaves I could see from the windows of the room looked like blue flames flickering in the heat-laden air. Everything in the outside world seemed to fade from reality, and his face had an unearthly, even uncanny, beauty about it. I'm convinced that all this resulted from the sorcery of the eye bandage.

Mr. Mizuno is an orphan. He has no blood relations to look after him with loving care. His parents were fairly well-to-do, but his mother passed away when he was a baby, and he was only twelve when his father died. After that the family business, a pharmaceutical supply store, declined. His two older brothers and an older sister were taken separately into the care of distant relations. At present, as the last child of the family, he is supported by the head clerk of his father's store, and goes to commercial school. I was afraid he must have had a rather restricted, lonely life, for he once confessed that his most enjoyable moments were when he went out walking with me. I also suspected that he lacked many personal belongings. He told me that he had promised to go swimming with a friend, but he didn't look happy at the prospect. In fact, he looked quite downhearted. That night I stole a man's swimsuit.

Quickly and quietly I entered Daimaru's, the largest store in my neighborhood. Pretending to look at this and that among the simple cotton dresses for women, I stealthily removed a black swimsuit from the counter, tucked it under my arm, and left the store. I hadn't walked more than five yards when someone called out, "You there!" I was so frightened I was ready to scream, and I ran like a madwoman. I heard a shrill cry of "Thief! Thief!" behind me, felt a blow on my back, and stumbled. When I turned around, I was struck across the face.

41

I was taken to a small police station. Quite a crowd of familiar faces from the neighborhood assembled in front of it. I noticed that my hair was in disarray and that my knees were showing beneath my summer kimono. I must have looked awful.

A policeman made me sit down in a cramped tatami room in the inner part of the office, where he interrogated me. He was a vulgar fellow, about twenty-seven or twenty-eight years old, with a fair complexion, a narrow face, and gold-rimmed glasses. He asked me my name, address, and age and wrote them down in his notebook one by one. Then suddenly he began to grin and asked, "How many times does this make it?"

I shuddered to think what he had in mind. I simply couldn't think of anything to say. Yet if I didn't reply, he would undoubtedly put me in jail and bring serious charges against me. I realized that somehow I had to talk myself out of the situation. Desperately I searched for explanations, but felt as if I were lost in a thick fog. I had never had such a terrifying experience before. When I finally managed to say something, it seemed clumsy and abrupt even to myself. But once I'd started, I raved on as if possessed:

"You mustn't put me in prison. I'm not bad. I'm twenty-four years old. I've been devoted to my parents all my life. I've looked after both of them with all the love in the world. Is there anything wrong about that? I've never done a thing that would make people point and whisper about me.

"Mr. Mizuno is a good man. He'll soon make a name for himself. I'm sure of that. I don't want him to be humiliated. He had promised someone he'd go swimming, and I wanted to send him there dressed like everyone else. What's so wrong with that? I'm a fool. A fool! But I'll make a fine man out of him, and present him for your inspection. He comes from a good family. He's different from other people. I don't care what happens to me as long as he goes out into the world and does well. Then I'll be happy. I have to help him.

"Don't put me in jail. I haven't done one thing wrong until now. I've looked after my poor parents as best I could. No! You can't throw me in jail. You can't! For twenty-four years I've tried my hardest, and just this once I made one stupid little mistake with one straying hand. You can't ruin these twenty-four years—my whole life, for that. It's wrong.

Why should you think I'm a thief simply because once in my life my right hand moved twelve inches without thinking? It's too much. It's just too much! One slip—a matter of a few seconds.

"I'm still young. I have a lifetime ahead of me. I can see it stretching in front of me—exactly the same sort of life I've been leading till now. Just the same. I haven't changed at all. I'm the same Sakiko I was yesterday. What trouble did I cause Daimaru's with this stupid swimsuit? There are crooks around who extort one or two thousand yen from people— no, worse than that, an entire fortune—and yet they're admired for it, aren't they? Who are the prisons for? Only the poor go to jail. I feel sorry for thieves. Thieves are just harmless little people, too weak and honest to go out and cheat other people so they can live in comfort. So they get backed into a corner, steal something worth two or three yen, and end up in jail for five to ten years. My God! It's grotesque. Crazy! I mean it: really crazy!"

I think I must have been insane then. The policeman had turned pale, and was looking at me speechless. Suddenly, I felt I really rather liked him. Through my hysterical tears, I made an effort to smile at him. He must have thought I was a lunatic. He escorted me to the central police station with great care, as if he were handling a bomb. I was kept in custody that night in the detention ward. The following morning my father came to pick me up, and I was released. All he asked me on the way home—and very timidly at that—was whether I had been beaten while I was there. He said nothing else the rest of the way.

I blushed to my ears when I saw the newspaper that evening. I was in the headlines: "ELOQUENT SPEECH MADE BY YOUNG DEGENERATE LEFT-WING WOMAN." That wasn't the end of my disgrace. Neighbors loitered near the house. I didn't know what it meant at first, but I soon realized that they were trying to get a glimpse of me and see how I was doing. It made me tremble. Gradually I began to understand how serious my small offense really was. I would have taken poison without hesitation had any been available; I would have gone and calmly hanged myself had there been a bamboo grove nearby. We closed the shop for a few days.

Before long I received a letter from Mr. Mizuno. It read as follows:

I believe in you, Sakiko, more than anybody in the world. But you lack a proper upbringing. You are an honest woman, but in some respects you are not quite upright. I tried to correct that part of you, but I failed. Individuals must be educated. I went swimming with a friend of mine the other day, and on the beach we talked for a long time about ambition. We were sure that we would eventually be successful.

Please behave yourself from now on and try, even in some small way, to atone for your crime by apologizing to society. We condemn the sin but not the sinner.

Mizuno Saburō

P.S. Be sure to burn this letter and its envelope after you read it.

That was the entire content of his letter. I suppose I had forgotten that his family had once been wealthy.

Days passed. I felt I was sitting on a bed of needles. It is now approaching early fall. Father said that he was depressed because the light in our six-mat room was dim this evening, and he changed the bulb to one of fifty watts. Beneath the new light the three of us had dinner. Mother kept saying that it was far too bright. She shaded her forehead with the hand that held her chopsticks, and was very cheerful. I served Father saké, too.

Mentally, I tried to convince myself that, after all, this was the sort of thing we find happiness in—putting in a brighter light bulb. In fact, I didn't feel miserable at all. On the contrary, I thought that, in the light of this humble lamp, my family was like a magic lantern, and I felt like saying, "Well, take a look at us, if you please. We make quite an attractive family, my parents and I." A quiet joy welled up in my heart, and I wanted to let it be known, even if only to the insects chirping in the garden.

MOON GEMS

Ishikawa Jun

Translated by William J. Tyler

". . . The breezes that stir the pages of the novel are very different from the gusts of the mundane world." (Fugen.)

A native of Tokyo born in 1899, trained in French literature and accomplished as a translator of André Gide, Ishikawa Jun made his literary debut with the publication of the "récits" Kajin (The Beauty, 1935) and Fugen (The Bodhisattva, 1936), works that represent his satirization and rejection of the Japanese "I-novel" and, simultaneously, his desire to create a "roman" on the order that Gide envisioned in Les Faux-monnayeurs. Ishikawa's career can be viewed as his struggle to introduce the concepts of European modernism into Japanese prose fiction, to search for their literary and philosophical correspondences in the indigenous tradition, and to create what subsequently he called the jikken shōsetsu, or experimental novel. This was a task attempted unsuccessfully by other members of his generation, most notably Yokomitsu Riichi (1898–1947), and not fully achieved by Ishikawa himself until the 1950s when he began producing his most experimental works, Taka (Hawks, 1953), Shion monogatari (Asters, 1956; tr. 1961), Aratama (Wild Spirits, 1963) and Shifuku sennen (The Millennium, 1965). These novels are highly fantastic—Taka speaks of a mysterious language called futurese; in Shifuku sennen crypto-Christians exploit the chaos attendant on the arrival of Commodore Perry's black ships to bring the Apocalypse to Japan.

While one may be tempted to treat such works as purely fictional constructions, Ishikawa's novels also incorporate elements of literary parody

45

and satiric allegory. This is apparent from the all-important seriocomic tone of the writing, which is heavily influenced by Edo period literature, especially the mystification style (tōkaiburi) of the literati, or bunjin, of the Temmei era (1781–88). Unable to escape Japan during the war years, Ishikawa launched upon a course of inner emigration that he refers to as his "study abroad in Edo" (Edo ryūgaku). In the "mad verse" of Temmei kyōka poetry, and the covert criticism of society that the kyōka coteries practiced through the medium of pure play (asobi) and parody of the classics (mitate), he found in Japanese tradition the incipience of a style and movement analogous to European modernism and the inspiration for a form appropriate to the modernist Japanese novel.

The present work, "Meigetsushu" (Moon Gems, 1946), represents the genesis of Ishikawa's postwar experimental fiction. It looks back to the paro-dying techniques of Kajin and Fugen (the watashi-shōsetsu in contradistinc-tion to the watakushi-shōsetsu), yet moves toward greater fictionalization and more fantastic treatment of the material. It is also a paean to Ishikawa's literary mentors, namely, the bunjin tradition that flourished in the Tem-mei era. This tradition was transmitted to twentieth-century Japanese let-ters chiefly by Nagai Kafū (1879-1959), who appears in the story as Mr. Gūka, "the Lotus," a play on Kafū's sobriquet of "Lotus Breeze." Gūka's "Liaison House" (Renkeikan) is also a play on the name of Kafū's Azabu residence, Henkikan or "Eccentricity House," which was destroyed in the bombing raid of March 1945. Like Ishikawa's short story, "Marusu no uta" (I Hear the War God Singing, 1938) which was banned by the military authorities, "Moon Gems" is a poignant allegory describing the tension be-tween aspiration and despair in the life of a writer who would defy his times but lacks the means to effect active and meaningful resistance.

Ishikawa's most recent novel is Kyōfūki (Record of a Mad Wind, 1980). Although too difficult a stylist to be a popular writer, Ishikawa has been the recipient of the Akutagawa Prize (1937) and other distinguished literary awards. Because of his singular erudition in Chinese, Japanese and Western literature, he is often referred to as "the last of the literati." Of late his experimental fiction has frequently been compared in the Japanese press with that of Nabokov and Borges.

New Year's Day, 1945. I rose early and went into the city to a certain Hachiman Shrine. I went to greet the new year and to receive a lucky arrow as a souvenir. As I stood in the crowd before the shrine and was bathed in the light of the rising sun spreading across the cold, windy sky, I composed a crude *kyōka* verse.

Though their gabled peaks
Are enshrouded in the mists
Of the New Year,
As ever I entrust
The sum of my hopes to the gods.

I returned to my lodgings at the edge of the city and stuck the arrow in the strip of molding that ran along the upper half of the room. Together with the three branches of holiday green that earlier I had arranged in a cheap vase, it became my sole concession to the new year in an otherwise drab bachelor apartment. Nursing my government ration of saké, I yielded once again to the temptation to compose another dubious *kyōka* poem—in honor of the saké, said to dispel all care with the sweep of its "jeweled broom," and the *senryō*, the holiday green which, bearing its felicitous red berries in the dead of winter, is worth a "thousand *ryō*."

Sweet elixir of the jeweled broom
And holiday green bedecked in red,
T'is a *senryō* spring,
And its light pours forth, glittering
Like a thousand thin pieces of hammered gold.

No doubt the great *kyōka* poets would chuckle at my feeble imitations of their famous Temmei style. My visit to the shrine, and the receipt of a lucky arrow, had been a matter of whimsy; and I had felt no need to celebrate simply because today was the beginning of a new year. Yet I was possessed of a secret longing and wished to secure for it a propitious resolve. The desire? I am under no obligation to keep it secret: I longed

47

to learn to ride a bicycle, and the sooner the better. It was in December that I conceived the idea of taking bike lessons, and I was determined to proceed with my plan.

By nature I am disposed to the quick and convenient although there is nothing about my person even vaguely suggestive of agility. My hands move only to let a ball tossed gently my way fall to the ground. Let a trolley stop across the street and my legs will not carry me the few yards to board it in time. Given this state of affairs, I must admit that I had little hope of initiating any movement that might prove equal to the harsh realities of our times. My profession too is devised to eliminate the need for nimble hands and feet, and so it has been my destiny to let them content themselves with inactivity.

Indeed, were one to seek the mathematical equivalent of this thing I call myself, it would be an exercise in the calculation of the square root of minus one. I think of myself as not inhabiting the face of the earth but rather a space one foot under, living in shame yet loath to abandon it. I know that I must rise, cast off this ignominy, and crawl out upon the ground, there to climb to the height of a single foot and make my mad dash through the reality that impinges on us all.

Were this longing ever to assume some concrete form, nothing would suit my needs better than the self-propelled mechanism of a bicycle. I could at least manage the cost of a used one; it would require no gasoline, and it ought to be relatively easy to operate since bikes are also ridden by women and children. What is more, the fulfillment of my wish lay readily at hand. I had only to obtain the bike and, with a contemptuous look over my shoulder at the crowded commuter trains, be off to negotiate the city. Moreover—the benefits are too many to enumerate—by and by my small coup might attract a particle of attention and lead to the desired movement. . . My heart leaped at the thought, but I had yet to master the rudiments of the vehicle.

Some time ago a friend gave me a letter of introduction to a certain corporation. He felt that I had a role to play in what he called "the essential business of the day." His intentions were well meant, and I rejoiced at this stroke of luck. Thinking that at last I had found a way out of the snake hole in which I lived, I set out one day late last year to call upon a gentleman who held an important post in the company.

It would be more correct to say that what I met was not the man but his boots. As he lounged in his chair with one leg extended casually over the other, the room was so overwhelmed by his pair of spit-polished, ox-blood red leather boots—so tight-fitting as not to show a single crease, so spanking new as to still reek of a live steer—that the man's face, poor fellow, seemed disproportionately small and insignificant, as though it had been relegated to the back of the room.

Admittedly, there was good cause for my being impressed by a pair of boots. For what I coveted second only to a bicycle was a fine pair of boots. Need I recite the litany of their praises? When the air raid siren goes off in the night, how much simpler it would to ease one's feet into a pair of boots rather than fumbling in the dark with puttees and getting them on inside out. Or, rather than cringing in the shadows and tiptoeing along a thief-infested street in an ordinary pair of shoes, imagine how boldly one could strut about in boots! Besides, boots are essential footgear for bicycles. They look stylish, and one pedals better. There need be no fear of brushing against objects along the way and scraping an ankle.

It may sound extravagant of me to speak of boots, however, when I have yet to attempt the bicycle. I shall content myself with a pair of plain, even slightly faded, black leather boots . . . although that too is a dream I only halfheartedly believe will materialize. But now that the man's boots appeared on the scene to make sport of the unprepossessing pair that I had only dreamed of owning, I ceased to recall what errand had brought me to his office in the first place. There was nothing for it but to submit to the beautiful shine of his boots, however intimidating that might be.

The résumé examined by the face at the far end of the boots was virtually blank. There was but one line to record, and that to distinguish me from the ranks of the unemployed and uncouth. It was a candid statement of my abilities that read, presumptuous as it may sound, "writer by trade." It did not appear to help the man much. The operation of the firm was divided, he said, between those who handled goods and those who moved papers, and his manner suggested that he would find a way to work me into the latter.

"No," I replied, "I'd appreciate being put in merchandising. That's why I've come." I was quite sincere. I wanted nothing to do with paperwork and its blurring profusion of figures and letters.

"Training in the business end of our firm," he said patiently, "begins with recruits of seventeen and eighteen years of age."

"But couldn't you let me do their work?"

No sooner had I asked my question than there flashed before my eyes the sight of young boys dashing about the city proudly conducting company business on their bicycles! Had I known how to ride a bicycle I might have pressed my case, but I felt a twinge of embarrassment, and it seemed to have crept into my voice. My request sounded weak.

It was then that "Boots" cut me to the quick.

"Can you ride a bicycle?"

His tone was pleasant enough, but he emitted a crude chortle as though he pitied me. He was every inch a man dressed in boots, and possessed a sharp, discerning eye. I was too devastated to speak. I blushed and backed from the room.

Thus the search for a job undertaken so lightheartedly came to an abrupt end after a three-minute interview. I had spoiled the goodwill of a friend, wasted three minutes of this man's busy day; and, in seeking the favor of both and pleasing neither, I had put myself to a great deal of trouble. I felt obliged to remonstrate with myself since this wretched state of affairs was due solely to my inability to ride a bicycle. As long as the bicycle eluded me, I was destined to similar failure should I in a nervous moment decide to crawl out of my hole and seek refuge in the "essential business of the day." The repetition of this failure would only deepen my shame and entomb me forever one foot underground. How unhygienic that would be!

As for lessons of any sort, the younger the age at which one starts the better. And how much more so for operations requiring physical dexterity. To be quite honest, I have reached an age that can hardly be called young . . . and a state in which, having inevitably started down the path that links physical time and the human life-span, I am helpless to reverse matters. Yet inasmuch as I am able to tie my obi and walk on two feet, it is imperative that I mount a bicycle without further delay.

Today, namely, New Year's Day, is the occasion of my first lesson.

To the rear of my lodgings is a small vacant lot. There one used bike and an instructor await me. The one who is to instruct me is a little girl who lives in the neighborhood.

"*Ojisan*, where are you? Aren't you ready yet?"

I can hear her voice outside the window. She has called me two or three times now.

I hurry to finish my saké and, pulling on my tired puttees and worn-out tennis shoes, I rise.

In a moment like this, who has time for comic verse?

Those familiar with the layout of the older, densely built-up sections of downtown Tokyo will recall how, if one followed the covers of the drainage ditches along a back alley, at the point where the alley narrowed and appeared to dead-end, one might discover a large vacant lot. These lots were often quite extensive in size, like those used by dyers for stretching kimono cloth. Today they can be found only in a few neighborhoods on the edge of the city. The back lot of which I speak, while not a dyer's lot, is one of the few remaining.

It did not appear to belong to anyone, and it saw little human traffic except in the hot summer months when a Sumo ring was improvised and the children of the neighborhood came for wrestling practice in the evenings. Thus it was a lively spot until the coming of autumn. At this time of year, however, the ring had been plowed under, and small fox-holes had been dug as bomb shelters alongside the vegetable patch planted by the neighborhood patriotic association. There was adequate space to practice riding a bicycle, and the plowing had the salutary effect of softening the earth along the edges so that one was unlikely to injure oneself in a fall.

My lodgings were at the back of the east end, and a small cliff overshadowed the lot to the south. To the north was the alley that led to the street where the trolleys ran; to the west, the back doors of the seven or eight houses engaged in the businesses that fronted on the main street. The bicycle shop was one of them.

The shop had long ceased operation, and its proprietor, now a civilian conscriptee, commuted each morning to an armaments plant located on the Chūō Line. All that remained in his shop was two used bikes. The fact that I was allowed to borrow one was due to the largess of this man who, despite his nearly fifty years, looked healthier and heavier—one wonders why—than the rest of us. Although the bike would have been better described as dilapidated rather than used, its age and rickety condition made it all the more serviceable for my purposes as a beginner. The owner and I agreed that, once I had mastered it, he would let the bike go—"at a special discount"—in monthly installments of ten yen. One could not have asked for a better bargain. Moreover, he had a daughter, aged sixteen; it was she who volunteered to take me as her pupil.

A spiteful person seeking to find fault with this child, innocent by nature and soft of limb, might have detected that her right leg appeared a fraction shorter than her left. She was not handicapped, although certain boors in the neighborhood complained about her being too lame to be inducted into the civilian girls' work corps.

Admittedly she dragged her right leg when she attempted to run, but the limp was scarcely noticeable and did not seem to trouble her in the least. Once she mounted the bicycle, her forte, she would throw her hands in the air and, like a cherry petal fluttering upon the breeze, go round and round, cutting smaller and smaller circles on the ground. She had the poise of an equestrienne. Those who have watched her ride would agree that the bicycle was her true set of legs.

A description of the events of that first lesson on New Year's Day brings no honor to my name. The girl's instruction was thorough and without fault. But since I was new to the task, I spent much of the time sprawling on the ground rather than mounted on the seat. The vehicle disdained me as a beginner and, no matter how often I rose undaunted by a spill—or how much I attempted, first, to mollify it or, growing impatient, to conquer it by force—it dumped me on the ground like so much unwanted furniture. I was at a loss to deal with its stubborn frame which would not yield to my entreaties. I perspired. My clothes became muddied. My hands were scraped and cut. At times I collapsed struggling to catch my breath. And, as if that were only the beginning of my torture, from every quarter of the neighborhood came children, forming a circle around me and greeting my every fall with noisy shouts of glee.

There were so many that one wondered where they had been hiding. A Frenchman I once knew would throw his arms into the air and shout, "Des gosses, des gosses," when exclaiming about the hordes of children that descended on him wherever he traveled in Japan.

Likewise, on this day a considerable number gathered, even though many children had already been evacuated to the countryside. Their presence was unwelcome, but the final blow came when the little girl on whom I relied also joined their ranks and, joyfully clapping her hands, made fun of me. She grabbed the bike and, letting her foot glide over the crossbar, began to ride. In her hands the recalcitrant machine seemed to breathe new life and went round and round as it was directed. I lifted my weary body from the ground and brushed the dirt from my clothes.

"Enough for today. Enough, enough. . ."

I persevered with the lessons, however. I went to practice in the back lot whenever the weather permitted. But my clumsiness persisted and I made no progress. The bicycle continued to make sport of me, but at least I mastered the art of falling without injury and suffered less.

As for the children, they soon stopped coming. The weather was cold, and their interest waned. Occasionally, one of their parents passed through the lot, but the adults were always in a hurry and they gave no heed to my lessons. The little girl patiently taught me the fundamentals of the art but, since she was under no obligation to stay continually by my side, I spent many hours struggling with the bicycle by myself.

Confronted alone, the bicycle assumed a sinister, almost lethal, air, and as I spat the dirt from my mouth, I knew that I was engaged in a life-and-death struggle. I had ceased to understand the purpose of spending an hour of each bright morning with it, or why I had originally imposed this task on myself. What I did know was that this hour had encroached upon the time I once spent sleeping, spread large upon my bed, and that it was propelling me in the direction of violent, almost murderous action. I would forget all else until I fell to the ground exhausted.

Ludicrous as my behavior may have seemed to an outsider, the back lot was a quiet place removed from the clamor of the world and I felt little embarrassment in practicing there. Although the lot served as a shortcut to the top of the cliff to the south, the north wind whipped across it and no one darkened the path where withered bamboo grass clung to the frozen and exposed earth. No one, that is, except an old man who appeared from time to time on the path atop the cliff.

Though I say old, there was nothing remotely old-fashioned about him. He walked tall, his back erect, a soft black felt hat making his silky white hair seem youthful. He wore a great black coat over what appeared to be the fine black tweeds that had been available before the war. On his feet were a pair of low clogs looking very worn. At times he carried an umbrella; at others, a Kodak leather bag, as he strode briskly through the dry grass. For the moment, I need only identify this elderly gentleman as Mr. Gūka, "the Lotus."

Gūka is a poet of great renown. His residence is located five or six neighborhoods away, at the end of a quiet lane. He calls it "Liaison House." Even the most common of men, who may know nothing of what Gūka has accomplished in poetry in the last decades, have heard the rumors about the Parnassian existence of the owner of this mansion—of how, loath to waste even a word of vituperation upon the sleazy claims of our society, he sealed his gates and refused categorically the traffic of the mundane. I too rank among the common lot who have heard them. Lacking any true profession, I have maintained appearances by proclaiming myself a "writer by trade," but all that I have authored is of questionable value, totally and completely; and since I am congenitally given to laziness and am no more than an impoverished dilettante, too indolent to rouse myself for a trip to a library to peruse Gūka's works, I have been content with knowing him secondhand. As the world would have it, the Lotus lives alone and is said to be engaged in the composition of a work to be kept from the eyes of men. He handles his own daily chores and, on the occasions when some philistine wanders beyond the gate, trespassing upon his yard, it is Gūka who goes to the door and sends him away with the words, "The Lotus is not at home."

If indeed this is his wont, I would not presume to peek through the trellis or tread the perilous space before his door, even though I live nearby; nor have I the curiosity. Whenever he has come my way on the street, I have expressed my respect inwardly. I have never addressed him nor been so frivolous as to doff my cap. We have never met, and on his constitutionals he has passed unaware of my lessons in the vacant lot at the bottom of the cliff, just as I have continued them with blithe unconcern for his opinions.

One matter troubles me, however. It relates not to Gūka's poetry but his clogs. I have heard that in better days he paid meticulous attention to the details of his dress and insisted that clogs be worn only with kimono. No chronology of an artist's life would gloss over the point at which he switched to wearing clogs with Western attire, but my random guess is that this innovation is of recent origin and that it is indicative of a sudden increase in Gūka's spiritual energies. As his clothes faded, and the clogs became chewed and worn, he began to move forward—in the area of literature at least—at a pace equal to the speed of light. At first the combination of a suit and clogs belonged to the realm of eccentric dress, and no doubt the world has had its laugh at his expense, but today fashion runs far behind, breathless in an effort to catch up with the tracks of Gūka's clogs. One can never be too vigilant, given the speed with which poets advance.

But as for myself, his junior, I run still further behind a world that lags behind him. I have only begun to take bicycle lessons and distantly approach the mastery already achieved by a child of sixteen. I feel profoundly ashamed of myself.

And yet, despite there being virtually no correlation between my existence and Gūka's, one could perhaps claim that the relationship between his clogs and my bicycle is not entirely tenuous. The course that he has run in a decade, I must compress into a few hours.

There is a Chinese maxim to the effect that cold and impoverishment make a man brilliant and agile. As for being cold and poor I have no peers; but, as for brilliance and agility, I have no confidence whatsoever. . . Were there a saying that cold impoverishment makes a man weary and ignorant, how appropriate it would be for me!

As I stood beneath the cliff and gazed at Gūka, was it merely false pride, the inability to admit defeat, that prompted me to say, "Damn you, Gūka"? From time to time I raised my eyes and studied the master of Liaison House. Was it an illusion? Did he stop and look down at me? Perhaps there is a link between us after all.

Yet, while his clogs fly across the face of the earth like the eight swift stallions of Emperor Mu Wang of the Chou, my bicycle has not described an arc even a yard wide. To close the gap between us, I needed to extemporize and, in my limited way, I conceived a plan of action. It was extremely simple: deep breathing exercises in the morning.

On the days when I awoke early, I would go outside at dawn and aerate my lungs. The little girl was asleep, and Gūka had yet to appear. I alone possessed the back lot. The city lay darkly frozen in the cold light of morning sunrise. As though to warm the very core of my body in their eastern light, the clouds swelled in the sky and gradually turned a bright, flaming red. Catching the wind as it whipped at me, I threw out my chest and took a deep breath.

There arose out of the dawning sky three stripes of blue, white and red which resembled neither wind nor light and which intertwined as they raced across the sky and, as though thrown with deliberate aim, poured into my mouth. No sooner had their cold seared my tongue and entered my lungs than my body became cool, and the impatience and irritation within me seemed to issue from the soles of my feet. This is what is known in the Chinese art of wizardry as *tai-su nei ching*, the Inner View of the Great Principle. What had I gained? My body became lighter, a most convenient state for a cyclist. For me, still unschooled in this Taoist art, the experience lasted only a few moments. But in that instant I had my sextant, so to speak, and by setting it I was able not only to learn how Gūka had made his dash through terrestrial time but to measure the agility with which the little girl rode.

Chance yielded yet another discovery. I happened upon the practice of riding my bicycle late at night.

These were the hours when the world lay asleep, though men seldom rested lightly upon their pillows. When the sirens wailed I too would kick back the covers and jump, winding on my puttees in the dark (no doubt inside out), and with fireman's ax in hand rush outside to crack the ice in the rainwater barrels. If the raid ended without mishap, instead of crawling back into bed I went to the lot and practiced riding my bike. I seemed to do it somehow better then, and would deceive myself into thinking that in fifteen minutes I had compensated for an hour of useless effort during the day.

One needed moonlight to practice at night, and for the first time I discovered how bright the moon can be. There is a famous *kyōka* verse in which the poet suggests that a man "dare not ask" (*mōshikane*) of life more than a full rice bowl and a moonlit night—only to add, in a facetious play on words, that "perhaps money" (*mōshi kane*) might also be desirable. Leaving the matter of money aside, there was not a soul living at the time who did not offer thanks for a bowl of rice and a moonlit night. Houses were blacked out early in the evening, the darkness so thick that one stumbled to find a foxhole.

One night, after rising from a brief sleep, I stepped outside to find that the moon had risen and the back lot was flooded with light. The old bicycle seemed rejuvenated. Even the spots where the black paint had chipped away shone with the look of the original lacquer and, while the chrome fixtures seemed icy enough to freeze and snag off a finger, I was reassured by the glitter and sparkle playing about the handlebars. I reached for them and pulled myself onto the saddle.

As I rode, the wheels streamed round and round like sprays of water circulating in a fountain. They spun and gained momentum until before long I began to wonder where the bike would carry me. Iridescent stones! Moon gems! How rare they are! The jewels I held in the small grip of my hands were shards of pure moonlight that fell upon the handlebars. How wonderful it would be to master this bicycle . . . at least half as well as the little girl . . . faster . . . one fraction of a second faster . . . it's been misery struggling with you, bicycle . . . let me ride smoothly, gracefully, naturally . . . we're no longer here . . . but long, long ago . . . once upon a time . . . even a poet from the West was warning . . . "Nothing is more likely to propel us headlong down the path to barbarism than a singleminded application to the concept of spiritual purity. . ."

"*Ojisan*, hold on. Hold on tight."

To my surprise my instructor had come into the lot and was calling me from behind. She urged me on. I felt so confident. Going round and round . . . round and round . . . unless one hand lost its balance . . . no, no . . . and I was dumped on the ground with a thud.

We had a great deal of snow this year; seldom was a winter as cold. Moreover, there were numerous fires; the heavens were often enveloped in flame. In spite of my determination, it was not possible to continue my lessons each night. January and February came and went and, by the beginning of March, I had grown accustomed to the bike. Physical object though it was, it came to treat me with more consideration. I reached the point where I could ride with no hands. As long as I maintained my balance, I managed to stay aboard for nearly an hour.

Moreover, the bike was in the process of becoming my own. I had spoken with the bicycle man and, in line with our earlier agreement, it would be mine for monthly installments of ten yen. I made my first payment on the first of March. According to him, I also needed to pay an additional ten yen each month for maintenance, which indicates how antiquated the bicycle was. It was the only conveyance I possessed, and I did not dare suggest that it was unworthy of the additional cost.

One night that first week of March, the wind blew hard as the hour grew late and, at the height of the gale, the air raid sirens began to whir. The neighbors jumped from their beds. We cultivated a sixth sense about such matters, and this did not seem a typical drill. A crowd had gathered by the time I reached the lot, and everyone was hard at work preparing for an attack. Belongings were carried into the air raid shelter and piled in a heap. The radio crackled in the driving wind. A fire hose stretched across the ground and a hand pump had been readied.

The horizon turned bright red above the city and, as we watched, the fire spread, narrowing the distance between us and the flames. We could see it dancing madly out of control as it was flailed by the wind. Nor were the flames confined to the city by now. Pockets of fire broke out to the right and left of us. The sky was filled with an ominous light, making the faces of those gathered at the shelter, and even the colors of our clothes, quite distinct. Sparks twirled about our heads.

I walked back to the rear door of my lodgings where I usually parked my bicycle, and stood ready to defend the building. The fire buckets were filled with water. I had no family heirlooms to remove from my room. Besides, I assured myself that the nearby flames would not spread within our reach. Preventive measures would work and the fire be confined to a small area. Still, it was too soon to relax one's guard.

Suddenly I realized that the little girl was standing next to me. She had stolen up from behind and, leaning on the seat, let the bike press against me. She said nothing as she looked deep into the sky. Although she seemed unafraid, what vague foreboding caused her shoulders to tremble slightly? It was then that I fully understood for the first time that her right leg was not normal. She was no longer the little girl who rode the bicycle with the greatest of ease but a pitiful young lady who would go through life handicapped by a bad limp.

I forgot my usual ineptitude and resolved then and there that should a crisis ever arise I was prepared to sacrifice to the flames the only real possession I had in this world, namely, the collection of rare and used books that I kept in my apartment. To save this child, I would put her on my bicycle and ride to the ends of the earth.

Fortunately there was no need to carry out this resolve. The fires in the vicinity were extinguished by daybreak, and our quarter had not reported a single casualty. That the color in the sky above the city gradually paled and died out was not due solely to the breaking of the dawn. The flames were dying out. I heaved a sigh of relief at the thought that the fire fighters had been victorious.

"We've won, *ojisan*, we've won. I promise to give you another lesson," shouted the little girl as she ran toward her house. Her step was smooth and self-assured; she had reverted to being the little acrobat of the bicycle.

"What's this?" I thought. "Doesn't she realize how worried I was about her?" I raised my hand in the air as though to bless her as she ran.

"Yes, we've won. I'll ask you again soon."

I returned to my room and collapsed on the floor. I had not meant to fall asleep, but it was nearly noon when I awoke. The neighborhood seemed changed. The sky had cleared but the air made one feel irritated and nervous. The relief I had felt at daybreak disappeared, and an indescribable anxiety swept over me. I could not bear to sit still and, going out, I grabbed the bike. Of its own accord it headed in the direction of the city and the shrine I had visited on New Year's Day.

This was my first excursion. Never would I have believed it would occur on a day like this and, lost in thought, I sped along untroubled by the mechanics of the bike's operation, pedaling madly in my old tennis shoes.

I had yet to obtain a pair of boots. Perhaps it was for the best. All my dreams would have been fulfilled, and I would no longer have known what to do with myself.

Presently I found myself in the vicinity of the shrine. I cannot remember in detail what I saw either there or along the way. Nor would I have wished to. The shrine had been obliterated. There will never be a *kyōka* verse appropriate to it again.

Hurriedly, I retraced the route I had traveled. As I entered the lodging house I realized that my clothes were covered with a thick layer of gray dust. I grabbed a brush, and, standing in the doorway, began to beat the dust from my shoulders. I choked on the odor that filled the air.

A scene floated before my eyes. It was not the scene I had witnessed along the road to the city. It was from a passage I had read long ago in a book . . . a description of the cremation grounds at Toribeno in Kyoto. Larks danced in the sky and the spring sun shone brightly, but columns of smoke drifted slowly from the pyres in the fields and an acrid smell hovered over the grasses and mingled with the shimmering heat. That was the smell that permeated my clothing. I stopped and, letting the brush drop listlessly to my side, fell into a wooden silence. My sadness knew no bounds.

I became anxious about the welfare of Mr. Gūka and his mansion. On my way into the city I had passed along the street that ran behind his house and, relieved to see everything in order, I had not troubled myself about his welfare. But hadn't flames shot up the previous night from the area in which he lived? The property may have appeared safe from the rear, but wasn't it possible that the front had been hit? I turned and started out again, this time on foot. I climbed the path running from the back lot to the summit of the cliff and took a shortcut through the adjoining neighborhoods. My feet hurried along only to come to a grinding halt. The quarter visible from the top of the cliff, the quarter where Gūka's mansion was located, had been leveled.

I walked amidst the ruins. Before the now nonexistent house, at what appeared to be the remainder of a gatepost, I stood on its small threshold stone.

Night was beginning to fall, and the dull light of the sun gave the whole area the look of a ravine bottom. Here and there victims of the air raid had fire hooks and were turning over the smoldering ash in an effort to salvage what they could. There was no sign of Gūka.

An elderly woman was sifting through the rubble that lay behind

Gūka's mansion. From time to time she looked up, as though aware of someone standing absentmindedly in the distance. Eventually she approached and, as though inviting an explanation, she studied my face in silence.

"This was Mr. Gūka's residence, wasn't it?" I said.

"Yes. As you can see, it burned down."

"What happened to him? . . ."

"He's safe. He escaped in time."

"I see. And his possessions?"

No sooner had I asked my question than I was embarrassed by its irrelevance. Her reply was firm, as though to emphasize her point.

"No, Mr. Gūka was not the type to bother with his belongings. This section was the last to burn but, even if there had been time, he wasn't the type to bother. He carried out a manuscript wrapped in a cloth bundle, and that was all. He walked to that small rise across the way and watched the house burn. He stood there until it burned to the ground. Until about dawn. He watched it to the end."

I knew nothing about the old woman but I found her direct and articulate manner refreshing. At the same time it reinforced my feeling that my question had been quite frivolous. There was nothing more to say.

"Toward morning a party came for him. I'm a neighbor and have known him for years. You know that he lived alone and was a quiet, retiring sort. When finally he got ready to leave, there was a little bread in the house, and since I know he is partial to bread, and I even had a little butter, I gave it to him. He was delighted. I expect he will return tomorrow."

I was no longer concentrating on what the old woman said. Instead there arose before my eyes the vision of a man stripped of everything but his manuscript, standing on the rise, blown by intemperate winds, bathed in a shower of sparks and quietly watching his house collapse in flames. I sought to capture in my mind this vision of a great poet, old but undaunted.

If a man draws a bow, let him draw it boldly. The bow that Gūka has drawn in the belles-lettres of our day is no ordinary one.

I thanked the old woman as I turned to leave.

That evening I went to the vacant lot and, wiping my bike clean of the dust that had collected on it earlier in the day, I gave it a polishing. Although the hour was early, the neighborhood was quieter than usual. The houses had turned off their lights and closed out the world. It appeared that the little girl would not be joining me tonight. The heat of the flames that had ravaged the city still hung in the air, but the moon rose in the sky, bathing the back lot in a cool, white light.

The mad winds had ceased to blow. The days were getting warmer. Had life been otherwise, we would have counted the days until the cherries blossomed. Polishing the bike bolstered my spirits, and I composed in my mind a *kyōka* which I entitled "Love Song for a Bicycle."

Although the bike ought not to have responded to polishing, at length it began to acquire a small shine. Perhaps it was the brightness of the moon. Instead of parking the bike under the eaves once I had finished my work, I straddled the seat and began to glide about the lot. In a single breath I rounded it six times, cutting a sweeping arc across the earth.

My movements were light and supple, as after doing deep breathing exercises in the morning. I had finally got the hang of it.

To tell the truth, my infatuation with the bicycle had begun to wane even as the machine was about to become my own.

If someone were to express a genuine desire for an old, used bike, I would be ready to make a present of it.

THE MAGIC CHALK

Abe Kōbō

Translated by Alison Kibrick

Abe Kōbō (1924–) was born in Tokyo, but he spent virtually all his youth on the outskirts of the great Manchurian deserts, an experience that in one critic's view has shaped his shifting conception of reality. Mishima Yukio once described Abe's fiction as being particularly low in the "humidity" content of most Japanese literature, and it is indeed as an author totally detached from his environment that contemporary Japanese readers understand his writings. Abe's defenders in Japan and the West consider him their only "international" author, by which they mean a writer free of essentially all the features that distinguish him as peculiarly Japanese. It has been suggested, in fact, that the Japanese language itself is an unsuitable medium for Abe—that he might be more at home writing in katakana, the phonetic syllabary designed for a hybrid vocabulary that is neither completely foreign nor completely integrated into native Japanese discourse.

Abe first attracted attention in Japan as the creator of avant-garde stories that were part Kafka, part scientific rationalism, part absurdism and part science fiction. Stories such as "Mahō no chōku" (translated here) and "Akai mayu" (Red Cocoon, 1950; tr. 1966) are based on logically absurd premises described with the most detailed and convincing logic, a mixture of Abe's training in medical school and an unrestrained literary imagination. While many of Abe's techniques and motifs can be traced to common roots in both Japanese and Western writing, the seriousness with which he ap-

63

proaches the nonsense of his narratives has proved intriguing to readers throughout the world.

Abe's most important novel, Suna no onna (The Woman in the Dunes, tr. 1964), appeared in 1962. Since its publication, he has struggled in a number of directions to expand or alter the vision he proposed in that renowned work. He has, in addition, turned to active participation in the theater, forming his own acting studio and producing his own scripts, often adaptations of his early stories. His best-known play is Tomodachi (Friends, 1967; tr. 1969), which received the Tanizaki Prize for literature. Most recently, Abe published a new novel after a seven-year silence in the genre: Hakobune Sakura-maru (The Ark Sakura-maru, 1984).

*   *   *

Next door to the toilet of an apartment building on the edge of the city, in a room soggy with roof leaks and cooking vapors, lived a poor artist named Argon.

The small room, nine feet square, appeared to be larger than it was because it contained nothing but a single chair set against the wall. His desk, shelves, paint box, even his easel had been sold for bread. Now only the chair and Argon were left. But how long would these two remain?

Dinnertime drew near. "How sensitive my nose has become!" Argon thought. He was able to distinguish the colors and proximity of the complex aromas entering his room. Frying pork at the butcher's along the streetcar line: yellow ocher. A southerly wind drifting by the front of the fruit stand: emerald green. Wafting from the bakery: stimulating chrome yellow. And the fish the housewife below was broiling, probably mackerel: sad cerulean blue.

The fact is, Argon hadn't eaten anything all day. With a pale face, a wrinkled brow, an Adam's apple that rose and fell, a hunched back, a sunken abdomen, and trembling knees, Argon thrust both hands into his pockets and yawned three times in succession.

His fingers found a stick in his pocket.

"Hey, what's this? Red chalk. Don't remember it being there."

Playing with the chalk between his fingers, he produced another large yawn.

"Aah, I need something to eat."

Without realizing it, Argon began scribbling on the wall with the chalk. First, an apple. One that looked big enough to be a meal in itself. He drew a paring knife beside it so that he could eat it right away. Next, swallowing hard as baking smells curled through the hallway and window to permeate his room, he drew bread. Jam-filled bread the size of a baseball glove. Butter-filled rolls. A loaf as large as a person's head. He envisioned glossy browned spots on the bread. Delicious-looking cracks, dough bursting through the surface, the intoxicating aroma of yeast. Beside the bread, then, a stick of butter as large as a brick. He thought of drawing some coffee. Freshly brewed, steaming coffee. In a large, juglike cup. On a saucer, three matchbox-size sugar cubes.

"Damn it!" He ground his teeth and buried his face in his hands. "I've got to eat!"

Gradually his consciousness sank into darkness. Beyond the windowpane was a bread and pastry jungle, a mountain of canned goods, a sea of milk, a beach of sugar, a beef and cheese orchard—he scampered about until, fatigued, he fell asleep.

A heavy thud on the floor and the sound of smashing crockery woke him up. The sun had already set. Pitch black. Bewildered, he glanced toward the noise and gasped. A broken cup. The spilled liquid, still steaming, was definitely coffee, and near it were the apple, bread, butter, sugar, spoon, knife, and (luckily unbroken) the saucer. The pictures he had chalked on the wall had vanished.

"How could it. . . ?"

Suddenly every vein in his body was wide awake and pounding. Argon stealthily crept closer.

"No, no, it can't be. But look, it's real. Nothing fake about the smothering aroma of this coffee. And here, the bread is smooth to the touch. Be bold, taste it. Argon, don't you believe it's real even now? Yes, it's real. I believe it. But frightening. To believe it is frightening. And yet, it's real. It's edible!"

The apple tasted like an apple (a "snow" apple). The bread tasted like bread (American flour). The butter tasted like butter (same contents as the label on the wrapper—not margarine). The sugar tasted like sugar (sweet). Ah, they all tasted like the real thing. The knife gleamed, reflecting his face.

By the time he came to his senses, Argon had somehow finished eating and heaved a sigh of relief. But when he recalled why he had sighed like this, he immediately became confused again. He took the chalk in his fingers and stared at it intently. No matter how much he scrutinized it, he couldn't understand what he didn't understand. He decided to make sure by trying it once more. If he succeeded a second time, then he would have to concede that it had actually happened. He thought he would try to draw something different, but in his haste just drew another familiar-looking apple. As soon as he finished drawing, it fell easily from the wall. So this is real after all. A repeatable fact.

Joy suddenly turned his body rigid. The tips of his nerves broke through his skin and stretched out toward the universe, rustling like fallen leaves. Then, abruptly, the tension eased, and, sitting down on the floor, he burst out laughing like a panting goldfish.

"The laws of the universe have changed. My fate has changed, misfortune has taken its leave. Ah, the age of fulfillment, a world of desires realized. . . God, I'm sleepy. Well, then, I'll draw a bed. This chalk has become as precious as life itself, but a bed is something you always need after eating your fill, and it never really wears out, so no need to be miserly about it. Ah, for the first time in my life I'll sleep like a lamb."

One eye soon fell asleep, but the other lay awake. After today's contentment he was uneasy about what tomorrow might bring. However, the other eye, too, finally closed in sleep. With eyes working out of sync he dreamed mottled dreams throughout the night.

Well, this worrisome tomorrow dawned in the following manner.

He dreamed that he was being chased by a ferocious beast and fell off a bridge. He had fallen off the bed. . . No. When he awoke, there was no bed anywhere. As usual, there was nothing but that one chair. Then what had happened last night? Argon timidly looked around at the wall, tilting his head.

There, in red chalk, were drawings of a cup (it was broken!), a spoon, a knife, apple peel, and a butter wrapper. Below these was a bed—a picture of the bed off which he was supposed to have fallen.

Among all of last night's drawings, only those he could not eat had once again become pictures and returned to the wall. Suddenly he felt pain in his hip and shoulder. Pain in precisely the place he should feel it if he had indeed fallen out of bed. He gingerly touched the sketch of the bed where the sheets had been rumpled by sleep and felt a slight warmth, clearly distinguishable from the coldness of the rest of the drawing.

He brushed his finger along the blade of the knife picture. It was certainly nothing more than chalk; there was no resistance, and it disappeared leaving only a smear. As a test he decided to draw a new apple. It neither turned into a real apple and fell nor even peeled off like a piece of unglued paper, but rather vanished beneath his chafed palm into the surface of the wall.

His happiness had been merely a single night's dream. It was all over, back to what it was before anything had happened. Or was it really? No, his misery had returned fivefold. His hunger pangs attacked him fivefold. It seemed that all he had eaten had been restored in his stomach to the original substances of wall and chalk powder.

When he had gulped from his cupped hands a pint or so of water from the communal sink, he set out toward the lonely city, still enveloped in the mist of early dawn. Leaning over an open drain that ran from the kitchen of a restaurant about a hundred yards ahead, he thrust his hands into the viscous, tarlike sewage and pulled something out. It was a basket made of wire netting. He washed it in a small brook nearby. What was left in it seemed edible, and he was particularly heartened that half of it looked like rice. An old man in his apartment building had told him recently that by placing the basket in the drain one could obtain enough food for a meal a day. Just about a month ago the man had found the means to afford bean curd lees, so he had ceded the restaurant drain to the artist.

Recalling last night's feast, this was indeed muddy, unsavory fare. But it wasn't magic. What actually helped fill his stomach was precious and so could not be rejected. Even if its nastiness made him aware of every swallow, he must eat it. Shit. This was the real thing.

Just before noon he entered the city and dropped in on a friend who was employed at a bank. The friend smiled wryly and asked, "My turn today?"

Stiff and expressionless, Argon nodded. As always, he received half of his friend's lunch, bowed deeply and left.

For the rest of the day, Argon thought.

He held the chalk lightly in his hand, leaned back in the chair, and as he sat absorbed in his daydreams about magic, anticipation began to crystallize around that urgent longing. Finally, evening once again drew near. His hope that at sunset the magic might take effect had changed into near confidence.

Somewhere a noisy radio announced that it was five o'clock. He stood up and on the wall drew bread and butter, a can of sardines, and coffee, not forgetting to add a table underneath so as to prevent anything from falling and breaking as had occurred the previous night. Then he waited.

Before long darkness began to crawl quietly up the wall from the corners of the room. In order to verify the course of the magic, he turned on the light. He had already confirmed last night that electric light did it no harm.

The sun had set. The drawings on the wall began to fade, as if his vision had blurred. It seemed as if a mist was caught between the wall and his eyes. The pictures grew increasingly faint, and the mist grew dense. And soon, just as he had anticipated, the mist had settled into solid shapes—success! The contents of the pictures suddenly appeared as real objects.

The steamy coffee was tempting, the bread freshly baked and still warm.

"Oh! Forgot a can opener."

He held his left hand underneath to catch it before it fell, and, as he drew, the outlines took on material form. His drawing had literally come to life.

All of a sudden, he stumbled over something. Last night's bed "existed" again. Moreover, the knife handle (he had erased the blade with his finger), the butter wrapper, and the broken cup lay fallen on the floor.

After filling his empty stomach, Argon lay down on the bed.

"Well, what shall it be next? It's clear now that the magic doesn't work in daylight. Tomorrow I'll have to suffer all over again. There must be a simple way out of this. Ah, yes! a brilliant plan—I'll cover up the window and shut myself in darkness."

He would need some money to carry out the project. To keep out the sun required some objects that would not lose their substance when exposed to sunlight. But drawing money is a bit difficult. He racked his brains, then drew a purse full of money. . . The idea was a success, for when he opened up the purse he found more than enough bills stuffed inside.

This money, like the counterfeit coins that badgers made from tree leaves in the fairy tale, would disappear in the light of day, but it would leave no trace behind, and that was a great relief. He was cautious nonetheless and deliberately proceeded toward a distant town. Two heavy blankets, five sheets of black woolen cloth, a piece of felt, a box of nails, and four pieces of squared lumber. In addition, one volume of a cookbook collection that caught his eye in a secondhand bookstore along the way. With the remaining money he bought a cup of coffee, not in the least superior to the coffee he had drawn on the wall. He was (why?) proud of himself. Lastly, he bought a newspaper.

He nailed the door shut, then attached two layers of cloth and a blanket. With the rest of the material, he covered the window, and he blocked the edges with the wood. A feeling of security, and at the same time a sense of being attacked by eternity, weighed upon him. Argon's mind grew distant, and, lying down on the bed, he soon fell asleep.

Sleep neither diminished nor neutralized his happiness in the slightest. When he awoke, the steel springs throughout his body were coiled and ready to leap, full of life. A new day, a new time . . . tomorrow wrapped in a mist of glittering gold dust, and the day after tomorrow, and more and more overflowing armfuls of tomorrows were waiting expectantly. Argon smiled, overcome with joy. Now, at this very moment, everything, without any hindrance whatsoever, was waiting eagerly among myriad possibilities to be created by his own hand. It was a brilliant moment. But what, in the depths of his heart, was this faintly aching sorrow? It might have been the sorrow that God had felt just before Creation. Beside the muscles of his smile, smaller muscles twitched slightly.

Argon drew a large wall clock. With a trembling hand he set the clock precisely at twelve, determining at that moment the start of a new destiny.

He thought the room was a bit stuffy, so he drew a window on the wall facing the hallway. Hm, what's wrong? The window didn't materialize. Perplexed for a moment, he then realized that the window could not acquire any substance because it did not have an outside; it was not equipped with all the conditions necessary to make it a window.

"Well, then, shall I draw an outside? What kind of view would be nice? Shall it be the Alps or the Bay of Naples? A quiet pastoral scene wouldn't be bad. Then again, a primeval Siberian forest might be interesting." All the beautiful landscapes he had seen on postcards and in travel guides flickered before him. But he had to choose one from among them all, and he couldn't make up his mind. "Well, let's attend to pleasure first," he decided. He drew some whiskey and cheese and, as he nibbled, slowly thought about it.

The more he thought, the less he understood.

"This isn't going to be easy. It could involve work on a larger scale than anything I—or anyone—has ever tried to design. In fact, now that I think about it, it wouldn't do simply to draw a few streams and orchards, mountains and seas, and other things pleasing to the eye. Suppose I drew a mountain; it would no longer be just a mountain. What would be beyond it? A city? A sea? A desert? What kind of people would be living there? What kind of animals? Unconsciously I would be deciding those things. No, making this window a window is serious business. It involves the creation of a world. Defining a world with just a few lines. Would it be right to leave that to chance? No, the scene outside can't be casually drawn. I must produce the kind of picture that no human hand has yet achieved."

Argon sank into deep contemplation.

The first week passed in discontent as he pondered a design for a world of infinitude. Canvases once again lined his room, and the smell of turpentine hung in the air. Dozens of rough sketches accumulated in a pile. The more he thought, however, the more extensive the problem became, until finally he felt it was all too much for him. He thought he might boldly leave it up to chance, but in that case his efforts to create a new world would come to nothing. And if he merely captured accurately the inevitability of partial reality, the contradictions inherent in that reality would pull him back into the past, perhaps trapping him again in starvation. Besides, the chalk had a limited life-span. He had to capture the world.

The second week flew by in inebriation and gluttony.

The third week passed in a despair resembling insanity. Once again his canvases lay covered with dust, and the smell of oils had faded.

In the fourth week Argon finally made up his mind, a result of nearly total desperation. He just couldn't wait any longer. In order to evade the responsibility of creating with his own hand an outside for the window, he decided to take a great risk that would leave everything to chance.

"I'll draw a door on the wall. The outside will be decided by whatever is beyond the door. Even if it ends in failure, even if it turns out to be the same apartment scene as before, it'll be far better than being tormented by this responsibility. I don't care what happens, better to escape."

Argon put on a jacket for the first time in a long while. It was a ceremony in honor of the establishment of the world, so one couldn't say he was being extravagant. With a stiff hand he lowered the chalk of destiny. A picture of the door. He was breathing hard. No wonder. Wasn't the sight beyond the door the greatest mystery a man could contemplate? Perhaps death was awaiting him as his reward.

He grasped the knob. He took a step back and opened the door.

Dynamite pierced his eyes, exploding. After a while he opened them fearfully to an awesome wasteland glaring in the noonday sun. As far as he could see, with the exception of the horizon, there was not a single shadow. To the extent that he could peer into the dark sky, not a single cloud. A hot dry wind blew past, stirring up a dust storm.

"Aah. . . It's just as though the horizon line in one of my designs had become the landscape itself. Aah. . ."

The chalk hadn't resolved anything after all. He still had to create it all from the beginning. He had to fill this desolate land with mountains, water, clouds, trees, plants, birds, beasts, fish. He had to draw the world all over again. Discouraged, Argon collapsed onto the bed. One after another, tears fell unceasingly.

Something rustled in his pocket. It was the newspaper he had bought on that first day and forgotten about. The headline on the first page read, "Invasion Across 38th Parallel!" On the second page, an even larger space devoted to a photograph of Miss Nippon. Underneath, in small print, "Riot at N Ward Employment Security Office," and "Large-scale Dismissals at U Factory."

Argon stared at the half-naked Miss Nippon. What intense longing. What a body. Flesh of glass.

"This is what I forgot. Nothing else matters. It's time to begin everything from Adam and Eve. That's it—Eve! I'll draw Eve!"

Half an hour later Eve was standing before him, stark naked. Startled, she looked around her.

"Oh! Who are you? What's happened? Golly, I'm naked!"

"I am Adam. You are Eve." Argon blushed bashfully.

"I'm Eve, you say? Ah, no wonder I'm naked. But why are you wearing clothes? Adam, in Western dress—now that's weird."

Suddenly her tone changed.

"You're lying! I'm not Eve. I'm Miss Nippon."

"You're Eve. You really are Eve."

"You expect me to believe this is Adam—in those clothes—in a dump like this? Come on, give me back *my* clothes. What am I doing here anyway? I'm due to make a special modeling appearance at a photo contest."

"Oh, no. You don't understand. You're Eve, I mean it."

"Give me a break, will you? Okay, where's the apple? And I suppose this is the Garden of Eden? Ha, don't make me laugh. Now give me my clothes."

"Well, at least listen to what I have to say. Sit down over there. Then I'll explain everything. By the way, can I offer you something to eat?"

"Yes, go ahead. But hurry up and give me my clothes, okay? My body's valuable."

"What would you like? Choose anything you want from this cookbook."

"Oh, great! Really? The place is filthy, but you must be pretty well fixed. I've changed my mind. Maybe you really are Adam after all. What do you do for a living? Burglar?"

"No, I'm Adam. Also an artist, and a world planner."

"I don't understand."

"Neither do I. That's why I'm depressed."

72

Watching Argon draw the food with swift strokes as he spoke, Eve shouted, "Hey, great, that's great. This *is* Eden, isn't it? Wow. Yeah, okay, I'll be Eve. I don't mind being Eve. We're going to get rich—right?"

"Eve, please listen to me."

In a sad voice, Argon told her his whole story, adding finally, "So you see, with your cooperation we must design this world. Money's irrelevant. We have to start everything from scratch."

Miss Nippon was dumbfounded.

"Money's irrelevant, you say? I don't understand. I don't get it. I absolutely do not understand."

"If you're going to talk like that, well, why don't you open this door and take a look outside."

She glanced through the door Argon had left half open.

"My God! How awful!"

She slammed the door shut and glared at him.

"But how about *this* door," she said, pointing to his real, blanketed door. "Different, I'll bet."

"No, don't. That one's no good. It will just wipe out this world, the food, desk, bed, and even you. *You* are the new Eve. And we must become the father and mother of our world."

"Oh no. No babies. I'm all for birth control. I mean, they're such a bother. And besides, I won't disappear."

"You will disappear."

"I won't. I know myself best. I'm me. All this talk about disappearing—you're really weird."

"My dear Eve, you don't know. If we don't re-create the world, then sooner or later we're faced with starvation."

"What? Calling me 'dear' now, are you? You've got a nerve. And you say I'm going to starve. Don't be ridiculous. My body's valuable."

"No, your body's the same as my chalk. If we don't acquire a world of our own, your existence will just be a fiction. The same as nothing at all."

"Okay, that's enough of this junk. Come on, give me back my clothes. I'm leaving. No two ways about it, my being here is weird. I shouldn't be here. You're a magician or something. Well, hurry up. My manager's probably fed up with waiting. If you want me to drop in and be your

73

Eve every now and then, I don't mind. As long as you use your chalk to give me what I want."

"Don't be a fool! You can't do that."

The abrupt, violent tone of Argon's voice startled her, and she looked into his face. They both stared at each other for a moment in silence. Whatever was in her thoughts, she then said calmly, "All right, I'll stay. But, in exchange, will you grant me one wish?"

"What is it? If you stay with me, I'll listen to anything you have to say."

"I want half of your chalk."

"That's unreasonable. After all, dear, you don't know how to draw. What good would it do you?"

"I do know how to draw. I may not look like it, but I used to be a designer. I insist on equal rights."

He tilted his head for an instant, then straightening up again, said decisively, "All right, I believe you."

He carefully broke the chalk in half and gave one piece to Eve. As soon as she received it, she turned to the wall and began drawing.

It was a pistol.

"Stop it! What are you going to do with that thing?"

"Death, I'm going to make death. We need some divisions. They're very important in making a world."

"No, that'll be the end. Stop it. It's the most unnecessary thing of all."

But it was too late. Eve was clutching a small pistol in her hand. She raised it and aimed directly at his chest.

"Move and I'll shoot. Hands up. You're stupid, Adam. Don't you know that a promise is the beginning of a lie? It's you who made me lie."

"What? Now what are you drawing?"

"A hammer. To smash the door down."

"You can't!"

"Move and I'll shoot!"

The moment he leaped the pistol rang out. Argon held his chest as his knees buckled and he collapsed to the floor. Oddly, there was no blood.

"Stupid Adam."

Eve laughed. Then, raising the hammer, she struck the door. The light streamed in. It wasn't very bright, but it was real. Light from the sun.

Eve was suddenly absorbed, like mist. The desk, the bed, the French meal, all disappeared. All but Argon, the cookbook which had landed on the floor, and the chair were transformed back into pictures on the wall.

Argon stood up unsteadily. His chest wound had healed. But something stronger than death was summoning him, compelling him—the wall. The wall was calling him. His body, which had eaten drawings from the wall continuously for four weeks, had been almost entirely transformed by them. Resistance was impossible now. Argon staggered toward the wall and was drawn in on top of Eve.

The sound of the gunshot and the door being smashed were heard by others in the building. By the time they ran in, Argon had been completely absorbed into the wall and had become a picture. The people saw nothing but the chair, the cookbook, and the scribblings on the wall. Staring at Argon lying on top of Eve, someone remarked, "Starved for a woman, wasn't he."

"Doesn't it look just like him, though?" said another.

"What was he doing, destroying the door like that? And look at this, the wall's covered with scribbles. Huh. He won't get away with it. Where in the world did he disappear to? Calls himself a painter!"

The man grumbling to himself was the apartment manager.

After everyone left, there came a murmuring from the wall.

"It isn't chalk that will remake the world. . ."

A single drop welled out of the wall. It fell from just below the eye of the pictorial Argon.

BAD COMPANY

Yasuoka Shōtarō

Translated by Kären Wigen Lewis

Yasuoka Shōtarō's characters are all clumsy, bumbling individuals who masochistically persist in challenging themselves even when they realize there is not the slightest chance they will ever succeed at anything. Failure has been such a consistent trademark for Yasuoka that he has had a great deal of difficulty coping with his enormous success as a writer. In the delight he takes in playing the failure, Yasuoka resembles Dazai Osamu, while in the earnest purity of his characters' endeavors, he is reminiscent of Shiga Naoya. Unique to his work, however, is a distorted critical sense that allows Yasuoka to view all the ridiculous acts of his characters with a wry, detached humor.

Yasuoka was born in 1920 in the island town of Kōchi, but most of his youth was spent in transit, following his army veterinarian father on transfers between Manchuria and various spots in Japan. The idea of a home is thus absent from Yasuoka's work, and the embarrassment his mother felt being married to a "horse doctor" was conveyed undiluted to her son. The many failures of his father's life, and the dotage of his mentally unstable mother, are important motifs in Yasuoka's fiction, and his finest work, the short novel Kaihen no kōkei (A View by the Sea, 1959; tr. 1984), *is a moving examination of the shattered relationships between these three family members.*

During the war Yasuoka was drafted and sent to Manchuria to fight, but he contracted a respiratory disease and had to be hospitalized for the duration of the conflict. Even after the war, Yasuoka had to spend six years

*in bed with Pott's Disease, a painful affliction that bends and constricts
the spine. From his sickbed, Yasuoka began writing agonizingly funny stories
about characters not unlike himself who were total disasters as human beings. He won the Akutagawa Prize for two such stories in 1953: "Inki na
tanoshimi" (Cheerless Pleasure) and the story translated here, "Warui
nakama" (Bad Company).*

*Since his early autobiographical success, Yasuoka has written with wry
perception about his war experiences in the novel* Tonsō *(Flight, 1956),
which anticipated the "M.A.S.H." view of war by a couple of decades. With
the stirring success of* A View by the Sea *Yasuoka began to turn from purely
humorous examinations of failure to more probing studies of the breakdown
of human relationships. A pair of novels on this subject,* Maku ga orite
kara *(After the Curtain Falls, 1967) and* Tsuki wa higashi ni *(The Moon
Is to the East, 1970), were followed by a translation into Japanese of Alex
Haley's* Roots. *Most recently Yasuoka has produced his own* Roots *saga,*
Ryūritan *(A Tale of Wandering Ancestors, 1981), a quest in Japanese history
for the home that was denied him, which received the Grand Prize for
Japanese Literature.*

*   *   *

The China Incident was just beginning to be one more commonplace
episode in our lives when my friends and I began to see our faces clearing at last of acne, that plague of the middle school years. It was our
first summer break after advancing to college prep school. I had turned
down an invitation from a classmate, Kurata Shingo, to visit his home
in Hokkaido and, having no plans of my own, had decided to kill time
by signing up for a summer session French class in Kanda.

One day I walked into the classroom to find someone else's belongings spread out on the front-row seat I always took. The desk hadn't been
specifically assigned to me, but I moved the books to the next empty
seat anyway and sat down, then went back out to the hallway for a
cigarette. But when the teacher came and I returned to the classroom,
a small kid in a blue shirt was sitting in my chair. He looked like a sissy,

77

with his skinny neck and an oversized shirt of a pastel shade that belonged on a woman's apron, but his looks only made his insolence all the more striking. I walked up to the desk and deliberately snatched my textbooks out from under him, but he didn't bat an eye. He simply sat with his wan face turned to the front, irritating me more than ever with the profile of his large, unsightly nose. I had no choice but to take another seat—not the empty one next to him, however, but one as far away as possible.

Presently the teacher began to call roll. Each student was supposed to answer with the French *"présent."* When our teacher, a thin blonde named Mademoiselle LeFolucca, looked up at the class over her spectacles and read off "Monsieur Fujii," the boy in the blue shirt shot up and practically shouted in a drawn-out, high-pitched voice,

"Je—vous—réponds!"

Then with a feminine flourish he sat down again. . . This queer response shattered the harmony that normally reigned in the classroom. The backs of the boy's ears turned bright red as he shrank in his seat and hid his face like a baby bird on its perch. "Idiot!" I muttered to myself. Fujii Komahiko told me later that he had been trying to flirt with Mlle. LeFolucca that day. I was stunned. She was an ugly, mean-tempered woman.

One day on the train home from school I happened to end up in the same car with Fujii. To my horror, as soon as he recognized me he came over with a big grin on his face and sat down next to me. My nostrils were immediately assaulted by a strange, abhorrent smell. He greeted me like an old friend, but with large, exaggerated gestures; as he warmed up he started flapping his arms around like wings, exposing in the process a pair of cuffs blacker at the wrist than any I have ever seen, and giving off even more of that horrible stench. Wondering how long it would be before I was rid of him, I asked,

"Where do you live?"

"Shimo-Kitazawa."

My luck—the last stop before mine. The whole way there he talked in a steady stream, telling me how his family was from Shinuiju in Korea; how he was now staying in his brother's apartment by himself, while his brother—who was a medical student—was home for vacation; how

78

this was his first time in Tokyo (his high school was in Kyoto); and so on, and so on. At the least response from me he would scoot forward and excitedly rub his thighs together, sending up a new wave of that rotten onion smell each time. . . By now I had quite forgotten my irritation at his having taken my chair in class the other day; all I wanted was to get away from that smell. Just as we came within one stop of Shimo-Kitazawa, he changed the subject and asked,

"What do you know about Kurt Weill?"

I was somehow flattered. In those days there wasn't anything that could have made me feel as proud as being asked a question like that. I immediately launched into telling him all about the man who had composed *The Threepenny Opera*. Despite the fact that he was now on the listening end for a change, Fujii's mannerisms remained as exaggerated as before. He nodded his head up and down emphatically at every word, and leaned so close to me he nearly rammed his ear into my mouth. But this time I wasn't dying to make my escape from an embarrassing situation. Besides, I wanted to show off my *pour vous*, rare items in those parts, and the programs and stars' photos I'd been collecting since junior high. So when Fujii started to get off at his station I invited him to come home with me. His answer was not what I expected.

". . . I'd be embarrassed, going to your house." His cheeks and eyelids flushed red, and he laughed weakly. Then he said, "Why don't you come to my place instead? It's that one, there," and he pointed to an apartment visible from the window. I didn't know what to make of his attitude, but I agreed to visit him later that afternoon.

I didn't take this promise to Fujii very seriously. When I reached home, a cousin from Den'enchōfu had come to visit. Now that she was engaged she hardly ever dropped in any more, unlike before. She also seemed to have started looking more like a lady. To tease her I did mocking imitations of her fiancé's Tōhoku accent, as well as of his table manners, his way of greeting people, and other quirks of his. Though I didn't quite understand why, the more this seemed to fluster her, the more I enjoyed my little game. . .

The next day, as soon as I walked into the classroom, Fujii bounded to my side and demanded, "Where were you yesterday?"

I said nothing. "I bought apples and bananas and sat there waiting for you," he said, staring straight into my face. . . The whole scene was somehow comical. But when I tried to laugh, no laughter came. There was something in his eyes that I couldn't identify, something I hadn't noticed until now. Mouthing a wordless reply, I realized that for the first time in my life I had let down a friend on account of a girl. "My old lady got sick and I couldn't come," I said.

That afternoon—perhaps out of guilt for having lied to him—I went straight from school to Fujii's apartment. Oddly enough, from that day on I was never again put off by his overpowering smell.

From our first get-together Komahiko and I quickly became close friends. With my father away, Komahiko seemed to feel less uncomfortable at my house than he had expected. I for my part was intrigued by his independent life in a one-room apartment, where inkwell, school cap and books lay side by side on a shelf with the frying pan and coffee pot. . . When I went to the apartment early in the morning, Komahiko would thrust one naked arm out from between the rumpled sheets and beg a cigarette. When I handed him the cigarette and matches, he'd open his puffy eyelids to a slit, look at me, and smile. . . At such times I found myself unconsciously acting out love scenes from books and movies. Komahiko was slight of build, and except for his nose being too big, his face had a kind of clear-eyed beauty. . . Not that I thought of him as a weakling. He had a measure of bravado that I just didn't have; I noticed it when he talked to his landlord or his neighbors. I had also seen him sit, unfazed, in a tiny, filthy restaurant and calmly—even with seeming enjoyment—proceed to eat a piece of fish that was covered with flies. . . But none of this had particularly impressed me yet.

There came a day, though, when I had to be surprised. The two of us were walking down the street together when we found ourselves saying how hungry we were. In the fanciful mood that camaraderie seems to conjure up, we started talking about *kuinige*—skipping out of a restaurant without paying the bill.

"Want to give it a try?"

Komahiko was already pushing open the door of a restaurant on a side street when he put this to me, though at the time I had no intention of actually going through with it. For me, eating away from home itself counted as an adventure, *kuinige* or otherwise. Moreover, in this kind of formal, European-style restaurant my head was soon swimming with such problems as whether to tuck my napkin in at my chin or lay it across my lap. . . The dining room was fairly crowded. The waiters hurried back and forth but always gracefully, flitting about like white butterflies. The two of us chose a table overshadowed by a large, hairy hemp plant, ordered two dishes, and had our meal. When we had finished, Fujii smiled and said, "Ready?" "Sure," I answered absentmindedly. Then Fujii took hold of one strand of the hemp plant and struck a match.

Suddenly there was a burst of light in front of me. In a flash the trunk of the hemp plant was a pillar of flame. Pandemonium broke loose. All the patrons were on their feet at once, and instantly the place was transformed into a classic fire scene. . . Dazed, I leaped up from my chair when above the din of breaking crockery I heard Fujii's voice at my ear and, snapping out of it, I dashed after him full speed toward the exit.

The whole thing had turned out so unexpectedly that I thought I must be dreaming. But what really amazed me happened after we lost sight of each other running down crowded back streets and became separated. . . As soon as I was by myself, I was seized with fear; this on top of the excitement and the running had my chest pounding alarmingly. I wandered restlessly in circles, not knowing where to go or what to do, greatly agitated, setting out to find Komahiko one minute and wanting to take to my heels again the next. The sunlight glared harshly off the concrete sidewalk, and though my back and chest were pouring sweat, a chill ran through my body. Hounded by fear and remorse, I had almost completely given in to my guilty conscience when at last I saw, up ahead, the familiar oversized blue shirt: it was Komahiko, the sun behind him as he strolled down the broad avenue toward me. . . My mood swung right around: I now felt flushed with triumph.

"Hey!" I could have hugged him.

"Hey!" he called back.

Full of my own excitement I started telling him all about the crowded streets I had run through, when I noticed a large mysterious package in one of his hands. "What's that?" I demanded. He mumbled nonchalantly, "Oh, miso, dried sardines. . ." I was shattered. Here he was telling me that within minutes of doing something as dangerous as that he had calmly stepped into a grocery store to do his evening's shopping. My sense of high drama was dashed. What had been a terrific adventure for me had been a purely practical affair for him.

I had always been intimidated by restaurant workers before, thinking of them as nasty "etiquette police"; but after this episode, I saw them instead as people just grown malicious from scurrying around serving other people for too long.

One day toward the end of our summer vacation, I went to Fujii's apartment to find wire, wire cutters, nails and whatnot strewn about the place and Fujii himself facing the window hard at work. . . As he fiddled with a hand-held shaving mirror, Fujii explained that he was setting up a periscope for seeing into the bathroom of the house diagonally across from his flat. I was thrilled with this idea, and let out a loud exclamation. Fujii reproved me. Then he asked, "Didn't you have a mirror at your place that was a little bigger than this?"

"I think so," I said, perking up again, and dashed out of the room. But when I got back with the larger mirror, the wire and the wire cutters were gone, the whole mess cleaned up, and Fujii himself was acting deliberately nonchalant. . . At a loss for anything else to do, I set about constructing a reflecting device of my own.

"Forget it. It's too dark to see anything now."

Something cold in his tone made me bristle. Fine then, I'll do it myself, I thought, and without a word I continued with my work. But sure enough, as the sun began to set, the light in my mirror all but went out; the bath, lit only by a single bulb, was also barely visible; and before long all I could tell was whether someone was in there or not. When I refused to give up even then and continued fiddling with the mirror, Fujii said tauntingly from where he lay,

"Do you really want to see it that much?"

"What about yourself?" I retorted.

"Why, me. . ." Fujii began, and then broke off with a snicker. I persisted. He said, ". . . Well, you know, until two or three days ago I could see straight into the bath right across the street. Shame they had to go and close the window."

I was furious.

"Why didn't you say something sooner!"

At this Fujii, still slumped across the bed, crossed his legs which had been spread wide toward me, let out a simpering laugh, and said, "I . . . I couldn't, especially not to someone like you."

In a flash of intuition I knew then that Fujii had had a woman. . . In that split second my image of Komahiko was turned on its head—a hidden something inside him, a secret domain so vast that the eye could not take it all in, suddenly stood bared before me. Feeling as embarrassed as if I had strayed by mistake into a stranger's house, I completely clammed up. . .

The truth is that I thought constantly about women. Whenever I daydreamed about the future, whenever I imagined myself in the kind of role I wanted to fill someday, inevitably there was a woman beside the hypothetical "me"; in addition, I entertained various sexual fantasies about women. But in spite of all this I had never once thought of approaching a woman in real life. To me, women were too distant to be anything but objects of fantasy. My several female cousins were somehow in a class apart from the rest of womankind, and all my other relationships with women were on the order of passing encounters on a bus or train: I could see them but I was cut off from them. . . So now, though Fujii lay right in front of me, I felt a sharp difference separating us. He was a man from an unknown world.

I went home that evening and thought about nothing else all night. In my exposure to Komahiko during the short space of this summer vacation, I had felt an attraction stronger than anything I'd ever experienced before. If I was still unable to go into the dingy restaurants he frequented, it was not out of any great scruples about nutrition or hygiene, but because the dark, damp gloom of the place scared the wits out of me. Likewise with prostitutes: it was more than a question of disease or morality; it was something harder to overcome that made me avoid even the thought of going to them. Nevertheless, now I was coming to believe that I would have to learn to love precisely these things that I had always avoided. . . Just as a man begins to perceive the woman he loves as mysterious, I began to think of Komahiko as a boy with awesome powers. The smallest detail of his way of life seemed to take on a whole new splendor. With the logic of a child who imagines a miniature orchestra inside a phonograph, I began to see a woman inside my friend. . .

From the next day on I tried on various pretexts to get him talking on the subject of women, but Fujii remained elusive, and I only grew more perplexed. Unfortunately, at this point I had no power to pressure him with. It wasn't until the day before he was to go back to Kyoto, as we walked the streets together that night, that I finally persuaded him to talk. It was the first time I had consciously played on his vanity.

"Listen, it's an incredible bore," Komahiko warned me. "You're bound to be disappointed, so I'd drop it if I were you." It turned out, however, that since coming to Tokyo Komahiko had gone to amuse himself several times without my knowledge.

Autumn came.

When Kurata Shingo, back from his family home in Hokkaido, first saw me at the start of the new term, he was taken by surprise. He seemed not to know how to respond to my subjects of conversation, my vocabulary, even a lot of my gestures and mannerisms. To me, on the other hand, this old friend and classmate seemed as dumb as a mule. . . It bored me to death now to sit around with Kurata, listening to records and nodding stupidly to the beat, or hearing him brag about his tennis. He talked eagerly, gesturing emphatically with his long neck, but I turned a deaf ear to almost everything he said.

Suddenly, at one of my mumbled replies, Kurata turned his long, sunburned face straight toward me. The conversation broke off as his voice trailed away. I too was silent. From the opening of his short sleeves came a scent like the sweet smell of dry hay. . . This was the smell of virginity, I thought, and that odor I noticed when I first met Fujii must have been the smell of experience. . . Which smell did I have now? I wondered. The day after I had said good-bye to Fujii, I had found my way, following the directions of a famous novelist who had written about the place, to a brothel across the river.

The shock I had received at Komahiko's hand was now to be passed on to Kurata. . . Only half aware of what I was doing, I began to retrace the course Fujii had marked out over the summer. *Kuinige*, stealing, voyeurism. . . The difference was that my actions were marred by

84

something that smacked of revenge, something that wouldn't be satisfied until I had forcibly shaken him up. With *kuinige*, for instance, the way I handled it was not to let him in on it ahead of time but to spring it on him out of the blue and force him to make a run for it. The only time I was a hundred percent successful was when I stole a spoon from a restaurant on the main strip of the Ginza. That time Kurata's admiration was spontaneous. . .

The pattern on this particular restaurant's teaspoons was an unusual combination of straight lines and circles, and I took a fancy to it. As we stood up to leave I pocketed mine. But as we were on our way out, the waiter ran up behind us and said, "Excuse me, sir, I believe you have one of our teaspoons. . . ?"

I turned slowly around. "You mean I'm not allowed to take this?" I asked taking the spoon out to show him. . . The waiter was flustered. Blushing, he waved me away, saying, "No, go ahead," and he actually went away beaming as if he had brought his customer some forgotten belonging. Kurata, who I thought was standing next to me, must have fled at some point, for the next thing I knew he was about eight yards away and staring at me wide-eyed. When we were outside the restaurant, he let out a sigh like a man confessing, and applauded my calm, saying, "That was superb." It was the first time I had impressed Kurata without contriving the effect. Just how impressed he was became clear as early as the next day, when he pulled the same stunt himself at a cafeteria near the school. His performance there was so good that the waitress ended up giving him a cutlet knife almost as big as a butcher's. This unwieldy token of her admiration was too large to fit in his pocket, and he couldn't very well ditch it by the side of the road, either.

In short, there was no mistaking that Kurata too felt an inexplicable fascination for adventures of this sort. Now the most important of these by far was undoubtedly my trip to the quarter across the river. But when this subject arose, the urge to advertise what I had done became entangled with my desire to lead him on yet awhile through a net of enigmas, so that in the end, every time I looked at Kurata, I couldn't help hesitating. . . True, perhaps I had been disappointed on returning from the other side of the river, as Komahiko had predicted. But "disappointment" in Komahiko's sense was precisely what I had set out to find. The indefinable dissatisfaction I felt had nothing to do with that. I had in fact had more than enough of this kind of letdown: for two or three days afterward, I couldn't look at a female without being overcome by the absurdity of it, so much so that I nearly found myself in trouble. . . But this wasn't what I'd had in mind. What I had been hoping for was some kind of token. Nothing visible to strangers, but something I could recognize as a sign—that's what I thought I would come away with. But if I had, it must have been stuck to the middle of my back, or hanging behind my ear. Though I followed in Fujii's footsteps, I was totally on my own. . .

"You really want to see it that much?" Sitting in the front row at the Asakusa Revue, I was planning to turn to Kurata and say this to him. But somehow when I was about to open my mouth it seemed that I was the one who wanted to see the show. . . What would Fujii have done in a situation like this? Wanting to make the same impression as he had that time, I rehearsed his glance and other mannerisms in my head. But nothing I tried would make me sound like that. This only made me more and more irritated, until I finally blurted out,

"Let's go. This is boring."

My saying this for no apparent reason when the show had barely begun, especially after I'd insisted so adamantly on bringing him here, made Kurata angry, but he didn't want to say we should stay, either, so he had no choice but to follow me out. . . When I finally recovered my own good humor, it was ironically through doing what I could to coax Kurata out of sulking over the bind I had put him in in the first place.

In short, the whole time I was with Kurata I thought only of Fujii. The more progress Kurata made from mulishness to normality, the more I became like Komahiko, or so I thought. So I took care not to treat Kurata like a dumb animal. . . Once in a while, however, though I was sure Komahiko was in Kyoto, I would be tormented by the nightmarish possibility of Kurata and Komahiko somehow meeting. If that happened, what would become of the image of myself that I'd been at such pains to plant in Kurata's mind?

This nightmare came true. Roused from sleep one morning by the maid, I went downstairs to find Kurata and Fujii standing together at the front door. They just happened to have taken the same train. Fujii had nothing with him except the raincoat he had thrown over his shirt.

"I was getting fed up with Kyoto—thought I'd come up here for a while," he said.

Yet this coincidence turned out to be not the disaster I had imagined, but a totally unexpected joy. The atmosphere was festive, and soon the three of us were feeling like old chums. The odd thing was that Kurata, who was generally withdrawn and rarely said a word to someone he had just met, acted as if he'd known Fujii for years. For he had already become familiar with another Fujii, the one inside me.

The conversation between the three of us was animated to an alarming degree. Now that the real Fujii had appeared, I had no doubt faded to a pale shadow in Kurata's eyes. This meant that at the same time that I was struggling for Fujii's approval, I also had to work to shore up the image Kurata had of the Komahiko in me. And what with Kurata and I outdoing each other to ingratiate ourselves with Fujii, he had to talk twice as much as usual in order not to lose either friend. . . With all of us trying to impress each other this way, the boasts grew by the minute. Finally, hoping to dump Kurata, I proposed that we go to the other side of the river.

As a scheme to upset Kurata, this completely backfired. Contrary to my expectation that he would blush and have to mull it over first, he immediately joined in. . . Thinking back on it, I can see now that this was the last thing I should have done. Kurata was like a man in a blazing house: he had that freak strength to perform incredible feats without feeling any pain. I had thrown away my most valuable trump card. And the worst of it was, I didn't have a bit of fun once we got there. What happened was, the three of us split up when we reached the place to seek our respective adventures, but almost as soon as I started walking I was picked up by a policeman on a juvenile delinquent beat. This after I had been trying to pass myself off as an old hand in front of Kurata.

Finally released from the police box three hours later, I ran across the street and was heading for a dark corner to hide in when someone called out,

"Hey. Over here."

It was Kurata and Fujii. My initial joy at returning to the fold was short-lived. It turned out that these two had stood in the shadow of a yakitori stand at the side of the road and watched for over an hour as I bowed to the crowd of policemen surrounding me, or raised my arms against threatened blows and pleaded for mercy. . . They told me all this with an air of the utmost concern.

Fujii left again for Kyoto. But I could not go back to treating Kurata like a mule. . . Fujii had stayed only two nights in Tokyo, but those two nights had been like two years of ordinary time, if not more. Like a guide on some whirlwind tour, he had led us from one place to another, seeking out his favorite spots—specialty seafood restaurants, coffee houses, theaters; we would hop in a cab to go some ridiculously short distance, and then traipse along on foot for hours and hours around a particular district that he liked. We needed no alcohol to intoxicate ourselves. Three abreast we strode through the back streets of the Ginza, Fujii in the middle, firing off our automatic lighters like pistols. . . The third day ended with the fanfare of a carnival.

Komahiko's image only grew larger as he receded. In Kurata's eyes I was now but a shadow of Fujii—even the incident with the spoon now seemed a mere imitation of Fujii's exploits. At first this was unbearable. But as the days passed each of us came to feel a certain pleasure in bringing out the Komahiko in the other. We walked the streets we had walked with Komahiko, we went into the coffee shops we had visited with Komahiko, we made a leapfrog game out of taking turns playing the part of Komahiko. . . We imitated even completely trivial things like the way Fujii held a coffee cup to his mouth. He never picked up a cup by the handle, but would always take hold of the cup itself, lift it slowly to his mouth, press it to his thickish lips, and then, extending his tongue slightly as if to lick the rim of the cup, let the coffee dribble slowly down his throat. It made him look greedy, as though he were trying to suck the last bit of flavor from every drop. Another thing was we both started unconsciously stooping our shoulders. Fujii, who was short, always walked erect, his chest thrown out and his head back, but in our efforts to imitate him, the two of us found ourselves doing just the opposite, rounding our backs. Again, while both Kurata and I had always been finicky eaters, now we outdid each other by eating anything Fujii had pronounced good. My mother couldn't work out why all of a sudden with the arrival of fall her son should develop an appetite for tomatoes. . . In all things Kurata and I served as each other's inspectors. Neither would allow the other to copy Komahiko directly. If Fujii had worn a pair of socks embossed with a fish design, for example, that specific design was out of bounds. A bird or butterfly pattern was the loyal as well as tasteful choice in a case like this.

The letters between Tokyo and Kyoto flew thick and fast. . . These letters were everything to us. With all the stunts we pulled, the thrill of the act itself was nothing to the pleasure of writing about it afterward. Fujii always compared and rated the letters from the two of us in Tokyo. His letters from Kyoto were invariably addressed in both of our names, and mailed to each of our houses by turns. When we showed them to each other, each of us would secretly judge the thickness of the letter sent to the other's place.

In this way our mental image of Komahiko grew more idealized every day. Even in our striving to outdo each other Kurata and I were united. And at every turn we'd think, "If only Koma were here." A bus crammed with passengers might break down in the middle of the road and be unable to move, and we'd look at each other and think, "If only Fujii were here. . ."

In Kyoto Fujii was killing himself with this correspondence. Almost every other day he had a letter to write. At least if his correspondent had been a woman, the work of letter writing wouldn't have been so grueling. All you have to do to satisfy a woman's interest is write down the same old things you've been doing every day of your life. With another man, though, it doesn't quite work that way. . . The letters arriving from these two friends one after another raised Fujii to a dizzying height before he knew what was happening. Looking about him, he could hardly find any explanation for it. In this precarious, intoxicated state, like walking on clouds, the one thing that was clear was the importance of stringing along for as long as possible the fellows who were helping to induce it. . . But Fujii was soon trapped by a misleading suggestion he himself had thrown out. To wit, like Kurata and I, he too started believing that the true source of beauty in his life was his intimacy with women. The result of this was that Fujii started making a veritable religion of frequenting the red-light districts. And all to stir up inspiration for his letters to us. . .

One day I arrived at Kurata's house in Harajuku to find him clearing his father's gold trophies off the ornamental shelf at the front of the hallway.

"What's going on?" I demanded, but he seemed highly agitated and wouldn't answer, hurling the cups one after another into a closet on top of his little brother's toys. "What's going on?" I demanded again, but looking into Kurata's troubled face, I suddenly felt like laughing out loud.

So it's getting to him, too, I thought. Kurata's family was much like mine. My father had gone off to North China with the military; his father was an executive in a munitions company, and toured the country to inspect regional plants. As a result, both of us were largely free to do as we pleased from one day to the next. But recently I had started to find my house somehow constraining, confining. It wasn't that anything in particular had changed at home, but that the pact between the three of us was starting to bind me even there. For instance, it wouldn't do to hesitate or be scared when you came in late at night. That was definitely a disgrace. It was also against the rules to wash your hands after going to the bathroom. There were a host of new injunctions like this binding us. Since the goal in all things was to achieve "beauty" (beauty being defined by Fujii's way of life), this outcome was inevitable. . . I had no choice but to be a complete slob at home. I happily let my clothes and my room get as dirty as I could. It was as if I were trying to bury the household mores I now found so oppressive in a heap of junk and garbage. . . But Kurata had another kind of pain to bear. While all I had to do was sit back and watch as dust and cobwebs covered the photographs of starlets I had pasted on the wall, Kurata's room was decorated with skiing equipment, a tennis racket, the tail of a broken glider, and even a sterling silver model of a naval bomber that he had secretly taken from the guest-room mantelpiece in his father's absence. These things had once been his pride and joy. Recently, however, like Jean Valjean's troubling tattoo, they had become a daily torment for him.

Now, to make his humiliation complete, in order to escape his friend's judging eyes he had come secretly to return the bomber to its original spot. . . His pent-up rage had finally exploded, and he had lashed out even at the trophies in the hall.

Once you start doing battle against a parent's hobbies like this, there's no stopping. Every inch of the house is their territory. . . For me, it started with my father's sword, which had been placed on display in the decorative alcove; then the hanging scroll and the flower vase began to irritate me; soon I reached the point where I couldn't tolerate things I had never even noticed before—down to the pattern on the sliding paper doors and the cracks in the pillars. Especially the food: it came to be downright ridiculous. Everything on the table irritated me. Even when I had my mother fix up a separate dish of something I had liked when I ate it with Fujii, it seemed to lose all its taste as soon as I took a bite of it at home.

Needless to say, both Kurata and I began to spend less and less time at home. We passed the better part of each day in a dingy little coffee shop. As our allowances tended to be on the low side for regular eating out, we came up with halfway measures such as spreading butter on baked potatoes we bought on the street, and this was the sort of thing we lived on.

In those days, Japanese society as a whole was behaving every bit as eccentrically as we were. Everyone in the country was suffering from a whole array of factitious observances which had their basis in the moral code of a "new" era. Once, for instance, when a line of people waiting to see a performance by some famous movie star had wound all the way around a certain movie theater, someone decided the crowd was being unnecessarily frivolous and turned a fire hose on them. Periodically troops in the signal corps could be seen riding around in the streets—more for display than for lack of any other place to practice. Suffering miserably under the heavy copper coils wrapped around their chests, all they managed to do was obstruct the traffic. . . Apparently on some kind of orders from somewhere, our school would hastily assemble the students on the playground for a lecture from the principal. The principal, wearing pale yellow gloves and standing like a bronze statue, would say something like, "The way to train a monkey to dance is to take it when it's still young

91

and make it walk on a red-hot sheet of iron. When it feels the heat, the monkey begins to prance about. This is the meaning of discipline. Now the same goes for you boys. . ." A number of us would be fighting hard to keep from laughing out loud. . . The idea of us being little monkeys! The deeper symbolic meaning of this story was utterly beyond us. Nobody—the principal included—had any idea what the sheet of iron stood for. . . Afterward, many of the students who had heard this speech were wounded or killed in combat. Among those who suffered burns was none other than the principal himself.

Already it was getting to the point where a person could be publicly reprimanded for anything at all. Surprisingly, it happened more often in reputable places like the coffee shops that sold nothing but pastries, places frequented only by the quietest students, than to those wandering through the red-light districts. Dim-witted students who had been spotted in front of a pool hall during school hours would be hauled off to the police station to get paddled and come back blubbering. . . We were completely in the dark about when this sort of thing would happen and what form it would take. The one thing we could be sure of was that when the day-to-day tedium was starting to kill us, when we began to get the feeling that we'd left something undone but were completely helpless to remember what it was—then these things would suddenly spring out at us. For when we fell into a mood like that (which we called "stagnation"), we were itching to pull something off ourselves.

We hit stagnation pretty often. Naturally the thrill of a dare wore off after the first time around; as the repetitions mounted, stagnation was sure to follow. The arbitrary punishments already mentioned helped us out at first. That topsy-turvy state of affairs had grown more remarkable with every passing day, until even the military police were drawn in to help round up juvenile delinquents. For us, the effect of all this was exactly the same as sitting in a chair and "traveling" by watching a panorama go by. . . But as these disciplinary actions, too, became commonplace, we gradually lost our nerve. Both Kurata and I skipped most of our classes, but we had no desire to do anything else, either, and we fell to spending whole days sitting in that grimy downtown coffee shop, staring at each other and feeling as if we were starting to rust away. Seeing Kurata huddled like an old man over the damp-smelling charcoal brazier, I would automatically think of Komahiko. I'm sure I provoked the same thoughts in Kurata. . . We would start in animatedly on the subject of our plans for a new round of adventures, knowing all the while that it was mostly a lie. But that too would as suddenly break off. . . For the figure of a soldier with a bayonet—on the prowl for some runaway comrade—had passed across the darkened window like the silhouette of evil.

The letters from Kyoto became more and more frenzied. Unaware that the pair of us in Tokyo were stooping to gross exaggeration in our competition to impress him, Fujii—determined not to be outdone himself—was pushing himself to the limit. . . His letters were full of wildly idiosyncratic theorizing, replete with dogmatic pronouncements, morbid images developed to an extreme, and nearly indecipherable leaps of logic, all written in an eccentric style. Then one day in the dead of winter came a letter bearing the following enigmatic poem.

Desolate as when I came—
Taking leave of Kyoto at springtime.

This was accompanied by the news that he had been expelled from school, was seriously ill, and was thinking of going back to his home in Korea.

The letter had come to Kurata first. Kurata arrived at my house in Setagaya panting like a post-horse, his breath a white vapor in the cold.

One look at the letter left me so dazed I could barely think. I was too afraid to read the whole thing through. Kurata was undoubtedly in the same state. Hastily we left the house. Trancelike, we walked for some time, stopping in the middle of nowhere, occasionally making loud, meaningless attempts at conversation. . . I didn't know what to do with myself. All our escapades of the past half year had seemed to take place in a dream. In fact, a real human life had been at stake in all these "dreams" of mine. . . And all the while, Kurata and I had been having a ball.

Is it because this is all too frightening that I actually feel cheerful? I speculated. The truth was, however, that another part of me refused to acknowledge that I was rejoicing at my friend's misfortunes. . . I was, at least, aware that there was something despicable in my reaction. I thought therefore I was saying the opposite of what I "really" felt, but paradoxically I spoke the truth when I cried out,

"We ought to celebrate. Let's go out and have a feast."

Kurata replied with apparent relief,

"You're right. Today Fujii sets out on his greatest adventure of all."

Together we picked the fanciest restaurant we could find. I decided that in a formal place we were likely to be so preoccupied with wielding our forks and knives properly—cutting a piece of meat without sending it flying off the plate, or carefully winding slippery spaghetti onto a fork—that we wouldn't have time to think about anything else. As we soon found out, however, self-inflicted suffering while dining did nothing to alleviate our inner pain.

"Let's at least send a telegram to congratulate him," I said, emerging from my private misery to make another jaunty suggestion.

"Good idea," Kurata answered.

But when we left the restaurant we went to the usual dingy coffee shop and sat there until closing time without any plans to do another thing. Until we separated that evening, not another word about the telegram passed between us.

That night I was upset—not over the business with Fujii but over Kurata's inscrutability. . . It was perfectly clear that if we carried on much longer the way we had been, we too would soon share Fujii's fate. I dreaded that prospect. Not that I would have known how to answer if asked to explain my dread. I could only have said that I was terrified of the uncertain, insecure future I imagined. . . Regardless of whether I had any intention of deserting Fujii in the end or not, I at least wanted to bring it up for discussion—though the only possible motive for doing so was in fact a desire to turn traitor.

Kurata was by nature the more withdrawn of the two of us. From the next day on, while paying lip service to Fujii's character and outlook on life, I began dropping hints here and there about the misery that awaited Komahiko in the life he was likely to lead from now on. . . If I could somehow maneuver Kurata into saying he was going to desert him, my plan was to follow in his footsteps.

The scheme worked. More than there being any particular force behind my warnings, the fact was that something in Kurata was waiting to hear them. . .

In the growing frenzy as final exams approached, deals were being made all over the classroom for the swapping of notebooks. "I hear more guys flunk the first-year exams than any of the rest." "Yeah, and they say if you fail the first time around you're stuck for good, too. . ." In our present state of mind this kind of talk, even from a crowd we normally despised, was enough to get through to us.

"Shall we go to F's grave and pay our respects?" I asked Kurata cynically. Every year on the birthday of the school's founder, the whole student body paid a visit to his grave; tradition had it that anyone who didn't go along would fail his exams. The two of us had been absent that day, as usual.

"Yeah, let's go," Kurata said, brightening. . . The day was clear, and it felt good to walk through the cemetery. Hoping to boost the effect still further, I worked to put him in a genuine class-outing mood. Before I knew it I was feeling like a regular doctor treating a sick patient. In fact, the pleasure of taking the initiative for once, and the prospect of seeing Kurata again, even made me leave for school the next day in time for the first class.

Kurata was not there. The second period arrived and he still hadn't shown up. At that point my suspicions started working on me. It dawned on me that Kurata was probably somewhere with Fujii. Sitting in my iron-legged chair listening to a boring lecture, I wished that I had slipped out before class had started. But as each lecture ended, I had a feeling Kurata would show up for the next one, so I passed up my chance and stayed in the room. Kurata didn't come to a single class even in the afternoon. . . I had never felt this impatient waiting for Kurata before. But then, was it really for his sake that I was waiting here? If I really wanted to see him, surely it would have been faster to go to his house, or to the café where we always hung out. Was I staying in the classroom only out of solicitude for my patient, Kurata?

When I returned home there was a note from Fujii. "Came up to see you before I go back to Korea. Staying at a flophouse in Asakusa. . ."

So I was right, I thought, with a touch of self-satisfaction at having guessed correctly, and not particularly surprised. A map in Fujii's distinctive handwriting accompanied the letter. I took a cold and cursory look at it. (It's too bad about him. But if I sit here feeling sorry for him, I'll end up going right down the hole after him.) By this time I had put Kurata quite out of my mind. . . Having sat around waiting all day already, I felt as if I were the one who had been betrayed by my friends. And since I thought I had fulfilled my obligation to the friendship in that gesture, I felt clean and clear, as though my demon had been exorcised.

I dare say this change of heart, this resolve to shape up and fly straight, was merely a matter of convenience. The proof of this came the next morning when I had already begun to backslide. In other words, my real desire—to take the easy way out—showed its true colors. Arriving in the middle of rush hour at the station where I had to change trains, I sat on a bench and let one train that would have taken me to school go by. As I smoked a cigarette there, I had a frighteningly vivid image of the cold iron chairs and concrete floors of the classroom, and let the next train, too, pass by. . . My attendance record was bad in the extreme. It was possible that missing today's class would mean I would fail for sure. These hours were far too precious to squander. But for that very reason, idling this time away became a special pleasure. . . When I had watched the last train that would have taken me to class on time pull out of the station, still full of commuters, I stood up and muttered to myself, "What's the difference, it's just one more day."

I myself couldn't see my treacherous heart for what it was. Like a habitual liar who believes his own lies even as he tells them, I too failed to see just what I was doing. Or more precisely, I made no effort to see it. . . Having given up the idea of going to school, I went instead to our usual café. The place was completely deserted this early in the morning, and smelled like a rotting kitchen drainboard. There was a dazed, vacant feeling to the place, like that of a man who hasn't had enough sleep. I tried to burrow my way into that state by sitting in the farthest corner chair and staring at the soiled curtains or the stains on the wallpaper, merely marking time. . . What was I doing there? Maybe a certain doglike element in me, the loyalty to run after a master even when left behind, was sustaining the way of life I had been living until a short week ago. But the rational part of me didn't notice that at all.

When it got close to noon, I started thinking about lunch, and though I wasn't hungry, I was just wondering what to have when suddenly I heard familiar voices advancing across the street toward the shop. . . It was Fujii and Kurata. I shot up as if yanked out of my chair, and as soon as I came to my senses I dashed out the back door and up a different street. The first thing I felt was an unspeakable terror. Discomfort and humiliation brought on by ruminating on my own cowardice followed soon after. . . While my mind wavered between retreat and return, my feet took me further and further away.

What had terrified me so? Like an overcoat lining exposed by the wind, the intentions I had been hiding from myself had appeared in a flash as soon as I heard their voices. If I turned back now, there might still be a chance. But fast on the heels of this thought was another one, that they were probably talking right now about my betrayal and about those intentions I had just seen exposed; it was now this fear that made it impossible to go back.

Walking blindly from street to street wherever my feet led me, stepping in the broken tiles and the puddles of washtub water that were strewn across my path, I tried to forget the two voices that still rang in my ears. . . They were not easily erased. Then I knew why: that was the last time I would ever hear them speak. . .

When I had come far enough to think I really couldn't go back, I stopped and looked over my shoulder. . . If I hadn't heard those voices, if they hadn't approached the coffee shop talking so loudly, I would still have been sitting in that chair. And if that had happened, the three of us would undoubtedly have become good friends again as before. . . I was sure of it—for something hidden in my heart was waiting for just that to happen.

In fact, the final act of my betrayal was yet to come. This was not to take place until evening, after I had gone home. As long as I stayed in the city, there was still some connection between us.

That night a woman in a black kimono jacket appeared at our house. It was Mrs. Kurata, Kurata's mother. . . My mother answered the door, then called me.

Mrs. Kurata had been worried sick about her son, who had left the house two days ago and had not been seen since; and today she had opened a dresser drawer to discover that the family's bankbook was missing. Besides that, two Boston bags, her husband's duck-hunting cap, a tiepin set with a precious stone, and even a large sum of cash were all gone. . . Searching through the diary and memos on her son's bookshelf and through the mound of letters, she had understood the gist of this appalling situation.

"I wonder where he went," I sighed, not without envy. Mrs. Kurata, however, interpreted this as the most obvious sort of subterfuge. . . She had suspected me from the start.

"Come on, I want the whole truth now. . . Where has my Shingo gone off to?"

I could only answer that I didn't know. At this, Mrs. Kurata suddenly broke into a strong Kyushu accent and lashed out at me, saying the basic fault was mine. A bead of spittle gathered at the corner of her clay-colored mouth. . . The woman's words only increased my determination. I looked over at my mother. She looked back at me. After the wasted, embittered face of Mrs. Kurata, I could hardly miss the flush of triumph on my mother's round face, the beaming pride of one whose son has been compared with another and won.

Seeing this, I knew it was safe to excuse myself.

"Well, I guess I'll go out and look for him then," I said, and after locking up my bookcase, just to be on the safe side, I left the house.

Night had fallen. Naturally, I had no intention of tracking my friends down, despite my promise to Mrs. Kurata. When, out of habit, my feet began to turn toward the coffee shop, I changed direction and walked down unfamiliar streets. I didn't know where to go or what to do with myself. A warm wind blew from a starless sky. . . On an impulse I stopped a cab and gave the name of one of the red-light districts across the river. Maybe I would run into them there. So I said to myself. But of course that wasn't what I was hoping for.

As the cab started up, I was lured by the car's speed into a heightened, sentimental mood. Looking at the lights reflected in the window as they went past, what I saw were the flickers, deep in my heart, of feelings from the time when I had loved my friends. . . But as the car picked up speed, the sheer joy of moving obliterated everything else.

Each time we crossed one of the numerous bridges, the midsection of the girders would float into view in the headlights, as soon to be buried again under the body of the car. . .

At some point I rose half out of my seat, put both hands on the back of the driver's seat, and slipped into a fantasy that I was moving under my own power. . .

That winter, a new group of nations joined the war against Japan.

STARS

Kojima Nobuo
Translated by Van C. Gessel

Kojima Nobuo, born in 1915 in Gifu, is a solitary figure on the contemporary literary scene, a novelist who has turned a bitterly satirical gaze upon himself and his contemporaries and found them all to be "partial cripples." His novels and short stories take a dark look at ineffectual characters thrust into a vortex of relativism and contradictions that render them unable to act.

The primary literary influence on Kojima has been the writings of Gogol, the master Russian satirist whose works Kojima encountered while studying English literature at Tokyo University. The experiences of his own life have tended to reinforce the view that human life is absurd: Kojima began teaching English at the middle school level just eight months before Japan declared war on all the major English-speaking nations of the world; after he was drafted into the Japanese Army in 1942 and failed officer candidacy tests, he was sent to Manchuria, where he worked alongside Nisei intercepting and decoding transmissions from U.S. Air Force units stationed in Asia.

Since his recognition as a writer with the publication of "Kisha no naka" (On the Train, 1948), an incisive account of the pandemonium of the early postwar days, symbolized by the masses swarming and jostling to board an express train, and the train's frantic rush toward Tokyo and a new, "modern" order; and "Shōjū" (The Rifle, 1952; tr. 1979), an erotic tale of an ambivalent soldier, Kojima has continued to write about morally handicapped individuals who search for, but never find, meaning in their everyday activities. Hōyō kazoku (Embracing Family, 1965), which won the

100

Tanizaki Prize, is one of the most harrowing of modern Japanese novels in its focus on an enfeebled intellectual, while the gentler story "Amerikan sukūru" (The American School, 1954; tr. 1977) is widely admired for its humorous study of a painfully proud yet insecure teacher of English in Occupied Japan. Kojima's most recent work is a massive, fourteen-hundred-page novel, Wakareru riyū *(Reasons for Parting, 1982), which critics in Japan are already calling a landmark in the evolution of the modern Japanese novel.*

"Hoshi" (Stars, 1954), translated here, is one of the more biting chronicles to emerge from the Pacific War. Kojima has created an essentially perfect literary emblem of spiritual ambivalence in George Sugihara, a Nisei educated in America but drafted by chance into the Japanese Army. Kojima has infused this character with much of the ambivalence he himself felt during the war years. The story concerns itself with the various "stars" by which men seek stability and guidance in their lives. For George Sugihara, who goes into the army confused and uncertain, there can never be any reliable stars; but he goes on searching for them anyway.

*   *   *

What man wouldn't feel an unusual surge of emotion as he gazed at the lone red star on the collar of a uniform hurled randomly in his direction? I for one felt dazed at that moment. It may have had something to do with the fact that I was an American Nisei without a jot of military training who was going to have to spend the rest of his life as a soldier. That demeaning insignia—the simple, worn, tarnished star buried in some threadbare red cloth—would cling forever to my collar, invisible to me but obvious to everyone else. A curse upon the man who thought up such a cunning mark! By its nature, that unlucky token exercised far less control over me if I made no conscious effort to remember it was there. That star pinned to my collar—I wore the lowliest of them all. For everyone to see. I was made to realize this every single day.

I found that I really knew nothing about the army up until then. When I thought of the long chain leading upward from private second class to general to field marshal, my eyes swam as though I were peering up a ladder to heaven. The gulf was so incredible; one could never skip a single rung of the nearly twenty steps above. And a swarm of single stars like an ocean surrounding me. Moreover, this miserable single star acquired new life as it became two, then three stars. Suddenly on the next level a stripe was added. Then a silver stripe was joined by a silver star. Next the design changed and was given lively borders. And thereafter. . . Thus, the higher you got, the more decorative and resplendent your uniform became. I suppose a conference must have been called to decide all this. One can imagine how inspired the delegates had been by the belief that the Great Ones must be suitably adorned. "No, that's a bit too pretty." "The balance is off." "Make that one a bit more humble— the way it is, it doesn't bring out the distinction enough."

So when I joined the army, each time I noticed someone gazing at me, I angrily returned the look, feeling this would let people know where I stood. But I realized that I'd been singled out by the senior noncoms as their plaything. Until then I hadn't known how feeble a look of hatred can be. They laughed uproariously at me because my body was built like an American's, because I wasn't very agile, and because of the solemn expression on my face. Then amicably they would tell me to look in the mirror. When I turned around, the "roasting" began. When they taunted me, they referred to it as "Western-style cooking" or "American sightseeing." I had to answer all sorts of questions about California and American women. "Speak some English," they'd jeer. "Sing some jazz." If I had performed to their satisfaction, they might have dropped these demands. But I refused to answer them, angered at the malevolence of this vegetarian race. Once I adopted that attitude, they shifted the direction of their interrogations. No longer did they treat me like a jester; now they were looking for excuses to beat me up. "Western-style cooking" came to mean frying me alive, and "American sightseeing" meant watching me double over in pain.

As a result, I became even more averse to looking in the mirror. I stopped even using one to shave.

A soldier named Hikida slept in the bed next to mine. He too was viciously beaten and abused. I stood by and watched while he was pummeled, and surprised myself by experiencing feelings of pleasure. He had done nothing to deserve this kind of treatment. Frankly I enjoyed watching him being beaten because I couldn't bear his ugliness. I realized then that I felt not the slightest affinity with him, and that I too was abusing him in my own special way.

His ugliness had little to do with his awkward posture, or the fact that his uniform was always in disarray because his spare time was all devoted to receiving upbraidings for his idleness. Rather I felt that the measly single star on his collar deserved a better setting than his tiny eyes and his long, pale, downcast face with its three moles. Indeed his looks were an insult to that star. Even one star was too exalted for him. He made me wish that someone had invented an even humbler insignia.

I couldn't bear thinking about the way others viewed me. But vaguely I sensed they felt that I was a disgrace to my own star, too. By insulting one star I was insulting every other star.

In our barracks once, we had a bottle of soy sauce that we'd brought over from the mess hall. Hikida asked me what he should do with it, and I told him to pour the stuff out. I thought that if we returned with what was left in the bottle, they would threaten simply not to give us any more—that was a bit of military common sense even I could figure out. Hikida did as I told him and poured the sauce down the toilet. Then we took the bottle back to the mess along with the other dishes. The cook was waiting there for us, wanting to know what had happened to the soy. Apparently, everyone from the other barracks had dutifully brought their leftovers back.

"You must have poured yours out," he insisted.

"I used it all," I replied.

"Liar! Where did you get rid of it?" He looked at me. "Hey, American! I bet you made him pour it out!" He had work to do in the kitchen and we had assignments of our own, but the cook detained us and thoroughly bawled us out. Normally I would have borne the brunt of the assault, but somehow when the cook's eyes fell on Hikida, he began stamping his feet as though in pain. From the expression on his face it was obvious he wouldn't be able to keep from attacking Hikida. I stood to one side, gritting my teeth. Hikida had his own unique way of taking a beating. Like a child, he covered his face with his hands, trying to deflect the oncoming blows from his head. Of course it would have been more natural and effective to roll with the punches. Hikida had the knack of making people want to beat him, and clearly sometimes his submissive posture only increased his assailant's anger. The cook was so inflamed as he disposed of Hikida that he forgot I was even there.

It dawned on me that if I stuck close to Hikida, it would be like wearing a cloak of invisibility. After all, there was no question that Hikida was my inferior.

Mentally I had moved up a step to some vague, undefined status. I have cited only one example, but I was gradually growing in confidence.

It may sound foolish, but I lived in fear of army horses. There were several horses in our signal corps, and we had to feed them, clean up their dung, and groom them. These were duties that had to be attended to even more scrupulously than the care of our weapons and equipment. The horses were, after all, living creatures. There was a danger we might be kicked, or contract some disease from them; mostly, though, I was afraid of their eyes. The army has a saying that goes, "Even horses can recognize rank." These creatures had been part of the battalion long before we came along, and had transported our commanding officer and our vital equipment. How could they possibly be inferior to us? In fact I was often asked, "Could *you* run with the commander on your back? Even if you could, he'd refuse to ride you. Do you think you could carry all that equipment, American? It takes four men just to lift it—five men the likes of you. Which is better—you or the horse?" As a consequence of many such interrogations, I had become convinced (though it still seemed a bit odd) that what they said was true: a horse really was vastly superior. I was amazed that it hadn't occurred to me before. But a soldier didn't have the leisure to ponder the question at length, and at the bottom of my heart I couldn't bring myself to believe that horses were so very exalted. This was borne out by the fact that horses had no stars. I knew they could give us some stiff competition, but their status as such was surely inferior. And yet, we were a sort of domestic animal ourselves, and as animals they could certainly hold their own. So, when I thought of them peering at my star with those cool eyes, that army proverb felt as sharp as the flick of a whip.

For this reason I dreaded my encounters with them even more than my associations with my human superiors. It wasn't so much the fear that they would recognize my star and just disdain me. It was more the apprehension that they would compare our relative positions and try to display their superiority by kicking or biting. Would you laugh if I confessed that I hid my collar insignia from the horses? Well, it's true.

Still, how do you keep a horse from seeing your star? Their necks are so long, they're going to get a look at it eventually.

We were not allowed to look after the commander's horse. Yet somehow one morning we found Hikida sprawled out with his chin kicked in, and it turned out to be the commander's horse that had done it. This chestnut horse, called Gorō, had made mincemeat out of Hikida and then fled unchallenged to the parade ground, where he cut a figure of enviable beauty. Whoever instructed Hikida to groom that horse must have had it in for him. All right. I'm the one who falsified orders and told him to take care of it. Stupidly, he didn't even know it was the commander's steed. He was actually supposed to groom the horse in the neighboring stall. Later on I was thrashed, of course; they found out I had lied. But I didn't dread beatings. I dreaded being humiliated.

I no longer feared even beatings in the middle of the night, so long as such treatment involved no humiliation. As a student in America, I was once part of a rowing team, and the experience came back to me vividly. We sat aft in the boat and had to practice several thousand strokes. As we approached, say, five thousand strokes, shouts of encouragement would pursue us agonized oarsmen. The same thing happened to me when I was beaten across the face. Every ten blows or so as we approached the ultimate goal—thirty, forty, or fifty, depending on the offense—the haunting jeers of encouragement from the onlooking soldiers seemed to swell in volume. The humiliation tortured me more than the chastisement.

In the dead of night I often passed Hikida some of my portion of bean jelly. To that end I patiently saved up some of my own rations. It gave me the creeps just being near him. And then he would start backfiring under his blanket. I ignored the demands of my own stomach and stored up my rations just so I could have the pleasure of hearing those sounds. I also gave him part of my rice. We were both singled out for hatred because of what we did, but it put me in a position of superiority over him. And over my persecutors also.

Confined to his bed after the episode with the horse, Hikida received less sympathy than he had when, in the past, a fellow soldier had knocked him down. I poured gruel down his throat and mashed up sweets to stuff into his mouth. I've never been so conscious of how disgusting a mouth can be. And performing these tasks was my sole delight in life.

The region just southwest of the village where we were stationed was surrounded by high mountains. We were sent out to climb them many times. Should the enemy ever come, they would storm down from there. Soldiers who wanted to make a name for themselves were very fond of climbing them. Even though we never fought a single battle, being the first to the summit with a heavy pack on your back was a sure way of attracting attention. I hated those mountains. I wasn't really weaker physically than the others, but I couldn't bear the thought of being in competition with soldiers who had once been woodcutters or charcoal burners. I had decided to make Hikida my hiking companion.

We set out in the middle of one night. By noon of the following day we had crossed over three large, bald mountains. Our formation crumbled, and as expected, Hikida with his short scrawny legs soon fell behind the others. I stayed with him, and before long the two of us had formed a rear guard on our own. It took no more than a glance at his pathetic figure to make me want to rip the star off his collar. It seemed so venomous, so green, so like a parasite. I began counting the number of times he stumbled against the rocks. I plucked his rifle from his hands and shouldered his along with my own. Even he knew what it meant to surrender your weapon to someone else, but he let me take it anyway.

Just an hour later Hikida was dangling upside down over a cliff.

The men who had gone on ahead had already reached the summit and were waiting there to lay into us. But when the sun began to set and we still hadn't caught up with them, they came back looking for us. There they discovered Hikida stumbling along twenty or thirty yards behind me, about to fall off the cliff. I knew what was happening to him, because time after time he had called my name: "Hey, Sugihara! Hey, Sugihara!!" If I'd felt any goodwill toward him then, I wouldn't have been able to ignore him. But I had myself to think of, which is why I stayed about thirty yards ahead of him but still behind the rest of the unit. I knew they'd beat up Hikida before they turned on me. And after all, I was carrying his rifle for him, wasn't I? Obviously he'd given up his weapon and was trying to get himself killed. There could be no greater insult to his superiors—to those majestic stars they wore. As a reward for his cowardice, two senior officers dangled him callously by his legs over the top of the cliff.

Hikida let out piteous screams before he was hoisted up and set on the back of the commander's horse. The commander himself ordered it. Naturally the horse was our old friend Gorō. Hikida hung his head, stealing occasional glances at me in the hope that I would help him.

Along the way there was a brief skirmish in which two of the enemy died. During the fighting Hikida remained on horseback, hiding behind a crag.

One of the dead soldiers, dressed in a sky-blue padded uniform, lay face down at the side of the path. One of our men nudged the body over with his foot and stared at it. There, in the same location on his neck, the dead soldier wore a single white star against the black of his collar. The meagerness of that enemy star—though it wasn't an absolute meagerness—made me feel close to the dead man. Or was it just because he was now a corpse? When I was in America, I attended the cremation of a Japanese acquaintance. As the bones were broken up and placed in an urn, I heard an American comment, "He was well built for a Japanese, wasn't he?" I'm sure I wouldn't have felt envy for my late friend if his bones had been small and fragile.

Hikida's ceremonious return to camp astride the commander's horse should by all rights have been compensated by increased abuse from the men. But instead he was taken to the infirmary with pneumonia. I ended up carrying his meals to him.

He had been an artist, the kind who paints scenes on umbrellas. When we were alone he showed me some pictures he had drawn on tissue paper, and he blew his nose in them and asked me to throw them away. His drawings of roses and morning glories were prosaic and lifeless. But the expression on his face when he sketched them was unique, and I tried not to look at him when he was that way. I had to wash out his hospital gowns. When I peeled them off him, he looked bewildered and unable

107

to express his gratitude. It was important to me that he feel like that.

It's unfortunate, I suppose, but it never occurred to me that he might have a family. He may have mentioned it to me, but I must have forgotten, because when he asked me to bring a picture of his wife and children from his locker, I realized for the first time that he was a family man. He tried to get me to look at the picture, but I lied and said I'd already seen it. To admit that Hikida had a family would be tantamount to regarding him as a fellow human being. I wanted him to remain a domestic animal.

And so I wept when I reported to him that he was the only man who hadn't been promoted from buck private. There was no way he could have seen through my act.

What is it about getting an extra star that wields such tremendous power over the mind of a soldier? What meaning does it have to receive just one more pitiful earthbound star? Like all other ceremonies, the promotion ceremony is carried out with great solemnity. From that day forward, soldiers become more diligent than before. They want to go out in the world. Go out on a foray and display their advancement to others. But just who do they expect to show off for?

I peered into a mirror again for the first time since becoming a PFC. I only deserved one star. Now I was locked into the system. Seeing myself, I was overcome with shame.

In his infirmary room, Hikida called me, "Private, sir!" He was due to be released soon, and he had some things he wanted to discuss with me. He had been able to relax a bit here in the infirmary, he said, but if he had to go back to the unit now, he would have preferred being persecuted without a break from it. I told him I was going to be serving as a sentry now, and that while I was on duty we would be by ourselves. At that word of encouragement, he buried his head under the covers. He seemed somehow afraid of me.

"No matter what happens, Hikida, you've got to give up trying to die."

He peeped out from under the covers. "I do? I wish I'd been born a woman. No woman would have to put up with the likes of these guys. Why, they'd come running after me!" he said with regret. He seemed to have spent his leisure hours thinking about his family and about dying. A chill ran down my spine. So far the suicides in our unit were limited

108

to men with one star; without exception they had all hanged themselves.

Hikida was indispensable to me. He was less a human being for me than a sort of star. He was an even more necessary existence to the senior officers. That much was evident, because once he was hospitalized a sense of desolation swept over the unit; the men tried unsuccessfully to turn me into their punching bag, and afterward they often inquired about Hikida's condition.

In any case, he and I ended up standing watch at the city gates. The city was surrounded by a wall two and a half miles in circumference, which had been standing for fifteen or sixteen centuries. One gate opened out at each point of the compass. We were to unbolt the rusted locks of the heavy gates at 5:30 each morning, and close them at 5:30 each evening. Once the gates were shut all traffic ceased. We began patrolling the walls after things had quieted down. When we were off duty we were frequently sent outside the city to steal melons. Without even noticing, I had started giving Hikida orders. I stood stiffly over him as I made him tear a melon off the vine, then found another ripe melon and had him pick it. He looked up at me sheepishly. This angered me and I was forced to shout at him. This had never happened to me before. When Hikida moved, I moved too. What did all this mean? When had this come about?

As sentries, Hikida and I had to check the papers of every Chinese who went in and out of the gates, and keep an eye out for forgeries. Not only were we left on our own here, but with our metal helmets on our heads and our bayonets in our hands, none dared ridicule us. Nobody even knew I was a Nisei. In a position like this, I thought, I could get to like these locals.

"What's your name? Birthplace? Age?"

"Do you have any children? How many?"

"Where have you come from, and where are you going?"

"How far away is that village?"

"Your daughter's going to grow up to be a beauty!"

I strung together what few Chinese phrases I knew and asked questions of this nature, even commenting on things that had nothing to do with my sphere of responsibility. When missionaries passed through I greeted them in English. I realized that Hikida was aping me and making all sorts of inquiries. He knew a great deal more about commerce than I, and there were many things he wanted to learn. The locals carried cotton goods, flour, bedding, household belongings, charcoal, and all sorts of other items on their backs or tied to mules. Ostensibly it was our cruel duty to jab at their packs with our bayonets, and sometimes even to dump out the contents to check for concealed weapons. Instead Hikida and I spent our time plying them with questions for our own edification.

Because these peculiar inspectors never seized any of their belongings, the Chinese always thanked us with a *"Hsieh-hsieh"* as they passed through. One evening, though, our superior officer stole up behind us, saw what we were doing, and gave me a swift kick that sent me sprawling onto the ground. I fell flat on my face like a squashed frog, still clutching my bayonet. I couldn't understand why I was singled out for such treatment, but since I was a PFC and responsible for both myself and Hikida, maybe it was to be expected. When I got to my feet I was booted to the ground again. The Chinese man who had been standing by me suddenly began showering compliments on my superior. Those who were still waiting to go through the gate cast wry smiles in my direction. They must have found it amusing that the frames of my glasses were broken and one of the lenses had fallen out. At once they seemed distant and hostile to me, accomplices of my superiors. I realize now that, in that moment, they were given a graphic demonstration of the relationship between one, two, and three stars. That alone was sufficient cause for laughter.

My dreams were shattered in that fleeting instant. I still think Hikida is the one who destroyed my illusions. After that day I ceased to feel any sense of camaraderie with the Chinese who passed before me. When I caught Hikida leering at the occasional man who went by with a pregnant woman, I signaled to him to cut it out. But he merely grinned at me. It was obvious that lately he accepted everything I told him to do, and even reveled in carrying out my orders. He trusted me, and depended on my protection. Why was it that I couldn't bear that buoyant look on his face? Was that what happened when you climbed up one step on the hierarchical ladder?

110

A path three or four yards wide ran along the top of the city wall. One night we patrolled that pitch-black path. Normally one soldier patrolled two of the four sides of the wall, but since we were still trainees, Hikida and I stood guard together.

During the daylight hours it was all I could do to keep from throttling Hikida. When we were on duty, though, he followed his usual practice of trotting along behind me, gazing down from atop the wall at the houses in the town. Twice he nearly slipped and fell off the wall as he did this. Enraged, I vowed he wouldn't get off so easily a third time.

The next time the fool began sliding off the edge, I grabbed him by the collar and dragged him up, then hauled him over to the parapet on the other side and pinned him against it. Forgetting my sentry duties, I shouted, "You're a soldier, you know!" and gave him a good whack. The pain he felt reverberated through my hand. It was the kind of pain, I suppose, that can only be understood by one who has been continuously beaten himself. What I had really wanted to say was, "You're the lowest of all stars, you know!"

Hikida resisted by covering his face with his hands. He had just learned during his most recent pummeling not to lift his hands to his face, but with me he did it again. I jerked his hands away and beat him further.

"Jōji! Please stop—I'll do whatever you want! I'll do your laundry—anything!"

"You think I could stand being fawned on by someone like you?"

I must have said something like that. I was caught up in the fury of my mood. Hikida turned his flat, tearstained, frantic face out away from the city, wailed bitterly, and then tried to scale the parapet and leap off the thirty-foot-high wall. Remembering how close to suicide he had seemed in his hospital room, I froze in horror. Then I dragged him down off the wall.

What had I done atop that city wall? Inside the town, the intermittent braying of mules outside the wall could be heard. From the eaves of the house just below us rose voices chanting sutras. The lives these Chinese led were wretched, but perhaps ours were even more miserable. My torment had driven me to the brink of madness, and as I clutched at the cold, ancient stones of the city wall, I saw a wreath of stars as-

111

cending from a point below me into the sky. It circled the sky and then disappeared behind the wall opposite me. For a long while I had forgotten that there were stars in the heavens.

I trembled, feeling desolation welling up within me. Hikida, still huddled on the ground, muttered petulantly, "You're not a Japanese after all. You aren't! You aren't!"

Once the unwelcome Hikida had been transferred to a unit in Southeast Asia, orders came for me to report to regimental headquarters to serve as an orderly to Captain Inoma of the district command. He was twenty-two or -three, with nothing special to recommend him aside from the fact that he was an officer. His chief claims to fame were the manner in which he could spit vigorously out his window each morning after I brought in his water, and the fact that he could drink the murky Chinese tea. He was, in short, a model officer. Bedecked in his officer's stars, he looked at least thirty years old. Strangely enough, when a man acquires two stars, his age seems to advance in concert with his promotion, as though even his years were subject to the rule of the stars.

Brought into close contact with these distant stars, I felt not hatred, but something more like adoration. I wondered if, as a result of all the anguish I'd been made to suffer in the midst of those inferior stars, I hadn't come to feel that life had greater meaning if I surrendered to the star system and regarded myself as worthless. I had indeed come to believe that stars had an intrinsic value to them—that a PFC was truly superior to a buck private, a lance corporal better than a PFC, a noncom greater than a common foot soldier, and an officer vastly more exalted than a noncom. I had become convinced that those of a higher rank than my own were an inherently different breed of human being. Particularly an officer. How could I even imagine that Captain Inoma— this lofty being for whom I washed laundry every day, delivered meals, and poured tea—belonged to the same species as myself? There was even a brief period when I embraced the peculiar notion that he was my superior by virtue of the fact that he belonged to a race of vegetarians. Perhaps I had fallen short of the mark because I had lived in America and been corrupted by the consumption of animal flesh.

112

More importantly, however, my advancement to two-star rank increased my faith in the stars themselves.

On one occasion the division commander inspected our regiment. When Captain Inoma barked, "Eyes right!" the soldier standing directly opposite me jerked his head toward the commander. In that instant it seemed to my apprehensive eyes that the soldier's face had stretched all out of shape. The commander marched briskly up to the soldier, placed his hand on the man's chin, gave a grunt, and moved on. The soldier stiffened his elongated face even more and stood unflinching. What had happened was that the officer had corrected the soldier's dislocated jaw in a flash. I was dumbstruck. The entire regiment wept tears of gratitude afterward, of course. Somehow the commander's majestic poise and magnanimity seemed well in keeping with the number of stars he wore. Thinking back on it now, perhaps there was nothing so special about this histrionic scene. Maybe he was just good at repairing dislocated jaws.

My duties as Captain Inoma's orderly were pretty much those of a chambermaid. If this very minute I were to bring out a captain's collar insignia and that of a PFC and ask a child to choose the better one, I have no doubt he would choose the captain's. I recognized the disparity between our positions and bowed low before Captain Inoma.

Since I had the lowest-ranking stars, I was sent to regimental headquarters to represent all the men from our office at roll call. First, however, I was supposed to put logs into five stoves, polish the twenty-odd yards of hallway and stairs with a rag, then take the captain's breakfast to him—BUT, only after I had taken him his washbasin, of course, and folded up his bedding. Even before all that, I had to go and get everyone's breakfasts and deliver them. I couldn't light the stove until I stole some coal from the kitchen. Strangely enough, I enjoyed carrying out this morning's worth of endless duties. As I scrubbed the floors, I found delight in the manner in which I wrung out the rags, and it was a challenge to try to miss all the nails in the floorboards. When I went to pick up meals for delivery, struggling to keep the slippers from flying off my feet and the soup from spilling out of the bowls, invariably a senior officer would be coming toward me in the distance, and I would have to muster a salute.

But I always experienced a pleasant afterglow as a natural offshoot of my trials. And it was somehow thrilling to be crawling along the floor with a rag in my hands and suddenly be able to stand up before the regimental flag, salute the sentry, and then return to my floor polishing. Our dust-covered flag was poised on a pedestal, guarded by a living soldier, and to it I offered my salutes.

The first time I met Captain Inoma, he wanted me to write out a *rirekisho*. Apparently he wasn't pleased that his new orderly wore only two stars and was, moreover, a second-generation Japanese-American. I'm ashamed to have to admit it, but I didn't know right off what a *rirekisho* meant.

"*Rirekisho. Rirekisho?*" I chewed the word over, until finally he explained what it was.

"Oh, you mean a 'personal history'!" I blurted out in English. That really exasperated him. But he seemed to consider it his duty to take what there was of this orderly and make a first-rate soldier out of him. In my personal history, I wrote that when I reached junior high age, I was sent back to California to be with my parents. After finishing college in the U.S., I returned to Japan to see my grandfather, and was at once drafted into the army. When he read this, the captain peered into my face as though examining some exotic animal. He admitted that I hadn't seemed completely Japanese to him, and he was kind enough to ask me all sorts of questions about California. I warmed to the occasion and began relating all manner of fond memories of the place, until suddenly he snatched up the résumé I had written, ripped it to shreds, and tossed the fragments into the stove.

"PFC Sugihara Jōji! You're going to have one hell of a time becoming a Japanese soldier. You will consider today the last time you have any past whatsoever," he ordered. He decided in addition that I was to write a daily "Journal of Self-Examination," which he would read to determine whether I was making progress toward becoming a true Japanese soldier. He also set out to teach me the fine art of Chinese poetic recitation. Subsequently he had me write out two new personal histories, but he tore these up as well. These facts were duly noted in my Journal.

If I wearied of ferreting out new material for my daily introspections, Captain Inoma did me the favor of pointing out my shortcomings.

Nothing made him happier than to see me covering sheets and sheets of paper with my self-examinings. He seemed highly suspicious that I might inwardly hold him in contempt, so I crammed my Journal primarily with rhapsodies declaring my profound respect for him. But eventually he came up with an unusual method of testing my loyalty. He had me prepare three separate collar insignia of captain's rank. While he slept at night, I was to rotate them on his uniforms every now and then. By doing that, of course, I was unable to forget even in my sleep that he was a captain. And naturally my Journal was also there to help me remember.

Perhaps because I felt humiliated as I carried out this penance of rotating his insignia, I let the notion grow in me that the captain was himself a star, and that stars had an innate grandeur about them. I had never felt quite that way before.

From my perspective now it is hard to believe that I once had such thoughts. But when Captain Inoma came walking toward me, my mind was riveted not upon him as a person, but on each of those cherished stars. The expressions on the faces of those three familiar stars were engraved upon my heart. Imagine it! Secretly I gave each of them a name. I called them Tom, Frank, and Kate, after the names of my two brothers and my younger sister. When the stars came my way, I greeted them inwardly with a "Hi, Frank!" and suchlike.

Once when I saluted Captain Inoma, I remember him asking dourly, "Private Sugihara, what exactly are you saluting?"

"Yes, sir. I'm saluting you, Captain, sir."

"You are not to salute me. You are to salute my eyes. Write that in your Journal."

On snowy days I felt sorry for Kate.

Frank was a rowdy boy and always getting dirty.

Brother Tom was always at his best at ceremonies.

These notions could not be written in my Journal, of course, so Captain Inoma had no way of knowing what was really going through my mind.

One day when I was attending the captain in his bath, he climbed out of the tub and plopped himself down in front of me. I felt as though a powerful electric shock had run through me. I couldn't shake off the peculiar sensation that Kate was still clinging to the nape of his neck. Why should I be so stunned to see the captain nude, without his uniform? Who in fact was this naked man before me? He was muscular, to be sure, but was there such a great difference between me and this man with the close-cropped hair when both of us were in the buff? After he climbed back into the bath, he launched into one of his recitations of Chinese poetry. I sat abstractedly holding his towel and soap. The sound of his chanting reawakened in me the realization that this was indeed Captain Inoma before me, and I returned to my senses. But I had a sluggish, uneasy feeling, as though a cog had slipped out of place. I wanted to get both the captain and myself back into uniform at once.

That was the first time I'd been in the bathroom with him. After that day, I was ordered to be his regular bath attendant. But each experience left me feeling more unsettled. Most disturbing, I started thinking there was something wrong with the way he gulped his tea, the way he re-filled his rice bowl, the way he snored in his sleep, and the way he spat out the window each morning. I grew pensive, something a soldier can-not allow himself to do unless he expects to be wounded or perpetrate some dreadful blunder. I began to worry that I might really put my foot in it.

One day when I accompanied Captain Inoma to Peking, I saw a string of hands across the way rise up in salute. Caught up in the movement, I too lifted my hand. Ahead of us an automobile came to a stop. The captain didn't move, so I followed his example and stood at attention, watching intently. The door of the automobile opened, and out stepped Chief of Staff Nawa. The captain at once shouted "Salute!" and I brought my hand up to the side of my head. But I was eager to see what was emerging from the automobile, so I peered out from behind the cap-tain's back, my hand still in midair. What should appear before my eyes but a full golden galaxy more sumptuous and dazzling than a million commonplace stars! I had never seen such splendor so close at hand. To what should I compare such an array of stars? The brothers and sisters I had doted on were no longer adequate metaphors—stars of this mag-nitude made those everyday varieties seem wrought of base materials. This officer seemed like a queen who had deigned to grace the city with her presence. By now I had forgotten all about my right hand. In nervous excitement I watched as the queen began her procession. Chief of Staff Nawa was advancing in my direction, so I took a step or two forward, until a stentorian shout rattled in my ears. I beat a hasty retreat.

I was informed that I had been disrespectful toward the chief of staff. That seemed impossible to me, but everything went black before my eyes as the captain dragged me back to the unit. An hour later I was standing looking the captain full in the face for the first time. Although Inoma claimed we had spent every single day together for some time now, it was true that recently I hadn't looked him in the face. The base of his nose was thick. His eyes were narrow but sparkling. His chin was angular, his mouth tightly clenched—though for several minutes now it had been restlessly opening and closing. I was still in a daze, unable to make out what he was saying.

"What kind of idiot gawks at a general like he's watching a peepshow? Especially right in front of that chief of staff! I'm going to have to finish you off with my sword."

He repeated this over and over again, but all I could do was look at him in stupefaction. I was totally stunned to think that words that had such great bearing on my very life could flow so casually from his mouth. All I could think of was that today I should remove Kate and pin Frank onto his uniform. His stars were crooked. It wasn't possible. . .

My memory grows dim at this point, yet I seem to recall the fact that Captain Inoma had been a classmate of this particular chief of staff, but was two ranks behind him when they received their commissions. Inoma had distinguished himself at the front line in an attempt to close the gap, but each time he attained some merit, his rival bounced up two more ranks. The captain was bitterly disappointed.

Captain Inoma seemed to have worked himself into a rage. He stripped me naked, then energetically tore off his own jacket. He made me sit facing the east, pulled out his sword and wrapped the blade with my shirt, then stepped up to me.

"Are you ready? Don't be a coward. Cut your belly open now, and I'll chop your head off for you. Don't worry about a thing."

I didn't have the impression that he was joking. But this was all too sudden to be really happening. I didn't even have time to feel sad. I gazed down at my stomach. My belly button seemed so forlorn, so alone. As I studied my navel, I blurted out:

"Look—a star!"

"What? What's that, Sugihara?" He peered forward.

"A star. It's a star!"

"You're right. Your navel does look like a star! What a—" The captain burst into laughter so raucous that I was astonished.

If this preposterous anecdote seems to defy all credibility, the fault lies in my inability to tell it properly. When one belongs to an army whose sole aim is to destroy other human beings, a sense of the preposterous is a requisite for survival.

Blessed are they who can doubt the truth of these sentiments!

I had spoken out of sorrow—sorrow over the fact that the lowest of all stars, that solitary star which I thought I was at long last rid of, had been hiding—of all places—in the center of my own belly. I was ashamed beyond endurance that my feelings had been revealed to someone else. From his roar of laughter it seemed that Captain Inoma had given up the idea of killing me and now regarded me as a lunatic, but in fact the innermost secrets of my heart had been exposed to his gaze. I was frightened to go on living.

Frantic to cover up my belly, I hurriedly put on the shirt that had been wrapped around his sword. Captain Inoma, still apparently in a state of excitement, reached for a jacket and slipped it on. But when he looked up at me, I nearly let out a cry of incredulity. The figure standing before me was "Private" Inoma. Not once had it ever occurred to me that Captain Inoma could be transformed into a private. I should have been bewildered and embarrassed, but instead a shudder of intense pleasure ran through my body. It had been careless of him to put on my jacket, when the feel of the material and everything else about it was so different from his own. Perhaps he had lost his wits.

He seemed to sense something was wrong from my expression, and he looked himself over. Turning a bright red, he removed my jacket and tossed it to me.

"There's no need to be switching insignia any more. You're confined to your quarters. Give serious thought to your behavior." With that he stomped out of the room.

He reported to headquarters that I was suffering from nervous prostration, and confined me to my room for ten days. But who can say that Inoma himself wasn't the lunatic for trying to decapitate me just because I was standing a few degrees askew when I saluted the general? I laughed out loud at the memory of how delighted I'd been to see Captain Inoma converted into a private. Why, I'll rip Kate right off his collar! . . .

Aiming for a time when he was in the tub, I sneaked into the bathroom. Not that I was eager to continue as his bath attendant, but having performed that duty for so long, it made me feel strangely desolate to think I might be relieved of the responsibility. Previously it had been my custom to call out through the fuel hole, "How is the temperature, sir?" I felt a prick of conscience as I crept in, but I stifled it and set my sights on the collar of his jacket.

No sooner had I set foot in the room than I had the impression that Inoma was shouting at me, and I turned tail and ran. When I got a grip on myself, though, I realized that the noise hadn't been a bellow directed at me, but rather his customary recitation, which he chanted as he made waves on the surface of the bathtub:

"Nature grows all the more desolate.
Another field of battle reeking of blood."

Taking advantage of the moment, I plucked Kate from the captain's clothing, put my insignia in its place, and fled.

I opened the double doors in the captain's room and slipped behind them, making sure I returned them to their original position. There in his room I perpetrated a certain act with great haste, then waited with bated breath for his arrival.

Before long through a hole in the paper sliding door I caught sight of him running this way, gasping for breath. He wore only his underwear, and carried a jacket in his hand. He burst into the room, flinging the jacket away. As I watched all this, he seemed like a petulant adolescent. Then he saw me, and retreated several steps without saying a word. When his back struck the door, he drew himself up and bawled at me: "You bastard! Isn't th-that my formal uniform jacket?!"

I said nothing.

I have the impression that I was looking into his eyes. He had, after all, once told me to do that. I couldn't have looked at his collar even if I'd wanted to, since he had on nothing but his underwear.

I was indeed wearing his dress jacket (I had, by the way, affixed Tom to the collar). I was stunned by my own appearance.

In that fleeting instant he seemed to recover himself, and suddenly his body loomed ominously over me. He thrashed me across the face.

"You rotten lunatic! You surprise even me. Madman! If we had more like you, an officer wouldn't be able to sleep in peace. It'd be the ruin of the army! I should have killed you back when I had the chance. Do you realize what you've done, you lousy American?!"

I was silent.

"Think about why you did this. Do you know? I'm sure you don't."

I said nothing.

"It's because you were brought up in a liberal country. Who knows—someone like you could end up switching a general's stars. If you did that, I'd never make major!"

Thereupon he unjustly bound me with ropes and locked me in the unit's uniform closet. I had no idea why he'd chosen such a place to incarcerate me, or how many days he planned to keep me there. I was disheartened. I quietly maneuvered myself into a seated position and looked around. Ironically enough I found myself surrounded by veritable mountains of collar insignia. Up until then I had seldom enjoyed a peaceful night's rest, but when I snuggled down into that mound of stars, I effortlessly dropped off to sleep.

Struggling now to organize my memories of that time, it seems that at some point I jumped to my feet, edged over to the window, cut the ropes that bound me with some broken glass, removed the window and leaped to freedom. As I made my escape, I think I muttered to myself something like:

"The following morning the chief of staff went to headquarters and the staff officers came in to pay their respects. 'My word, he *is* looking

seedy this morning, isn't he?' 'Wait—that isn't the general! It's a buck private!' 'What's a private doing strutting around here?!' 'But, no—better
keep quiet about this.' And so everyone at staff headquarters kept their
mouths shut. On the second day, the general. . .'"

Assuming that I did wander about daydreaming in this way, I must
have been trying to turn Captain Inoma's prophecy into reality. Just
then someone behind me shouted, "Humming jazz, are you?!" and with
overwhelming force tried to pin me to the ground. Clearly it was one
thing to chant Chinese poetry, but quite another for a soldier to sing
some jazz. I was infuriated, though that's no explanation for what I
did. I sank my teeth into my assailant's hand and knocked his arm away,
adding an uppercut to his jaw. It was then I realized that my attacker
was Inoma.

I left him on the ground shouting something about the brute strength
of a lunatic. In a frenzy I leaped a fence and came out on a road. I have
no idea how long I walked, where my feet led me, what I did, or even
if I was really in Peking. I had the feeling I had fallen off the planet
altogether. I dropped to the ground and cried out: "Army Private Sugihara
Jōji! Where are you? Get me out of here!!"

When the war came to an end, Captain Inoma announced that there
was no reason the hostilities should cease. Certainly he had the initiative
to go on fighting alone. And if the captain were to continue, how could
I as his orderly avoid going along with him? Before too long, though,
the captain declared his resolve to commit suicide. Then a short while
later he announced his intention to enlist in the Chinese Communist
Army, and invited me to follow suit. When you join the communists,
he reported, they let you skip three ranks—a captain like himself would
become a colonel, and I could end up a noncommissioned officer. The
invitation was very tempting. I was ready to cast my lot in with the Reds
if it meant hopping up three ranks; the fact is worth recording. After
the defeat, I was ordered to do liaison work, translating communications
from the interior into English so that they could be transmitted to the
U.S. Marines. I knew therefore that some units in the interior had already
surrendered to the communist forces without waiting for the northern
advance of the Guomindang Army, and that their main motivation had

121

been to get such promotions. Units that had refused to surrender had been annihilated.

"Do you really think I could become an NCO?" I asked Inoma, worried that perhaps only the captain would advance to colonel, and that I would be left as a common foot soldier. He seemed little interested in my problems, and replied, "Even if they don't promote you right away, I'll see to it that you get your advancement."

At that point I wore a mere two stars. But now that the war was really over, that pair of stars became as important to me as the captain's insignia were to him. They were imbued with my memories, my experiences. In that sense, I probably prized mine more than the captain did his. And because they meant so much to me, I had the strange notion that I wanted to continue living the sort of life in which stars would play a part.

Captain Inoma was directly responsible for my reinvolvement with English. One day he angrily shouted at me, "Starting today, you're going to remember all your English! Understand? No matter what it takes, you must remember every word of it. A man can do anything if he sets his mind to it."

"How should I go about remembering it, sir?" After all, it was Captain Inoma himself who had impressed upon me day and night that I was to forget every vestige of my American experience. This new command had come from the same Inoma who just a few days earlier had contemplated a one-man resistance against the enemy, then switched to a proclamation of suicide, and was perhaps even now considering the possibility of desertion.

Besides my duties as interpreter and translator, I was invested with the lofty responsibility of teaching interested officers how to converse in English. I received orders from Captain Inoma that I was not to wear my army uniform when I performed this noble function. I was told I should be happy I didn't have to wear a uniform; but I was more humiliated than I had ever been as a green recruit. I couldn't expect Captain Inoma to comprehend my humiliation. They (the chief of staff, for instance) could go on wearing their uniforms. But they insisted that I wear civilian dress. Had they let me keep my two stars on, it would have been their stars that bore the brunt of the shame. And why were they studying English anyway—a language that even I felt was better forgotten?

Once he began his English course, Inoma seemed to drop his plans of enlisting in the communist army.

In any case, they dressed me up in one of their civvy suits and forced me to sit in front of them for several hours at a stretch, for days on end. From my window I observed generals, captains, and lieutenants streaming down the tree-lined road to the headquarters building and into the conference room, each of them clutching the handouts I'd printed up for them. They still wore their swords. Soon Captain Inoma came to take me to the conference room. It was as though he had come to escort a prisoner. For the first time in my four years of army duty, I wept sloppy tears.

"I am Army Private Sugihara Jōji. It is a great privilege to teach you English conversation."

Of course, Captain Inoma took me aside after class and criticized the way I had introduced myself. "All you need tell them is the name your parents gave you—Sugihara Jōji. In fact, just plain Jōji is good enough."

Yet an unendurable sadness gripped me when I thought that, while units were at this very moment sending radio messages to report that they were surrounded by Red troops, the starry generals who controlled the fate of tens of thousands of soldiers in North China were seated in front of me like so many floor samples of the insignia of rank.

In consultation with Captain Inoma (rather, I should say it was he who composed the Japanese text), I printed up the following items in English:

—Days of the week, names of months, military ranks, names of weapons.
—"You are an American soldier, aren't you? I am Captain Inoma Goroku of the Japanese Army."
—"That is untrue. I cannot believe it."
—"Where did you hear that?"
—"Welcome. What can I do for you?"
—"You're welcome."
—"Our troops were brave. So were yours. Everything is my fault."
—"So-and-so is the guilty party."

—"X number of forces from the unit remain in x position."
—"We have provisions." "We do not have provisions."
—"Would you care for some saké?"
—"How will you deal with prisoners?"
—"I am not a war criminal."

These phrases are merely those I am able to recall now. I had them recite the sentences over and over again, correcting their pronunciation. But you can hardly expect proper pronunciation from men used to shouting everything in an officer's bark. I worked with them individually (this too on orders from Captain Inoma), drumming into them their names and ranks in English. The chief of staff couldn't for the life of him remember all the titles of military ranks.

Then Captain Inoma wailed, "I'm not letting anybody beat me at grammar," and he applied himself more diligently than anyone else. He outstripped all the others in language proficiency. In his room he produced a typewriter he had commandeered from an American merchant several years earlier, and had me teach him how to use it. He pounded away on the keys with clumsy fingers. Remarkable. In spite of all this, when he set one foot outside the classroom he became a stickler for ceremony. Even though he had become my student, he was punctilious about having me salute him. If I hesitated, he poked at my chest and berated me. Only when I wore street clothes was I impelled to speak openly, and only during that restricted period was he not on guard about my discipline. He devoted his time in the classroom to absorbing what I had to offer.

We were all promoted one rank en masse. Like fleeing bandits. Come to think of it, maybe the high command did it because they were afraid we'd be overwhelmed by the Chinese army, and all the insignia in the uniform closets would be confiscated.

I became a "Potsdam" PFC. Even now the name has a certain cynical ring to it. Cynical perhaps because we knew the absurd motivation behind the issuing of promotions at a time like that, and because we were delighted by the advancement even though we saw through the whole charade. Captain Inoma became Major Inoma. He changed his insignia himself. I was released from duty as his orderly, but everything else remained the same. Nothing could have been more awkward than this pairing of Major Inoma and PFC Sugihara.

When I went to Inoma's room to announce my promotion, he remarked, "This is good news for both of us," then asked me if I could find him a job, or see if they would take him on as a laborer on my father's farm in America—if, of course, it hadn't been confiscated by the government.

"Please don't ask that, sir. I want to go on thinking of you as a major. I can't cope with this."

"Don't you have any pity? Certainly if it were possible I would want things to continue as they are now. All right, I won't ask for your help. I've been greatly humiliated, Private Sugihara. I guess I should've killed myself, shouldn't I, Jōji?"

So saying, Major Inoma wiped away his tears with the palm of his hand.

The autumn sunlight that shone through the trees from the vast Peking sky made his platinum stars shimmer. The sight made me remember something I had forgotten for a long while—the stars and bells on a Christmas tree. I felt as though I could hear voices singing "Merry Christmas!" somewhere. What a bizarre association to make, I thought.

Despite this emotional scene, Major Inoma continued to implore me for assistance at every subsequent opportunity. When we boarded the LST for repatriation to Japan early the following year, his entreaties grew desperate.

My original unit had joined up with a Chinese Communist Army division in Shansi Province and fallen under the command of a famous Chinese general. As a result, I was sent along with Major Inoma to join a separate unit for repatriation. Our vessel was a transport ship laden with tanks. A thousand of us were crowded into the hold where the tanks were stored. We were in the prow of the ship and away from the boiler room, so we could hear the waves beating against the hull, and nearly enough water to sink the ship poured in on us. I was an interpreter, a sort of unofficial officer, but now that I was away from the officers' quarters and crouched here in the hold of a ship, I had a hard time believing that the thousand soldiers huddled around their knapsacks were being sent back to Japan in defeat. I had the deluded notion that we were setting out to Japan to fight. Before our departure, the men who were sensitive to emblems of rank had picked out and put on the highest-quality items from the uniform closets. That was only natural, since whatever remained would end up in the hands of Chinese soldiers.

Not a single man wanted to remove his uniform.

Every man wanted to return to his hometown wearing his insignia. What was the meaning of it?

Their attitudes were both touching and disagreeable, yet I shared the same feelings. I wanted to wear my uniform back to Japan and then have it on when I showed up at my parents' home in America.

Someone tugged at my left sleeve as I was immersed in these thoughts. I looked up to see a small, scrawny soldier with no collar insignia. "Come with me. I want to talk to you for a minute," he said. The moment I saw his face I shuddered, for he reminded me of Hikida. He wasn't Hikida, of course. That soldier without a unit had probably been transferred from one division to another all over Southeast Asia until he finally died somewhere. After all, he had been the sort of fellow who made you want to do all sorts of terrible things to him; even God had forsaken him. My initial impression that this man resembled Hikida was prompted by his dark, somehow idiotic face. I followed him onto the deck, where he spoke in forceful tones unsuited to his gawky frame.

"You're an interpreter, right?"

"Yes, I am."

"We're gonna beat up all the officers on board. We don't want any Americans coming in while we're at it. You either gotta make 'em let us do it, or else keep 'em occupied."

"Why don't you wait until we land?"

"We gotta do it while they're still wearing their stars. It wouldn't be any fun doing it after we got back home. You must know how we feel, having the number of stars you do."

"If you mess around with the system, we'll all end up losers."

"Once we reach Japan, everybody'll be in a hurry to get back home, and no one'll wanna beat 'em up then."

"What's wrong with that?"

126

He seemed so agitated that he might make trouble for me if I put up any further resistance, so I decided to humor him and said I would go at once to talk with the staff sergeant in command of the transport unit. I had taken no more than one or two steps in that direction when he let out a peculiar laugh.

I concluded from the fact that he'd been deprived of his stars that he must have been a prison guard or the like, and that as a result he had developed a personal antipathy toward symbols of privilege. He seemed to be the ringleader in the plot to assault the officers. I couldn't imagine all the soldiers on board joining in at his bidding, but there was no telling what might happen under the circumstances.

The American staff sergeant, his feet propped up on the desk in his cabin, was more than happy to chat with me. He became incredibly cordial when I told him that I had lived in Fresno for ten years. Initially I felt comfortable with him, but then he cocked his head and remarked how unusual it was for a man with a college degree to be nothing more than a PFC. He treated me as though I were part of the American army. Before long I could clearly read in his eyes that he too had begun to look down on me. As I jabbered on, I grew increasingly incensed that even this man was caught up in the system of rank.

"Georgie, would you mind giving me your PFC insignia? I'd like to take it back with me."

"What would you do with a PFC's stars, Mister Brown? You can get as many as you want down in the hold."

"No, I want yours."

I ignored his request. "Listen, would you please let my parents know I'm all right?"

He stared longingly at my collar while I wrote down my parents' address. He stuffed the paper into his pocket. When I told him about the men's plan to attack their officers, he exploded at me as though I were its instigator.

"An officer is an officer. This absolutely cannot be permitted, Sugihara!"

Besides his fear that order would collapse among the Japanese troops, his face indicated that he had an emotional distaste for the plot. He dragged me off, ordering me to point out the soldier who had spoken to me. I was greatly disappointed in him. Staff Sergeant Brown hid himself behind me, and after he had ascertained which man was the guilty party, he snapped his fingers, disappointed that his target looked so ineffectual. He called me into his room, and told me to give the soldier some gum, chocolate, and cigarettes as a bribe, then to reprimand him. He added a warning that none of it was to be eaten on board the ship, though the cigarettes could be smoked in the WC.

I did as Staff Sergeant Brown directed. I told the soldier, "If you're not careful, you'll never make it back to Japan." He took the items, but gave no reply. From the fragile, hastily constructed WC on deck (which tipped precariously toward the ocean each time a breeze blew) came a lavender stream of smoke that was whisked skyward by the wind. The toilet had no roof, and the men stood in line to use it, so he might as well have done his smoking in the hold. I did in fact reprimand him, but inwardly I hoped he would do something or other down below. I couldn't see us landing in Japan and then dispersing without *something* first taking place. Besides, I must have longed to atone for my treatment of Hikida by hoping that the soldier would raise a riot for which I would be punished.

Major Inoma was serving as commander of the makeshift unit on board, but I stayed down in the hold trying to avoid him. He searched me out anyway. I was amazed at how delighted he was that the ship was approaching Japan, and he declared that he was going to visit my relatives there. Once again he asked me to find him a job. I hoped that a certain *something*—having nothing to do with employment—would soon transpire between the two of us, but I was saddened as I looked at the major, who suspected nothing.

I latched onto another soldier and questioned him about the man who resembled Hikida. "Him? He's a madman. Didn't you know?" was the reply. He screwed his index finger against the side of his head. "They let him run loose because there aren't any rooms to lock him up in." Feeling desolate, I climbed up on deck to look for the lunatic. He was still tamely puffing away on a cigarette in the WC. It was true—a red strip of cloth denoting a mental patient had been sewn onto the back of his cap. That, I suppose, was his star. Now that I had been alerted, I did notice that his eyes jerked about irregularly. If he was a madman, though, I had greater contempt for those considered sane.

On the morning of the second day, after we had finished off our single daily ration of gruel and slumped down on our knapsacks, five or six American marines came sauntering in with their hands in their pockets. A few were whistling and cracking jokes. They appeared to be a pleasant enough group, but from their eyes it was obvious they were planning something, so the Japanese soldiers watched them closely. They divided up and started walking through the crowds of seated Japanese. They paid no attention to where they stepped, treading on knees and ankles here and there. Before long, I realized that they had their eyes riveted on the soldiers' necks. That seemed odd, but in the next instant one of the marines ripped the insignia off the collar of the sergeant seated just beside me. Then he stepped over me and pulled off the stars of the staff sergeant behind me. He stepped back over me and came to a halt in front of the staff sergeant seated in front of me. Comparing the two insignia he held in his hand, he flung the first across the floor as if he were playing hopscotch.

"What are you doing?" I asked him.

"You speak English? We're taking these as souvenirs. We forgot to bring any back from Okinawa."

"Do the repatriates always have their stars taken away like this?"

"This is our first voyage. I don't know what anybody else does."

"Does Sergeant Brown allow you to confiscate stars?"

"He wants them more than anybody."

"What happens if this leads to trouble among our men?"

"This!" He pretended to be firing a machine gun.

I learned from this experience that badges of rank were taken as souvenirs of battle, in the same way that enemy heads and ears had once been taken as the spoils of war.

Nearly all the NCOs' stars were appropriated by this band of marines. They then lined up the stars and chose the prettiest among them. While this was going on, I spotted some Japanese who looked as though they wished it were their very selves that had been snatched from them. I could no longer bear to watch this humiliation. Amidst cheers and screeches, the marines gleefully arranged the stars in several rows down the passageway.

Finally they marched off in triumph, heading next perhaps for an invasion of the officers' quarters. Something like a sigh filled the hold. This was followed by the sound here and there of stars being yanked off uniforms. But the men seemed at a loss what to do with the plucked stars. Then one man tossed his into the air, and the others began to follow suit. Some even chuckled as they did so. I kept my eyes on the mad soldier, but he had fallen back and was staring blankly at the ceiling. His lethargy seemed to stem only partly from the fact that he had no star to toss.

Unable to endure the spectacle any longer, I stood up and shouted, "You mustn't tear off your stars. They're priceless! Stop it!!" I repeated the words again and again, until those around me stopped hurling their stars about and gathered around me. One of them cried, "Who is this bastard? I'll get his!" He lunged and ripped off my insignia, then trampled on the three PFC stars with his boot and knocked me to the floor.

I climbed up onto the fiercely rolling deck. Inoma, bereft of his stars, stood there smiling.

"George! Brown took my knapsack and boots."

In their place he wore a pair of American army boots. Suddenly I recalled that his feet were larger than average.

. . . Inoma and the other soldiers were now looking for new stars.

With a list of its prow and a blast from its whistle, the LST entered Sasebo Harbor. Hills came into view through the morning mist. Their color seemed so familiar I became almost frantic to identify it. I paced back and forth on deck, wanting to ask people, "What color is that?" Then I stopped in my tracks. I realized that the hills were the color of the khaki uniform I wore.

ARE THE TREES GREEN?

Yoshiyuki Junnosuke

Translated by Adam Kabat

Yoshiyuki Junnosuke belongs to that line of sensual writers stretching back to Ihara Saikaku in the seventeenth century and including Tanizaki Jun'ichirō and Nagai Kafū in the modern period. Generally considered by his contemporaries to have the finest-honed literary style today, Yoshiyuki has persistently focused on the physical relationships between men and women in his quest for an unsullied emotional purity. Most often that bond is discovered in the associations men have with prostitutes, relationships uncluttered by egotism and unfulfillable demands.

Yoshiyuki was born in Okayama in 1924, but raised in Tokyo. Exempted from military service by ill health, he studied English literature at Tokyo University for a time, but opted for a journalistic career midway through school. Plagued by respiratory problems (like so many of his fellow writers in Japan), Yoshiyuki was in the hospital when he received word that his story "Shūu (Sudden Shower, 1954; tr. 1972) had been awarded the Akutagawa Prize. Although a few of his novels have won recognition, including Anshitsu *(The Dark Room, 1969; tr. 1975) and* Hoshi to tsuki wa ten no ana *(The Moon and Stars Are Holes in the Sky, 1966), Yoshiyuki's best work has been done in the short story, and in a peculiarly Japanese genre of fiction known as the* rensaku—*a cycle of stories linked by theme and character but more loosely bound together than a novel. Yoshiyuki's best work in the* rensaku *form is* Yūgure made *(Toward Dusk, 1978), a Noma Prize-winning book about a middle-aged man who seeks obsessive-*

ly for an emotional rather than physical virginity in his mistress.

The present story, "Kigi wa midori ka" (Are the Trees Green?), was published in 1958.

*   *   *

Iki Ichirō came to a stop on the overpass, and turned to face the twilight streets spreading out below him.

Every day he would leave for work at the same time. And every day he would stand still on top of the bridge and look out on these streets.

The town was half sunk in a kind of mist. It was hard to tell whether this was a genuine mist or rather the smoke rising from the numerous tall chimneys of the area, forming a layer that covered the streets. In any case, the town was always shrouded in mist.

When he looked out on the shrouded town, he would experience two different emotions. One was a feeling of ennui at the thought of having to go down into the town. It was oppressive just to think of the monotonous work waiting for him there. How much better if he could retrace his steps from the bridge, return to his room, crawl under the bedding, and go back to sleep.

The other was a stimulus at the thought of descending into the unfathomable, shadowy depths of the mist. He would have one or the other of these feelings, varying with the day.

Whichever one he experienced would serve him as a barometer to measure his own mental state. He would, therefore, purposely come to a stop on the bridge.

Today he could barely conjure up any desire to go on into the town below. For a while Iki remained standing on the overpass.

Since the small overpass straddled high, bulldozed cliffs, the people walking on the streets below looked about the size of cats and dogs.

For the most part the scenery viewed through the mist was made up of numerous parallel and intersecting railway tracks, glistening leadenly. One rectangular freight car, as if left forgotten on a siding. Gas tankers squatting blackly in the space beyond the tracks. Countless chimneys looking as if they had been cut out of gray paper and pasted on. Further back, a faint glimpse of the sea. The twilight sun gleaming dully.

Today the scenery affected him badly. On a day like this the thought of descending the long, narrow stone steps clinging to the cliff made him uneasy. The steps formed a path to the town below. He wanted to turn back. But he started down the steps after all.

The stone steps were crumbling. Halfway down, a junior high school student was sitting, memorizing vocabulary cards. When he walked around him unsteadily, he could make out the student's mutterings as he stared at the cards.

"Con . . . gra . . . tulations, congratulations." Congratulations, hmm, *omedetō*.

Simultaneously, the faces of a group of young men and women floated before Iki's eyes. In half an hour Iki would be addressing these faces. He was a high school teacher for a night school class.

"Hey, Ichirō. It is Ichirō, isn't it? I haven't seen you for ten years."

The owner of the voice was right in front of him, thrusting out his own face and peering into Iki's. A man about fifty years of age, wearing white overalls and sandals. Iki was momentarily at a loss. But from beneath those worn and wrinkled features a younger face soon came back to him.

"Oh, Mr. Yamada. You've aged a bit."

"Life's been rough."

His brow darkened as he searched his pocket, brought out a cigarette, and stuck it in his mouth. His hands, covering the lighted matchstick while he brought it to his mouth, were trembling violently.

Iki's eyes fell on these hands. As the smoke rose from the cigarette, the man threw away the matchstick irritably and dug both his hands deep into his coat pockets. It seemed as if he was nervously trying to hide his shaking hands. The cigarette still in his mouth, he spoke as though pushing the words out.

"It's from drinking too much bad alcohol. Anyway, it certainly doesn't affect my work."

While talking, he kept staring at Iki's hatless head.

"You've turned into the spitting image of your late father. The shape of the head is the same too. That's not an easy head to work with. I was

133

the only one who could cut your father's hair. Who's doing yours now?"

"No one in particular. I go to whatever barbershop's around."

"You can't just go to any barbershop, you know. Look how untidy your hair's become. I'll cut it for you. Why don't you come with me now? My shop's close by."

The barber looked worn out, and seeing his hands shake so, Iki felt incapable of refusing his offer.

Iki's usual route would have taken him a short way along the street below the stone steps, until he came to the station; instead he walked with Yamada in the opposite direction, cutting through the bulldozed cliffs. After covering a fair distance, they reached a spot where shops lined both sides of the road. They had already come as far as the next section of town.

The barbershop's red and blue pole was turning round and round. Yamada came to a halt in front of the shop.

On the glass front door the name HANDSOME was written in gold letters. Yamada turned and smiled in embarrassment.

"It's not a very good name, is it? The owner here chose it. Actually, he's a pretty impressive fellow. A long time ago, he even had a prince for a customer once. By the way, I'm planning on having my own shop again soon, just like before."

"I had no idea you were back. I've been living here for a while too."

"Ten years pass and I'm back near where I started. Well, come on in."

The two had both lived in the same town, but their houses had been burned during the air raids. It had been a while before they could return home.

The moment Iki sat down in front of the mirror, Yamada started vigorously combing his hair. Yamada's hand, holding the comb, was shaking as violently as it had been before. He dug the trembling comb deep into Iki's hair and then yanked it through.

Iki became uneasy. He was imagining these hands wielding a pair of scissors or a razor.

But as soon as Yamada raised the scissors in midair the trembling stopped completely. His other palm was already fluttering effortlessly around Iki's head.

"The more I look at it, the more your head resembles your father's.

The back sticks out and the top is flat. It looks just like a blimp seen from the front. I'm the only one who can cut this shape of head."

Along with the chatter of the glistening scissors, Yamada went on talking nonstop.

"How many years is it since your father died?"

"About eighteen now."

"Time goes by, doesn't it? Since he died when he was in his mid-thirties, he'd still be quite young if he was alive today. And yet he managed to do more in his life than most people have by the time they're eighty. Everyone said so at the time."

"They say he had double a man's share of food and women."

"That's for sure. Don't ask me why, but just before he died he used to invite me out specially and take me around. At that time I knew your father better than anyone. Anyway, he had quite an extravagant way of living."

Iki would sometimes—quite frequently, actually—run into people who had known his father. Each had inside him his personal image of what his father had been like. There were also people who, without ever having known him in person, had concocted their own impression of him.

Without exception, each of these images concealed a thorn of some kind. A thorn that pierced Iki.

Iki had always felt at a loss when asked what his father did for a living. From acquaintances of his he'd heard various accounts.

An artist.

A stockbroker.

Didn't I hear that he made perfume once?

A libertine.

Now the barber Yamada had described him as a man with an extravagant way of living. And as far as Iki could tell there was no hidden sarcasm behind his words.

"It's funny, isn't it? Why would somebody with all those friends end up spending his last days with me?"

He said it in a tone of simple boasting. It occurred to Iki that Yamada was somebody with whom his father would have felt comfortable. And the very fact that his father chose someone like Yamada to be his sole

135

companion during his final days was, for Iki, a clue to the weakening of his father's spirit.

This wasn't the only thorn hidden in Yamada's portrait of Iki's father. In between the sounds of the scissors, Yamada's words rang harshly in his ears.

"Anyway, what are you doing now?"

"I'm a night school teacher."

"Hmm."

For a while Yamada kept quiet.

Iki knew exactly what the barber was thinking: "A night school teacher sounds pretty unexciting. He's nothing like his father. He's probably irritated by the fact himself." Such thoughts were a bother to Iki. The feeling of having to explain that he wasn't irritated was in itself a source of irritation. Moreover, when Iki thought that the explanation wasn't likely to be understood—how useless it was—he became all the more irritated.

There was just too big a difference between Iki's image of his father and Yamada's.

Yamada, silent for a while, started chatting again.

"How old are you?"

"Thirty-three."

"Single?"

"Nope."

"Hmm, any children?"

"One boy, in the second grade."

"Hmm. When your father was your age, you were already in middle school. Anyway, your heads are like two peas in a pod. I know how to cut your hair. When you think about it, time flashes by, doesn't it? I cut your hair from the time you were in grammar school. So, why not bring your son with you on your next visit."

While sitting in the barber's chair, Iki recalled his father's face as it looked twenty years ago, and Yamada's face too. Both seemed youthful, daring.

As a boy in grammar school, Iki Ichirō had kept his hair long, and for a certain period at that time, it had been painful even to think of Yamada's barbershop. This was directly related to his long hair.

One winter vacation, Ichirō and his father spent some time alone together at a hot spring resort situated in a countrified, backward area. It was a mystery to Ichirō why his father, who had such a restless personality, should choose to stay at this place. The whole time there his father was in a bad mood.

Ichirō, always at his side, became the perfect vent for his ill humor. All of a sudden, he started taking the boy to task for one thing or another.

"Ichirō, your hair gets in the way of your eyes. You should get a crew cut. Let's go to the town barber."

Ichirō shook his head stubbornly. His father responded in an angry tone.

"The year after next you'll be in middle school. It's the rule that all middle school boys have crew cuts, so you might as well get used to it now."

From as far back as he could remember, Ichirō had had long hair. He couldn't stand the thought of having it cut off. He continued to refuse, even more stubbornly. Then, suddenly, his father's mood changed.

"I suppose there's nothing I can do about it. I'll let it pass this time. But as soon as we get home I'm taking you to Yamada's barbershop."

In time his father completely forgot about the matter.

But occasionally he would remember. He would remember with a surge of impatience, and would try to drag him there.

A year later, in summer, his father revived the issue with a violence that Ichirō finally found impossible to resist.

Yamada held his hair between his fingers, as Ichirō sat in the high barber's chair.

"So it's finally time for your crew cut. Don't take it too hard now."

He was looking at Ichirō's face in the mirror, grinning.

"I'm fine."

Ichirō smiled back, but the smile stiffened a bit. Yamada pressed the cold blade of the hair clippers against his forehead. Then he briskly began cropping off his hair.

In five minutes Yamada had cut off all the hair on just the right side of his head. He put down the clippers and lit a cigarette. After a few long puffs, he wandered into the back of the shop.

Reflected in the mirror was a grotesque head, on the right side a blue crew cut, on the left the remaining long hair. Ichirō, feeling impatient and embarrassed, waited for Yamada's return. The barber remained out of sight.

At one end of the long mirror in front of Ichirō the street outside the shop was visible. In the street inside the mirror floated the reflection of a young girl. She was wearing sandals, and coming slowly toward him. The girl was known for her good looks, and she and Ichirō knew each other by sight. His body stiffened under the large white barber's cloth as he imagined her peeking through the window. Only his hideous head poked out above the white cloth.

If she did peer into the shop, Ichirō had resolved to stare back at her deliberately, open his eyes wide, and stick out his tongue. Clowning like this was the only means he could think of to protect himself. But Ichirō was also aware that such behavior was alien to him. He knew that he was a melancholy, introverted, unchildlike child. In the end he prayed that she wouldn't look into the shop.

Finally Yamada reappeared from the back. What remained of his cigarette was short enough to burn his fingers. He rubbed it out in an ashtray, and gave himself a good stretch.

"Well, shall I cut off the rest?"

At that moment, Yamada's pale, hollow-cheeked face was reflected in the mirror. His close-shaven beard had a bluish tinge. The words "a heartless handsome youth" floated into Ichirō's head. It was hardly an expression one expected from a sixth-grader. He had probably remembered it from some magazine story.

About twenty years had passed since that day.

As he sat in the high barber's chair, Iki noticed that Yamada's face had wrinkles that hadn't been there before. Nor was there any trace of the sharp lines that had once suggested a certain heartlessness.

Moreover, the man who had caused the young Ichirō so much suffering—namely, his father—had already left this world. But as the memory faded, he muttered to himself, "I've still got to watch my step, even if he isn't alive."

Yes, at all costs Iki had to watch his step. And yet, submerged in his memories, he had already slipped.

In between the sounds of the glistening scissors, he could make out Yamada's mutterings.

"I'll have to cut off more here."

Before Iki's very eyes his head began to take on a new, strange shape.

"Oh, I wouldn't make it too short there."

This diffident resistance was immediately crushed beneath the barber's confidence and enthusiasm.

When the clicking of the scissors stopped, Iki saw reflected in the mirror the shape of a schoolboy's head.

Iki was flustered. "How can I possibly appear in front of a class looking like this? What a mess," he muttered. But this wasn't the only reason Iki was flustered on seeing his haircut.

The other reason didn't come to him in any clear shape. Or rather, he hesitated to look directly at what it was. He only focused on the fact that his haircut didn't suit a teacher.

Yamada was energetically sharpening a razor on a leather strop. When he returned to Iki's side, he said,

"There. Now you look like two peas in a pod. So from here you're going to your night school, are you?"

When Iki stared at his face in the mirror—the face that Yamada had likened to a pea in a pod—he turned to his father and asked: "Even though you've been dead now for eighteen years, did you still want to take me to Yamada's barbershop?"

The face in the mirror rose straight to the ceiling and disappeared. Yamada had suddenly tipped back his chair.

Yamada started shaving his face.

"Your father was quite stylish. I used to shave his sideburns at a slant," he said in a nostalgic tone. Iki was annoyed at being placed in this situation. He said loudly,

"Shave me that way too. Shave my sideburns at a slant."

The nostalgic glisten in Yamada's eyes turned to an inquisitive shine. Finally, he answered dispiritedly:

"That style isn't fashionable any more, so I wouldn't recommend it. Besides, you're a schoolteacher. Anything too fancy would look strange."

When Iki left the barbershop his head felt cold. The chill went all the way down his back.

The lights were already on in the winter streets. From the loudspeaker of a radio store, music flowed out into the road. As he passed the shop, he could make out a man's voice singing.

Even though he was walking slowly, it wasn't long before he could no longer hear the music. He had only caught a small part, but he was vaguely familiar with the song.

The lyrics were fairly saccharine.

On a dark evening, a man stands alone on a cliff. Suddenly he feels a pliant breast in the palm of his hand. The flesh is so full it pushes its way between his open fingers. It is an illusory sensation. A moment later, the breast begins to melt before his very eyes, and turns into a milk-colored mist that flows through his fingers to merge with the pale twilight. The man, alone, stares at his empty palm as he stands on the cliff.

A young girl floated into Iki's mind. He shook his head in an effort to throw off the illusion.

He was moving his neck unsteadily right and left. His head felt light and cold. A clear picture of this head with its schoolboy haircut hovered before his eyes. Paradoxically, this made it all the harder to shake off the image of the girl that now clung to him.

The reason he had been so upset on seeing his head in the barbershop mirror was directly related to a girl called Kawamura Asako.

When he arrived at the school gate, the second period classes had already started.

Iki crossed the schoolyard and walked toward his classroom. The corner of the yard where people left their bicycles was too small for all the vehicles that lay scattered about. The night-class students rode to school on various vehicles they had used at their jobs during the day. There were scooters, small trucks, and even one bicycle from whose side hung a gaudy advertisement for a painting service.

As soon as Iki walked into the classroom there was a commotion among

140

his students. Ordinarily Iki had no problem discerning the real reason for this: it came both from students who were disappointed that the class wouldn't be canceled after all, and from the more serious individuals who were annoyed that the teacher's lateness had caused a loss of valuable time.

But tonight Iki felt that the commotion was their response to his haircut.

Iki was standing alone on the dais as all the faces in the room turned in unison toward him. The experience was one familiar to every teacher, but he felt as if fate had played some absurd trick on him.

He looked down, opened the textbook on his desk, and asked one of his students to translate. As the boy began, the many eyes that had been turned in Iki's direction all looked down at their respective books.

When the boy's voice stopped, a girl suddenly got up. Iki tensed when he realized it was Kawamura Asako. She almost never came forward with a question. What on earth was she going to say? Iki waited with bated breath.

What emerged from her mouth was an ordinary question.

But once again all the eyes in the room looked up from their books and turned in Iki's direction. In fact, it seemed as if they were comparing Iki and the girl.

Until Iki had looked at his newly cropped hair from Yamada's barber's chair, Asako had been nothing more to him than a girl who had vaguely caught his eye. Or at least he had made himself believe that this was so. One could even say that he'd convinced himself that he had no alternative but to believe so.

"When you fall in love with a young girl, you want even your hair to look like a schoolboy's, do you?"

Iki found himself thinking that a voice had said this somewhere in the classroom. In fact, the voice had first come secretly to him as he was sitting in the barber's chair. The mirror image of his head had seemed to Iki as if it were his own heart laid bare.

Growing louder, the voice had clung to him, following him as far as the classroom.

Once again the fact that all the faces in the room were turned toward him forcibly entered Iki's consciousness. He found it difficult to endure.

Suddenly he felt his job no longer suited him.

It had been quite a while since Iki had known this overwhelming feeling. He had been teaching ever since he'd graduated from college; before then he had worked part-time while going to school. It had taken him twice as long as usual to graduate, and during that time he was frequently prone to such feelings about his work.

In those days it was easy for him to abandon whatever job he had and find new employment. But now he was no longer a college student working part-time. Now he had to search carefully inside himself to see whether he could simply drop what he was doing or not.

A certain scene floated into Iki's head. This small incident also focused on his dead father.

It was seven or eight years ago. At that time he was working for a small publisher.

He was outside a station, waiting for the actress Hanamura Hanae. He was wearing his black school uniform with the stiff collar. His job was to escort the actress to the hall where his publisher was holding a symposium.

Hanae was married to an American and lived in an area where it was difficult for Japanese to get in, so it had been arranged for him to meet her by the station. Since it was their first meeting, she had no way of recognizing him. It was up to him to keep his eyes open for the middle-aged actress, whose face he knew from photographs.

Hanae made no attempt to hide her displeasure when she realized that no car had been laid on. The editor of the poor publishing firm had advised him as follows: "Her husband is an American so she'll probably come by car. If she walks, then you might as well take the train."

Iki searched for a taxi, but it was almost impossible to find one in those days. Having no choice in the matter, he handed her a train ticket, apologizing profusely.

As they were going down the station stairs he realized that Hanae was pregnant. She seemed to be deliberately extending her stomach as she walked down the stairs.

Hanae's mood went from bad to worse. There were no empty seats on the train.

Iki knew something about her. He had heard that she had once been in love with his father, though it didn't seem to have been a very deep relationship. Moreover it was a long time ago. It occurred to him that if he told her he was Iki Akio's son, it might possibly touch a chord in her.

He hesitated for a while. But when he looked at Hanae's clearly angry, frowning face, he couldn't endure the discomfort any more.

He tried to make small talk, but she would answer bluntly and immediately revert to her original expression.

Finally he brought up his father's name. In matters of the heart there are things a third party cannot be aware of. There was the danger that mentioning his father's name would hurt her feelings. If that was the case, then so be it, he decided. He could no longer put up with the present situation.

Hanae's stiff expression crumbled immediately. Her attitude softened to a degree that was surprising even to him. He felt relieved and, at the same time, ashamed of having done something rather uncouth.

"Is that so? You should have said so earlier."

With the words "you should have said so earlier," he felt once again an extreme sense of failure. It was more than he could bear. And as a result he was suddenly overcome with the feeling that his work no longer suited him.

Invariably other people's portraits of his father concealed sharp thorns for him—even when these portraits were favorably drawn.

Hanae turned to look at Iki as if gazing off into the distance. She said, "Actually, you do look rather like him."

As Iki stood on the dais, her voice came back to him.

"Your heads are like two peas in a pod."

Hanae's voice overlapped with the barber Yamada's, and his recollection broke off.

Iki shook his head unsteadily right and left. His head—newly cropped by Yamada in a boyish style—was cold.

The next day, Iki stood on the windy platform, on his way to his night school class.

Three trains came heading in the opposite direction, but his still hadn't arrived.

As the wind got stronger, he felt as if his weak, malnourished body were fluttering in the wind. His head, with its new haircut, was extremely cold. He couldn't dispel the image of this haircut. For the second time, from out of nowhere, a voice came ringing in his ears. "When you fall in love with a young girl, you want even your hair to look like a schoolboy's, do you?" Iki flinched at the thought that a short time from now in his role as a teacher he'd be entering the classroom where Asako would almost certainly be sitting.

Again a train came going in the opposite direction. Its many windows, dyed yellow by the light inside the cars, flickered past him, until the train came to a halt.

The yellow light from the windows seemed warm. Without thinking, Iki got on the train. When the train started moving, he decided to visit his old friend Yui Jūji.

The company where Yui worked was located near the heart of the city. When one made one's way through the narrow streets caught between ferroconcrete buildings, and crossed a bridge, the scenery changed dramatically.

The roads were crumbling and uneven. The smell of deep-frying oil floated through the air. A group of housewives, wearing aprons and carrying baskets, stood in front of a butcher shop.

Yui's office was on the second floor of a small, wooden building sandwiched between a store selling weights and measures and a noodle shop.

Yui was working behind his desk. A young woman wearing a red sweater at the corner desk was folding paper designs out of small squares of wax paper from caramel candies. Two or three cranes, the size of peas, were lined up on her desk.

"Hey, Iki. It's been a long time."

As Yui looked up and spoke, he glanced at the wall clock.

"Already six, is it? Hey! Bring us some tea, will you."

The young woman went downstairs.

"She's new, isn't she?"

"They make me do all the piddling work, so I insisted they hire someone to help me with it."

"But don't you feel bad about it, speaking to her so roughly?"

"You've got to be kidding. Until now she's been working at some greasy

144

spoon. She's told me herself that it makes her nervous to be treated any other way. She was orphaned by the atomic bomb, so she's suffered a lot. There's a lot of good in her. Then again, because of what she's been through, there's a lot of bad in her too."

The girl returned, carrying three steaming teacups on a black tray. She placed the teacups in front of Iki and Yui. Holding the remaining cup in the palms of her hands, she began to sip the tea, standing in her corner of the room.

Yui spoke to her.

"You can go home now. Or do you want to go back with me?"

Then he turned toward Iki.

"Whenever she's alone with a man she feels there's something wrong if he doesn't try to seduce her. It seems to be a habit with her. Once in a while I have to bring it up. Anyway, Iki, what do you think of her tits? She deliberately wears sweaters to show them off."

Suppressing her laughter, the girl started getting her belongings together. Then, out of the corner of her eyes, she glared at Yui. Her eyes had a coquettish gleam.

"Do you mind waiting thirty minutes while I finish up this work? Let's stop for a drink on the way back."

At the small drinking spot that Yui had taken him to, Iki was feeling the effects of the cheap alcohol.

"You've really changed, haven't you? You've become as tough as leather."

Yui stared at Iki for a while. A strange look flitted across Yui's face, and he flung out a reply:

"I'm just tired."

"But, for example, the way you act toward the girl in the red sweater—I'm jealous. You're so casual."

Yui looked taken aback. He seemed to have realized he had made a miscalculation.

"Hey, you're in love with somebody, aren't you? I've no idea who it is, but I'm sure it's a young girl." He looked carefully at Iki's face. "Is that why you had your hair cut like that? Is that what happens when you fall in love with a young girl?" Yui burst into loud laughter.

The words were identical to those that had been echoing around Iki's head since the night before. But Yui, in fact, was the first person ever to have said them aloud.

There was no denying that Iki was interested in Asako. Yet he had never thought that he was in love with her.

He had met the barber Yamada by accident, had felt obliged to get a haircut, and now Yui had actually come out with those very words. All this provided fuel for the passion Iki was now feeling for Asako. It was as if the love that had been hidden until now had been exposed during these last two days.

But what did he really know about Asako? Iki asked himself. The two of them had never even talked alone together.

"What kind of a girl is she?" he heard Yui's voice say.

"She works at a cheap bar."

Iki's answer wasn't a lie. Asako worked in a small bar in the old part of town. The reason Asako was going to night school was not because she was working during the day. Rumor had it that it was because she hated the family business, and if she went to night school there would be just that much less time to help out at the bar.

No, Iki's answer hadn't been a lie. What he didn't tell Yui was that Asako was a pupil of his. In this case, the word "pupil" had something unsavory, corrupt to it. Suddenly a scene floated into Iki's memory. A field in summer. He was a middle school student. By the bus stop near the fish pond a group of grammar school students had gathered. They were waiting for the bus going to the lake.

A male teacher, in his thirties, was in charge of the group. He was sitting on a large tree stump by the side of the road, holding one of the girl students on his lap. The palms of his hands were slowly stroking the girl's body, through her clothing. Just when they seemed about to reach her legs, they would return to her flat, weak chest.

The teacher's eyes were slightly bloodshot, as if he had been drinking heavily. He half closed his eyes suggestively as he continued moving his hands. From a short distance away, Iki was standing as stiff as a stick, watching the scene intently. It seemed as if the grammar school students didn't understand what was really going on. A fourth-grade boy said in a loud voice,

146

"Hey, that's unfair. Yōko's getting all the teacher's attention."

A faint smile hovered about the teacher's lips as he went on stroking. The girl on his lap made no attempt to get away. On her childish but rather classic features floated the gloating expression of a woman in her prime who has managed to capture the affections of a man in power.

"She works in a bar, you say? Let's go there now, then."

Yui's voice brought Iki back from the past. Iki did know the location of Asako's bar. But he felt reluctant about going there. He couldn't bear the prospect of walking into Asako's bar as a customer and having Asako wait on him. He also felt that it would be painful for Asako.

"Let's go," Yui insisted.

"Why don't we do it some other time?"

"But why? If it's because you don't have any money, I've got enough on me."

"It's nothing to do with money."

"Then why?"

Yui would never give in unless he clearly came up with a reason. Iki regretted visiting Yui. He regretted getting on the train going the wrong way. He told his friend hesitantly,

"The truth is she's one of my students."

"Your student? What difference does that make? You're probably a regular there."

"I've never been there."

Yui stared hard at Iki's face. The doubt in his look finally vanished, and he smiled faintly.

"You really are in love, aren't you? Is your heart still there?"

Yui stuck out his finger and thrust it into the left side of Iki's chest.

"I'm surprised myself. A man of thirty shouldn't feel this way."

Iki spoke in a defensive tone, as if countering an attack. When he realized how he sounded, he added somewhat disgustedly,

"But isn't it better than losing your heart altogether?"

"I haven't lost my heart. My heart is right here."

Yui lifted his arm, twisted it, and tapped his elbow.

"My feelings toward the girl are probably the same, then. My heart's in my elbow as well."

"Is that so? Well, let's go there and make sure that's the case."

Iki now felt it would be too much trouble to refuse Yui. Besides, without being dragged into the situation, he would never, in the end, have an opportunity to visit Asako and see her at work.

"Let's go."

Iki stood up with a burst of energy.

It was after ten. By this time Asako should have returned from night school and be at work.

Iki entered the bar as if being pushed inside by Yui.

"Oh, it's Mr. Iki."

The moment he stepped inside the bar, he collided with this lively voice. Iki felt flustered as all the customers turned simultaneously toward him.

More than this, it was Asako's appearance that flustered him. He had imagined her lingering in the corner of the bar, her face bare of makeup, looking indifferent and bored. But Asako danced lightly up to Iki's side. When she sat down next to him, she brought her lips close to his ear and whispered,

"What a surprise. This is the first time you've come here, isn't it?"

Her mouth was painted with a deep red lipstick that seemed to escape its borders. Her skin was completely hidden under a thick layer of makeup.

"I wasn't planning on coming. My friend lured me here."

She reacted, as if covering up for his clumsiness:

"Are you saying there's something wrong about visiting the bar where your student works? If that's the case, I'll quit school. Then you can come all the time."

Asako spoke in the manner of a bar hostess used to dealing with men. He couldn't help staring at her face.

The thick makeup didn't make Asako ugly. If anything, her face was even prettier, more charming than usual. And yet there was too much of the artificial about her. There were times when a mature expression— or, more exactly, the expression of a forty-year-old woman—seemed to flit momentarily across her face. For Iki, the face seemed an enigma, thrust right before his eyes.

148

Yui was silently observing Asako. His eyes were shining. Iki had no idea what Yui was thinking or feeling, either.

"Does your father have a beard, by any chance?" Yui suddenly asked the girl.

"My father died when I was in grammar school. No, he didn't have a beard. Why do you ask?"

"When I look at your face, I can't help thinking so. Hey, Iki, you know the girl in the red sweater at my company? When you look at her face, can't you see her father with a beard? With a big moustache like a paintbrush. But her father died when she was three. Her mother was killed in the atomic bombing, leaving her an orphan. But her father had died before that. I've tried any number of times to make her remember. But you know the memory of a three-year-old. She did recall something about how, when her father hugged her and rubbed his cheek against hers, it felt scratchy and hurt. But that's no good. It could be the scratchiness of unshaven stubble, and anyway, there has to have been a full moustache or else it doesn't count. A big moustache like a paintbrush. There aren't any photographs either. And there's nobody who remembers her father. Even if he didn't have one, it's better to know for certain. It's not knowing either way that makes me uneasy."

"But what does this have to do with anything?" Iki asked. Yui gave his usual weak smile.

"I'm so bothered by it, I can't sleep with her. I can't even kiss her."

Then Yui caught Asako's eye.

"I could sleep with you."

Iki, taken aback at Yui's words, failed to catch Asako's reaction. He had wanted to see whether a girlish embarrassment at Yui's unexpected, improper remark would show on her face.

As far as Iki could tell, the only expression floating on Asako's face was the look of a bar hostess fending off a customer's joke.

"You're quite a character, aren't you," she replied.

When he looked at the girl's heavily made-up face, Iki began to feel flustered again. An ominous feeling was mixed in with his embarrassment. He had fallen into this selfsame mood before. When was it? Iki groped within his memory.

149

He followed a faint, vague, frail thread. The face of a bar girl with heavy makeup. There was something next to her. The angry face of his grandmother, his now dead grandmother, who for many years had been confined to her bed. It was when he had turned to face her, perhaps. No, that wasn't it.

Suddenly it came back to him.

"I remember now. It was the face of a kangaroo."

"What's that about a kangaroo? Mr. Iki, you're drunk."

"No, it's about my dead grandmother," Iki corrected himself, at once surprised by what he'd said.

"Your grandmother? Is it something to do with your childhood?"

"Umm."

"They say that when you fall in love you start getting nostalgic," Yui said in a teasing tone.

Ichirō was a first-grader at the time. A circus had been set up in a nearby field. A big tent had been raised, and around it, to attract customers, various animal cages had been lined up.

A black panther with glistening eyes was crouching in the back of a dark cage; a lion was shaking its mane as it paced about.

Next to one of the cages a notice had been posted: KANGAROO BOXING FOR THOSE INTERESTED. NO ADULTS ALLOWED. Inside the cage, a kangaroo, wearing gloves on its forelimbs, was standing erect on its tail and hind legs. There were a conspicuous number of children around the cage, but none of them would come forward to box with the animal.

When Ichirō looked at the ridiculous yet unsettling figure of the kangaroo, wearing gloves and standing upright inside the dark cage, he could no longer suppress his curiosity. He hesitated for a long while, but finally resolved to take up the challenge.

A circus man, wearing a colorful uniform like a toy soldier's, put the gloves on Ichirō's hands. He was led inside the cage. When he was face to face with the kangaroo, he found the animal taller than he was. The kangaroo was just standing still. But when Ichirō thrust out his fist, the animal followed suit, waving its gloves instinctively.

Ichirō's eyes met the kangaroo's. The kangaroo's eyes were a pleasant shape. They were eyes that looked dazed, that expressed almost no feeling. One might have expected to see hatred or fear of the person striking out at it. But there was nothing beyond a dumb look of amazement. He began to feel more and more uncomfortable looking at them. The smell of the caged animal suddenly assailed him. Ichirō, in an effort to shake off this unease, desperately continued to strike, but the kangaroo simply waved its arms about.

He must have seemed just a cheerful child to the crowd outside the cage, now watching and laughing merrily. But Ichirō, as he faced the kangaroo's head, was trapped inside this sense of unease.

The feelings that floated inside Iki now, as he confronted Asako's painted face, were the same feelings he had experienced so long ago.

"What do you make of it? It's as if she's become a completely different girl from the one I know at school," Iki said to Yui after they had left the bar. "I heard that the reason she was going to night school was because she hated helping out with the family business, and she wanted to make her hours that much shorter. And yet. . ."

"She's like a fish in water in that bar," Yui answered.

"I can't understand it. Her makeup was so heavy it looked as though you could take it off all in one piece—like a mask. Perhaps she's trying to hide her real self behind that painted mask."

When Yui heard this, he gave a hoot of laughter.

"You're crazy. If you're going to be so sentimental, you'll end up getting badly hurt before long. Haven't you sobered up yet? She had the charm of a well-polished prostitute."

"I haven't sobered up at all. But it's all so pathetic."

"The ending for a man in love is always bad. Anyway, what made you fall for someone you knew almost nothing about?"

"Who ever falls in love with people they know well? It's all the fault of the guy who cut my hair."

Iki left it at that, and said no more.

Was it that Iki's love for the girl, brewing secretly all the while somewhere deep in his heart, had suddenly come floating to the surface the moment he had seen his hair cut like a boy's? Or was it, rather, that the shape of his hair, unexpectedly cut in such a style, had drawn out an illusory love for a girl who had been lurking in his memory? At this point, Iki could no longer tell.

Iki tried to remember the face of the girl he always saw in class. For the second time the face of a large kangaroo floated before him, and superimposed itself on a girl with heavy makeup.

The image of the kangaroo now led him to his grandmother and another painted bar girl. Iki's grandmother, paralyzed from the waist down and bedridden, would experience violent emotional ups and downs. For a long time she had been living apart from his grandfather. Her hair was abundant and black, and there was still a youthfulness left in her unpowdered face. People told her again and again that it must be awful to be referred to as granny. Their words were meant sincerely, but were also meant to flatter her.

In grade school Ichirō was often put out by his grandmother's sudden changes in mood. She would read to him at length from a picture book. She seemed to enjoy doing it, so the following day Ichirō would approach her with the same book in hand, feeling sure this could only cheer her up. But the old woman's temper would suddenly turn sour.

"Act your age. You can read a picture book by yourself," she would say cuttingly.

Ichirō's father was sometimes brought home in a drunken stupor by a heavily made-up bar girl. His grandmother's attitude toward the woman would be completely different, depending on the day. A few days after Ichirō boxed with the kangaroo, the bar girl stuck her hand into the lion's cage at the circus, and beckoned to it. She must have been dead drunk. The lion leaped at her hand and tore into it with its sharp claws. Apparently, white bone peeped out from the ripped flesh.

There was something indecipherable about his grandmother when Ichirō was that age. There were times when her features seemed to merge into those of the kangaroo he had confronted in the cage.

But now Iki could easily understand the old woman's capricious moods. The key was clearly in his hand. He still didn't understand about the kangaroo.

Both his grandmother and Asako were human beings. The kangaroo was a kangaroo.

"I'm going to spend more time alone with Asako," he resolved, as he walked side by side with Yui down the night-dark road.

"I've got to be careful whenever my father or grandmother reappear," he murmured suddenly. He gave his head a good shake, as if to dispel the illusion. His head, with its boyish haircut, still felt cold in the night air.

The next day in class, Asako turned to Iki, her face as usual, without makeup.

What is it about her that attracts me? Iki asked himself.

Her eyes are nice; they have a rich color.

A rich color, but what color? Shining strongly, then suddenly losing their shine—changing over and over. Sometimes they gleam pathetically. A pathetic gleam? Yui's laughter echoed loudly in the empty air.

Suddenly Iki realized that until now he had never once seen Asako laugh. Last night the heavily made-up Asako was laughing constantly. But he had yet to see the unmade-up Asako laugh.

When he realized this, Iki's desire to try approaching her alone suddenly dropped away.

After a few days had passed, Iki finally decided to pay Yui another visit at his office. He thought that he would invite him out to Asako's bar with him again. He couldn't imagine entering the bar by himself.

That evening, too, Yui was at his desk, working. The girl in the red sweater was sitting at the corner desk.

Lying about on Yui's desk were numerous, severed pieces of a nude photograph. The photograph had been cut along the outlines of the body, and then divided into any number of smaller parts. By the side of a breast lay half an arm, and beside that a thigh—all scattered about on top of the desk.

"What are you doing?"

Yui turned to him, holding a large pair of scissors in his right hand.

"She's really come apart, hasn't she? This way I do two pages of color layout for free. A poor company like this has no money to spare for layouts. How does this look?"

With the tip of the scissors, Yui moved a picture of an upper arm with a palm attached so that it joined one of an arm cut off at the elbow.

"We're going to ask the reader to fit the pieces back together properly. The plan is to print the original photograph on the reverse page."

Yui rummaged through the muddle of papers on his desk and dug out a photograph. When Iki looked at the print, he couldn't help being shocked. It was a nude shot of the girl in the red sweater, in a horizontal pose.

"It's her. She has a good body—she boasts of it herself. You see, we save money on the model's fee."

Iki looked at the face of his old friend. His profile was exactly the same as in the past. It seemed blank, devoid of all identity. One felt as if a needle would never pierce it—as if it were a big glass ball polished to smooth perfection.

Was this, perhaps, a mask which even now could be removed from Yui's face? Or had it become part of his own flesh? Iki tried to recall the Yui he had known in his student days. Even if Yui had had a face like that, it must have been a mask back then. But now. . . In the end, he had no idea.

Inside Iki's mind, as he stared at Yui, floated one more face—the face of a painted Asako laughing coquettishly. Her expression, too, he found impenetrable.

In any case, Iki decided that he had to see Asako again.

STILL LIFE

Shōno Junzō
Translated by Wayne P. Lammers

Shōno Junzō was born in 1921, the third son of an Osaka educator. He began serious pursuit of an interest in literature during his student days at the Osaka School of Foreign Languages and Kyushu University, but his first tentative efforts at writing were interrupted when the intensification of the Second World War brought an end to draft deferments.

As soon as the war was over, Shōno took up his pen again while working as a middle school teacher in Osaka, and over the next few years he was able to have several stories published in Kansai-area literary journals. In 1949, he received encouraging attention from established literary circles in Tokyo for "Aibu" (Caresses), a story about a young housewife and the feelings of emptiness and despair she experiences as she becomes increasingly disillusioned with her husband. Following this, he produced a number of stories in a similar vein, probing the emotional and psychological turmoils of young married couples who are faced with a variety of marital and financial crises or have otherwise become disenchanted with different aspects of their lives together. When one of these, "Pūrusaido shōkei" (Poolside Vignette, 1954; tr. 1962), won the Akutagawa Prize in 1955, Shōno's literary future was assured; he was able to leave the broadcasting company where he had worked since 1951 to devote himself exclusively to his writing.

"Seibutsu" (Still Life, 1960; winner of the Shinchōsha Literary Prize) is an early work, and one of the most important, in a long series of stories Shōno has written centering on a certain family of five. It is made up of

eighteen separate episodes detailing the kind of commonplace, everyday occurrences that tend, especially in fiction, to pass unnoticed or to be quickly forgotten. Since most of the highly diverse episodes are entirely self-contained, the story offers very little by way of continuous narrative development. It derives cohesiveness instead from the juxtaposition and repetition of related imagery, and from thematic associations that emerge when the various sections are read not only literally but metaphorically. The title itself is suggestive, for "Still Life" is in many ways more a picture than a story: the reader's mind must play over the episodes as his eyes would play over the objects in a painting, moving back and forth between one set of relations and another or between the individual objects and the subject as a whole. Much of the power of the work rests upon the subtle gradations of light and darkness resulting from the interplay between shadowy background and vividly highlighted foreground.

The family of five that appears in "Still Life" and its numerous sequels is virtually Shōno's own, and the conversations and activities described are closely modeled on real-life occurrences. His work is thus rooted firmly in the "I-novel" tradition that has played such a prominent role in modern Japanese literature since the beginning of this century. Where many other contemporary I-novelists have written of the disintegration of the family, however, Shōno's concern is often with the little things in life that hold— or at least can hold—a family together. In extraordinarily simple language and with a remarkable eye for detail, Shōno shows us the essential beauty and significance of the most mundane of human experiences—experiences that may seem trivial and meaningless but are in fact the very fiber of life.

*　　　*　　　*

"Can we go to the fishing pond?" the boy pleaded.

It was a beautiful, windless day in early March, and spring seemed just around the corner.

"You don't want to go fishing," his father said. "You know you'd never catch anything."

"I do want to too. All the kids go. Masuko caught five the other day."

"What were they?"

"Goldfish."

"Oh. Goldfish." The father's voice showed his disappointment. "It's not much fun if all you get is goldfish."

"It is fun too. Some of the kids even catch big ones."

"Oh?"

"You'll catch something too, Dad. You will." The boy would be entering the second grade in another month.

"I don't know," the father said. "It'd be my first time. The only fishing I've ever done was in the ocean. I've never been to one of those artificial ponds." Even to him the excuse sounded rather feeble.

"You should try it," chimed in his daughter, soon to be a sixth-grader. "Who knows? You just might catch something. And so what if you don't? It'll be fun anyway."

"I suppose you're right," he said. "I'll never know if I don't give it a try."

"If all three of us go, maybe at least one of us'll catch something," the girl said, seeing that her father had abandoned his reluctance. She often spoke to him like this, in an encouraging tone, when he seemed hesitant or worried about something. It was a remarkable way she had with him.

On the morning of the accident so many years before, this girl had lain in the corner of the room with her stuffed dog, alone like an orphan, oblivious to the possibility that anything could be wrong. She had been just over one year old then.

"Have a good time!" the mother called after them. "Come home hungry now, all of you." The three-year-old boy had to stay behind. He was too small to go fishing.

As they left the house, the father had a pleasant feeling inside. It always felt good to set out on something he had never done before. And the children's enthusiasm was contagious.

The boy had brought along the tin bucket he used for his water projects in the yard. As they walked, the father watched it swing back and forth at his son's side. He should get out and do these things more often, he told himself. It was better to go along, to stop making excuses. It didn't really matter whether or not they caught anything. They had set out, bucket in hand—that was the important part. It seemed a little thing, perhaps, but little things often made the biggest difference.

To begin with, anything was better than just sitting around doing nothing. All he ever did on his days off was loaf about the house. He never made plans for a Sunday outing, much less went anywhere when Sunday finally came. Sometimes he felt sorry for his family. But he had been this way for a long time now, and the children had grown used to it. So far as they were concerned, holidays were for staying at home and playing by themselves. They had fun enough.

Still, it wasn't good for him to be so lazy. After all, the fishing pond was hardly ten minutes away.

Down the road, the pond came into view, surrounded by rice paddies. Beyond it rose the slope of a wooded hill. There were two ponds, actually—one stocked with small fish, for beginners, and the other with larger fish, for more experienced fishermen. As might be expected on a Sunday, both were crowded.

"One adult and one child," the father said, as if he were buying tickets for the train. He didn't know any differently, since this was the first time he had come. He paid for an hour and got two fishing poles and some bait. But the last person to use one of the poles had returned it with the line badly tangled. No doubt he had gone home in a huff after failing to catch anything. The father couldn't tell where to start, so he asked the lady at the gate to unravel it for him.

"There you go." She handed the pole back to him with a smile.

"It's fixed?"

"Yes, it should be okay now."

Too eager to wait, the boy had run on ahead, but now he was back. "C'mon, Dad, hurry up," he shouted. "I found a good spot. Over there." The place he pointed to, however, was at the pond for experienced fishermen. Not one of the people there was using the sort of flimsy pole the three newcomers had rented. It was also more expensive to fish there.

"We can't go over there," the girl said.

"But you should see. There's lots of big ones."

"No," the girl said softly. "That pond's too hard for us. Beginners have to fish here."

"Oh."

After the lady had shown him how to bait the hooks, the father joined the children at the beginners' pond. There were quite a few adults fishing there, too—men fishing alone, young married couples fishing together.

The three of them shared the two poles, but they failed to get so much as a nibble. Whenever someone else caught something, the boy ran off to have a look, and each time he would call back in a loud voice, "It's better over here, Dad."

"Listen," the father admonished. "Whether you catch anything or not, you're better off staying in one place. When somebody over there catches something, you might think it's a better spot, but it isn't really. It just seems that way. Some people are good at it and some people aren't, but even the good ones have to wait and be patient and not change places all the time if they want to catch anything. You'll never have any luck if you don't sit still."

His own words reminded him of a story he had read in English class in junior high school. It was called "Stick to Your Own Bush." As he remembered it, several children go off into the woods to pick wild raspberries. They spread out among the raspberry bushes scattered here and there, and before long shouts of "I found some! I found some!" ring out, first from one direction, then another. One of the boys, who has yet to find a single berry, races about from place to place pursuing each new shout. When all the others have filled their baskets, he has only a few berries. "You'll never get very many that way," he is told. "Stick to your own bush." And that was the moral of the story—that it's the same with everything we do.

As a boy he had found it a dull and uninspiring story. But now he was a father, and here he was, telling his own son the same thing.

The scolding put an end to the boy's shouting, but, with no change in their own luck, he still darted off periodically to examine the fish that other people caught.

From where the father was sitting he could not actually see the fish in the water. He had to admit there might not be any there. Nonetheless he stuck to his own bush.

"I guess this isn't our day," he said to his daughter beside him. "It's not so easy after all." She went on gazing at her float.

Every now and then women with shopping baskets passed along the road in front of the pond. Some of them stopped briefly to watch the fishermen. The father had been observing these movements on the road when he turned around to find his float bobbing up and down. He raised his pole with a jerk. On the end of the line was a tiny orange glimmer.

"We got one!" cried the girl.

The boy, who had been watching an older boy fish, heard her voice and came running.

"We got one! We got one!" he clamored.

"Simmer down. Don't make such a racket," the father scolded. But his face beamed. It was indeed a tiny goldfish that had come up on the end of his line, hardly any bigger than a guppy.

Now for the first time they had a use for the bucket the boy had brought along. The little fish swam about in the pail as if to belie the fact that a moment ago it had been caught on the tip of a hook.

"W-w-when they've tried it once," the elderly doctor said, "they get so they try it again and again."

"That's what I was afraid of," the young husband sighed. Never had he imagined that only three years after his marriage he would feel so beaten and discouraged.

"At least that's frequently the case."

Would it happen again? he had asked disconsolately. Was she likely to try it again?

"T-t-t-t-taking it hard, are you?" The doctor burst into a boisterous, stuttering laugh. But there was a measure of sympathy in his voice. This distinctive laugh of the doctor's had long been familiar to the young man.

"Once is enough, I suppose?"

"It certainly is."

The doctor reached for the bottle and poured some more whiskey for his guest. The young man watched as the dark liquid rose inside the glass.

"These things can happen. You just never know," the doctor said. He picked up the pitcher and mixed a little water with the whiskey. "It's like trying to find your way in the dark."

The old doctor's sitting room was an annex of sorts, built on a level slightly higher than the main section of the house. He spent most of his time alone here, apart from the rest of his family. When he needed something, he simply clapped his hands. He never left the room except to see a patient.

The two sat facing each other, the bottle of whiskey on the table between them. Somehow, the young man always felt reassured when he talked with the old doctor like this.

The young man had been born and raised in this town, and his earliest memory of the doctor's clinic went back to when he was in the third grade. One day he was playing in a field near his house with a friend, running about barefoot on the grass, when all of a sudden he stepped on a piece of wood with a large nail sticking through it. His friend rushed off to get his mother, while he sat there crying. It had seemed an eternity before she appeared at the edge of the field.

The next thing he remembered was lying on an examination table in a dimly lit room while the doctor removed the nail. Tense faces peered down at him from above.

That had been his first visit to this place.

"H-h-how's her foot coming along?" the doctor asked. "Where she burned it."

"I think it still hurts her to walk on it."

"Yes, I'm sure it does. The burn's right on the bottom of her foot."

"She claims it doesn't bother her any more though."

The doctor gave him a sympathetic smile, then lowered his eyes.

"I was practically in a state of shock myself," the young man said after another sip of his drink. "I didn't realize the cloth had come loose."

"Of course, of course," the doctor laughed with his usual stutter. "It was hardly the time you would notice something like that. Not even your wife noticed, and it was her own foot."

The young man remembered the chill he had felt when he touched his wife's arms and legs. At first he had still been able to detect a slight warmth, but gradually her body had turned colder and colder. Frantically, he had filled three hot-water bottles with piping hot water and put them in her bed: one on either side of her chest, the third at her feet.

Later he had held her—first one way, then another—for the doctor to examine her. Beads of sweat had dripped from his forehead. He couldn't tell exactly when she had been burned; the cloth he had wrapped around the hot-water bottle must have come loose when her legs moved.

The doctor reached for the whiskey and poured himself another glass. "This kind of burn can be a real problem. I've had cases before: people go to bed with a hot-water bottle and don't realize they've burned themselves until the next morning."

"So it happens often?"

"I guess if you're sleeping soundly it doesn't hurt enough to wake you up. They take a long time to heal. The damage goes a lot deeper than other burns."

In his mind the young man pictured his wife still limping a little from the accident as she made her way about the quiet house.

"'Eight-year-old Suzie died three days after coming down with the flu,'" the father read from the paper. He had found an article among the news from America that he thought the others might like to hear. They were all sitting around the breakfast table, eating.

"Suzie is a little black girl," he explained before reading on. "'Many friends and neighbors came to express their sympathy to the grief-stricken parents. The funeral service took place without incident. But then, when it came time to lower the casket into the grave—'"

"Did something go wrong?" the girl broke in.

The father answered her interruption with a sharp look that said "Let me finish," then continued the story. "'When the parents raised the lid of the casket for a final look at their daughter, Suzie opened her eyes and said, "Mommy, can I have some milk?" The entire town went into an uproar.'"

"She came back to life?" the girl asked. She seemed anxious to have her father say it in so many words.

"That's right, she came back to life."

"Weird," the older boy said, and flopped backward onto the tatami. The three-year-old promptly followed suit.

"Imagine what a shock it would have been!" the father said. He tried to form a mental picture of the small southern town where Suzie and her parents lived, though, of course, he could not really tell how the houses or streets would look. The cemetery would be on the outskirts of town, no doubt, but what was the surrounding area like?

"What an awful story!" his wife said.

"Why? What do you mean?"

"Oh, I don't know," she said, looking very ill at ease. "I mean, my goodness, the child was supposed to be dead when all of a sudden she wakes up and starts talking. If I were the mother, I'd have been terrified." Her husband stared back at her but said nothing. "Wouldn't *you* be scared?"

Suddenly a strange voice filled the room: "Mommy, can I have some milk?"

It was the girl. She had leaned back against the wall and was gazing blankly into space, pretending to be Suzie at the moment she came back to life.

What would it sound like? the father wondered: the voice of someone who had all but entered the realm of the dead and then returned suddenly to the brightness of this world.

"Ohhh, don't do that," the mother scolded the girl. "It gives me the shivers."

The goldfish from the Sunday excursion was given a place in the children's study. It swam about happily in its glass bowl on the sill of the bay window.

"What a healthy goldfish!" the mother often exclaimed. She was the one who looked after the new family pet most of the time—changing its water, feeding it little scraps of bread, and giving it a pinch of salt every now and then.

When the father and children had come home with their tiny catch in the toy bucket, she had remarked on what a nice shape it had. It was true, the father had had to agree: it might be only so big, but it did have a nice, sleek body.

An almost invisible tinge of red showed here and there on its stomach and fins as well as on its head.

"I caught it when I was looking the other way," he had said. "We'd better take good care of it."

The study held quite a few things besides desks and bookshelves for the two children who were in school. Their mother's dresser was kept here, together with her sewing machine. In one corner was a basket containing some wooden blocks, the base of a ring-toss game, a baseball glove, and several other items—the few toys the children had not yet broken. In another corner stood two large suitcases, one on top of the other. They had seldom been used; most of the time they merely took up space.

To call it the children's study, then, was something of a misnomer. It was the room where they put everything that didn't fit anywhere else.

On the wall were two pictures. The one entitled "Star Children" had been done by the girl as a vacation project several summers before. Two little girls were holding hands and floating in a light blue sky, a star made of silver paper atop each of their heads. Their clothes had been cut from scraps of leftover fabric, and bits of yellow and gray yarn had been pasted on for hair. The second picture, entitled "Cowboys on the Plain," was a crayon drawing done by the older of the boys. One of the cowboys, a rifle at his shoulder, had just shot a large bird in a tree; the other was about to lasso a runaway horse. A bull came charging toward them and a rabbit was scampering by.

Two rattan chairs had also found their way into the room. Since they would block the doorway if set side by side, they were usually stacked on top of each other. The children liked to hitch these together with their desk chairs to make a stagecoach. One of them sat on the coachman's seat and the other two would get inside. Then, with many a shout and crack of the whip and clatter of the wheels, they would be off, racing full tilt along some old highway.

Such was the room into which the goldfish had come. It hardly seemed a safe place for a fragile glass bowl filled with water. There was no telling when a ball or some other toy might land in it, or when one of the children would get pushed against it and knock it over.

But incredibly enough, nothing happened. The children were no better behaved than they had ever been, yet somehow the bowl survived. As the days went by it blended in with the other things in the room, and no one worried about it any more.

Still, the father could never quite get over the feeling that someone would break it yet, someday.

"Good night, Dad!"

"Good night, Mom!"

"Good night, everyone!"

The echo of the children's voices seemed to linger in the air. Only a short while ago they had been racing to see who could put on his pajamas and make it into bed first. Now, with the hush of night settling over the house, only the father remained awake.

He contemplated the figure of his wife sleeping beside him. This woman, lying on her side, facing him—this was the woman he had married. For fifteen years he had slept with her, in the same bed, every night.

As a child he had slept alone, and in the army he had slept alone. But from the day he was married, he had started sharing a bed with another person. Two people who scarcely knew each other had begun to sleep together, just like that.

There had in fact been a short time when they did not share the same bed. How long had it been? Three months? Not even that, probably. They had slept in separate rooms, his wife with their baby daughter, who had just turned one. But the arrangement had come to a quick end. After the accident they had gone back to sleeping together. And they had done so ever since.

Awake alone in the stillness, the father thought back to their wedding night. He remembered the bright moonlight shining through the window, illumining his wife's face as she slept quietly beside him. She had hardly seemed to breathe. There was a small ribbon in her hair.

That was our first night together, he thought to himself.

The book he had been reading slipped from his hand. He picked it up again and started looking for his place.

"Here it is," he mumbled. "No, wait, I've read this already." He turned several more pages. Was this it? No, he remembered this part too. Where could it have been?

Choosing a page at random, he forced open his heavy eyelids and began to read. Within moments they drooped shut and the book fell from his hand.

"I forget if it was England or America, but I read a story about a boy who found a duck's egg and made it hatch," the boy told his father in their evening bath.

"He *hatched* a duck's egg?"

"Un-hunh."

"Where did he find it?"

"I don't know."

"Somewhere in the country?"

"Un-hunh, in the country."

"Near a stream or pond, I suppose."

"Maybe. Anyway, he wanted to make it hatch, so he tied it to his stomach with a piece of cloth."

"Where?"

"Right here." The boy cupped his hands at his side. The father could tell that he had picked the spot arbitrarily.

"He kept it warm like that all the time for twenty days or so. Even at school, and even when he went to bed."

"For twenty days?"

"Un-hunh, something like that, I don't remember exactly. Anyway, the egg finally hatched right in the middle of class, and the teacher and everyone was really surprised."

"That's amazing," the father said. "It actually hatched during class?"

"Un-hunh."

"And it surprised everyone?"

"Un-hunh."

"Is this something you read at school?"

"Un-hunh. On the bulletin board in the hall. There's a big paper with stories from all over the world."

"Was there a picture?"

"Some of the stories have pictures, but this one didn't."

"When did you read this story?"

"A long time ago."

"Back in first grade?"

"Un-hunh."

"And you happened to think of it now?"

"Un-hunh."

The father wondered what had made him remember the story. "You'd think he would've broken it," he said. "I wonder how he had it tied."

166

"I bet the egg wouldn't last a day if I did it," the boy said. "I'd forget about it when I was playing. Do you think you could do it, Dad?"

"No, I doubt it. Probably not," he said. "All right, ready to get out?"

"Yep." He jumped out of the tub.

"Just a minute," the father stopped him. "Did you wash your face?"

"My face?"

"If you have to think about it, you obviously didn't."

"Yes I did."

"Ohhh no, you can't fool me. Your face isn't even wet. Since when do you take a bath without washing your face? Come on. Stop stalling."

"Okay." The boy took the lid off the soap dish and filled it with hot water.

"Hey, no playing around now. Just wash your face."

"I will, I will." He laid his washcloth over the soap dish.

"Come on."

"Just a second." With a slow and deliberate motion he rubbed soap into the washcloth. Then, bringing the cloth to his lips, he blew on it gently. A soft bank of suds began to form.

"See."

"So that's what you wanted to do."

"Watch. They'll get bigger and bigger."

"Fine, fine. They're plenty big already."

"Isn't it neat?"

"Sure."

"You wanna try it?"

"No. You've shown me your little trick now, so hurry up with your face."

"Just a little more."

The heap of suds quivered gently as it swelled. Before long the boy's face was completely hidden.

"I wonder if you remember that movie we saw," the father said to his daughter. She was sewing a blouse for her doll.

"What movie?"

"When you were in the first grade. Or was it kindergarten? No, it wasn't the year we moved, but the year after, so you would've been in first grade."

The family had moved here from another city when the girl was in kindergarten. The older boy had just begun to say a few words; the second had not yet been born. The father could still remember the long train ride and his first glimpse of their new house standing by itself in the middle of some open farmland.

The following year, in winter, he had taken his daughter to see a movie.

"The foreman at a construction site falls into a pit being filled with concrete."

"Oh yeah, I remember," the girl said.

"How much do you remember?"

She stopped stitching. "The man was a carpenter, wasn't he?"

"Well, yes, he built houses. He laid bricks, though, so I suppose you'd call him a mason. He was in Italy at first, but then he got on a ship and came to New York."

"He was really poor."

"That's right. That was why he came to America. He couldn't make a living in Italy."

They had seen the movie in a theater at the back of a short alleyway, just off the main thoroughfare in front of the station. Even with their overcoats on, it had been chilly inside.

"He was sick or something and couldn't go to work."

"I think he had hurt himself," the father said, still trying to retrieve the details from his own hazy memory. "That's right. He becomes foreman of a demolition crew tearing down an old building, but then something goes wrong between him and his men and they don't get along very well any more. First the men stop speaking to him, then they walk out on him. So he has to work all by himself. Pretty soon a wall falls over on him and his leg gets crushed."

"That's why he couldn't work?"

"Something like that."

"Oh, I remember now. It's when his leg finally gets better and he goes back to work that he falls into the hole they're filling with concrete. He

168

screams for help but there's too much noise and no one hears him. So the concrete keeps getting higher and higher."

"And in the end only his head shows."

"I covered my eyes, it was so scary. But I couldn't help hearing his screams."

"What happened next?"

"His wife comes out with kind of a blank look on her face, and someone's talking to her."

"Right. Since her husband was killed on the job, she's supposed to get paid a lot of money. Someone asks her what she plans to do with it, but she only shakes her head to say she doesn't know. Or maybe she means she hasn't even thought about it. Do you remember anything else?"

"Unh-unh."

"No? How about the book I bought you before we went into the movie?"

"Unh-unh." She picked up her sewing and began stitching again. Her father watched the way her hands moved.

As he remembered, it was a picture book, but he couldn't recall the title. He had bought her the book to try to make up for dragging her along, on their one day off, to a movie that *he* wanted to see. Not only was it a foreign film, but the things he had heard about it suggested that it might be a bit heavy-going for a six-year-old.

The first few scenes were mild enough. One of the mason's friends at work tells him he ought to get married, and suggests a girl he knows. The mason starts seeing the girl and falls in love with her. And she falls in love with him.

"But what about a house?" she asks. "I can't marry you if you don't have a house." Her family, too, had emigrated from Italy. She knows what it's like to be poor. She knows how miserable life can be for a couple who marry without a house of their own.

The mason tells her that he has a house, believing this is the only way he can get her to marry him. The wedding is held. Immigrant families from the neighborhood gather for a joyous celebration.

Everything was fine up to this point. But then the bride finds out that

169

the house she thought was theirs belongs to someone else. Her happy smile vanishes. She had always been a cheerful, lighthearted girl, but now she sinks into gloom.

They begin their married life in a small, shabby apartment. On the wall they carve little notches with a knife, a record of their determination, no matter what the sacrifice, to save enough money to buy a house. Then a child is born.

As the movie continued, the events unfolding on screen became more and more harrowing. Early one morning the mason comes home drunk, having spent the night with another woman. On his way up the stairs of the apartment building, he decides to punish himself. He swings his open palm down on the pointed tip of the newel-post.

No! The father caught his breath and quickly turned to look at his daughter. The book he had bought her on the way to the theater was raised in front of her face. She had instinctively lifted it from her lap, as though merely closing her eyes would not be enough to block out the scene. Clever girl, he thought, breathing a sigh of relief.

The mason continued to suffer one misfortune after another, and with each frightening scene the book on the girl's lap rose, then fell again. Each time, her father let her know when the scene was over. "It's all right now," he would whisper. "You don't want to miss this part."

Near the end, when the mason fell into the pit, the father stole another look at his daughter. Once again she was hunched tensely behind her book. This time the book remained up throughout the scene, while the roar of the falling concrete and the sound of the mason's screams filled the theater.

Suddenly the screen fell silent, and the girl peeked tremulously from behind her book. The mason was nowhere to be seen. His bereaved wife stood all alone, utterly stricken.

"Did . . . did he die?" the girl asked in a tiny voice.

"Yes," he answered.

The father recalled all this as he watched his daughter work at her sewing. That book had really come in handy then, he thought. It had helped her get through the movie without having to watch the scary scenes.

In the same way, his daughter had been spared knowledge of the accident that took place in her own home. She was still an infant at the time, and could not have known the meaning of her mother's deep sleep. An invisible hand had gently covered her eyes.

"Hey Dad," the boy said. "Tell us something that begins with S."
"Something that begins with S?"
"Un-hunh. S-T."
"S-T?"
"S-T-O-R-Y. A story."
"What about a story?"
"We want you to tell us one."
"I don't know any stories," the father protested.
"You do too."
"I can't think of any."
"How about the wild boar story?"
"But I've told you that one lots of times."
"That doesn't matter."
The father had run out of excuses. "During the summer," he began, "boars always sleep. They stay at home in their dens, lying on big soft beds made of thatch, and all they do is sleep and sleep and sleep. Thatch—that's what the old hunter who told me this story called it—is a plant that grows in the mountains. Besides using it for beds, the boars make roofs out of it, to keep off the rain when there's a storm and to shade themselves on hot sunny days. It works very nicely, both ways. So the boars just lie around sleeping in their cozy little thatched houses, day in day out, all summer long. If that isn't the easy life!" he exclaimed enviously, glancing from the older boy to the younger.

"The old hunter told me, though, that you can't eat boar's meat in the summer. It doesn't taste good. So I guess maybe it's not such a good idea to sit around doing nothing after all. You see, when they butcher a summer boar, there's always a layer of fat as stiff as a board right under the skin. In fact that's what the hunters call it—a 'board.' And they say a boar with a board isn't any good because you can't eat the meat. But actually the 'board' has a special purpose. It helps keep the boar's energy inside its body so that it can sleep the whole summer long."

"That's why badger's fat is better, right?"

171

"Right. Badgers are the opposite of boars. They sleep through the winter, which means they have a lot of fat then and almost none in the summer. Badger's fat is really good. If you take some from just under the skin and heat it in a pan, you get a smooth, clear oil. Oh, by the way, there's another special name the hunters use: 'cukes.' That's what they call baby boars, because they have patches of fur on their backs that look just like big fat cucumbers."

"That's kind of neat," the older boy said.

"That's kinda neat," the younger quickly repeated.

"Mmm, I thought so too. Now, one of the boar's favorite foods, of all things, is earthworms. To think that an animal that big would go for worms—when they're known to gobble up a whole patch of sweet potatoes in a single night! The old hunter was really shaking his head over this one. He never could understand why such a big eater would take a liking to little earthworms. And they like spiders and mud snails, too. They dig up the snails with their snouts, just like the worms, but it's a mystery how they eat them because they never leave any shells behind. They must either take them home to eat, or else they swallow the whole thing, shell and all. The hunter said he didn't imagine snails would taste very good with the shell on them." The father tilted his head thoughtfully, then shrugged. "Who knows what they do?"

He went on: "Hunting for boars can be pretty rough, I guess. When you walk through the snow looking for tracks, your feet get soaked and clumps of snow fall on you from the branches overhead, and after a while your stomach starts to growl. An important thing to know when you're looking for tracks is that boars always travel the same paths. Maybe they're just the methodical type, or maybe they're actually afraid of something—I don't know. But in any case they always follow exactly in each other's footsteps. So no matter how many boars have gone by it looks like only one. That's how consistent they are.

"One time a terrible thing happened because of this. At the power station in the mountains there's a sluice for the water that turns the generators, and it has a log lying across it for a bridge. One snowy morning the workers at the plant found three dead boars washed against the sluice gates. They went up along the sluice to see if they could find out what had happened, and when they got to the log they discovered there was an icy spot about halfway across. What had happened was the first boar to come along that morning had slipped on the ice and fallen into the water. Since the sluice is made of concrete and the sides go straight up and down, the boar had no place to climb out and it got swept away by the current. Then the second one came along, and, because it followed the first boar's tracks onto the log, it slipped at the same place. After a while a third one came and fell into the water just like the others. Poor things. The men couldn't tell whether the boars had come one right after the other or a long time apart, but they could see what had happened from the way the tracks ended in the middle of the log."

"They should've watched out better," the older boy said.

"They should've watched out better," his brother echoed.

"That's right, they might have been okay if they had only stopped to think, 'Hey, wait a minute. The tracks don't go all the way across.' But they didn't, I guess. Well then, let's get on with the story about the old hunter meeting up with the wild boar."

The boys leaned forward. This was the part they had been waiting for.

"When he was in the mountains one day, the hunter came across a boar's den—made of thatch, as I said. He went home and told three of his hunter friends about it, and without letting anyone else know of their plans they got ready to go back for the kill. You see, you have to have at least three or four hunters to get a boar. If you try to do it alone, the boar will always get away. On the day of the hunt—remember, this all happened before the hunter was as old as he is now—the four of them set off for the mountains early in the morning. As it turned out, there was another group of hunters that had somehow got wind of their plans and had left even earlier. But the old hunter and his friends didn't know this yet, and they hiked on and on through the underbrush toward the boar's den. They came to a small cliff, and started climbing it, when all of a sudden they heard a panting sound and *boom!*—"

Pretending he was the hunter crawling up the side of a cliff, the father jerked his head back.

"Just as the old hunter started to pull himself over the top, he found himself face to face with a giant boar. Talk about being caught off guard!

173

They had all assumed the boar would be fast asleep in its den! The hunter immediately ducked down and reached for the rifle slung across his back. And the startled boar retreated, too, almost as quickly."

Now the father acted the part of the wild boar, first leaning forward as if poking his head over the edge of the cliff, then hastily pulling back.

"The hunter thought the boar had decided to run back the way it came, and if he didn't hurry it would get away. He started to scramble up after it. But *whoosh!*—the boar suddenly went flying by his head, landed with a tremendous skid at the bottom of the cliff, and went crashing into the underbrush below. By the time the hunters turned around, all they could see was the broken branches where the boar had disappeared, and, farther on, the churning of the undergrowth as it ran off."

"Wow!" the older boy exclaimed.

The younger boy sat speechless, his wide eyes glued to his father's face.

"What had happened was the other hunters, the ones who had gone earlier, had already shot at the boar and put it in a panic. That's probably why it made such a desperate leap. So when the old hunter thought the boar had taken off in the other direction, actually it had only backed up a little way to get a running start for the jump." The father broke into a laugh for a moment, but then finished the story with a straight face. "The hunter said someone else finally shot the boar a week or so later. And that's the end of the story."

Their uncle came to visit them from the town where they had lived before moving to their present home. He brought with him a bag of walnuts for the children.

"What a nice gift," the father said afterward. "We couldn't spend money on nuts for ourselves—they're too much of an extravagance. But as a gift for someone with children, they're perfect. A real treat. A chance for the children to have something we couldn't normally afford."

But how would they divide up the nuts? The mother decided as follows: the girl could have seven, the older boy five, and the younger boy three. That would still leave two, so she and her husband could have one each.

The older boy went to get the hammer and quickly finished off his share. The younger boy ate all of his, too, after his mother had helped him crack them open. The mother waited to eat hers until the following afternoon when she was at home alone with the younger boy. The father slipped his into his pocket; he still had it when he went to work the next day, but lost it somewhere the day after.

The girl decided to save hers for a while. She put them in a drawer in her desk, and took them out one at a time to polish them with a piece of felt. She wanted to bring out their best shine.

A few days later she told her friends at school, but only her two best friends, about the nuts. "They were a present from my uncle when he came to visit," she explained. "Do you like walnuts? If you want, I'll bring you some tomorrow."

"Sure," they said. They both liked walnuts.

Should she give them each two, or only one? she wondered. If she gave them two, they could rub them together in their hands to make a grinding noise, and they'd have more fun with them. But if she gave each of them two, that would leave her with fewer than half of her original seven. She wasn't sure she liked that idea. She enjoyed watching the walnuts roll around when she opened the drawer, and it just wouldn't be the same with only three nuts left. To give two would be better, of course. There was no question of that. But even one was better than nothing.

When she was getting ready for school the next day, she took four walnuts from the drawer and dropped them into the pocket of her skirt.

At school she ran into one of her friends. "I brought the walnuts," she said, reaching into her pocket. She still hadn't made up her mind whether she would give one or two.

"Here." She held out a single walnut.

"Thank you," her friend said gratefully.

That afternoon she walked home with her other friend, Ikuko. As they passed through the school gate she handed her a walnut.

"Thanks," said Ikuko.

"Try this. It's fun," she said, taking the other two nuts from her pocket and rubbing them together.

"That's neat," Ikuko said. The girl lent Ikuko one of her walnuts. Ikuko rubbed the nuts together for a while as they walked, then gave back the one she had borrowed.

"Not very long after that," the girl later recounted to her father, "we went by a place where some men were working on the road. We still had the nuts in our hands, but I guess I wasn't really paying attention because all of a sudden Ikuko said, 'Hey, you dropped one of your nuts.' So we turned around to look for it right away, and guess what. We hadn't gone back more than five or six steps when one of the construction workers said, 'I bet you're looking for your walnut, aren't you?' and started laughing. He said he'd already eaten it and showed us the shell broken right in half."

"And the nut was all gone?" her father asked.

"Un-hunh."

"Was he still chewing?"

"No, he wasn't. He'd already swallowed it. It couldn't have been more than a couple of seconds."

"Mmm."

"What I want to know is how could he have cracked that hard shell? With his teeth? We told him he was mean and just came on home, but we were really mad."

"I can imagine," her father nodded. After a pause he said, "I guess the nut must have rolled right in front of him—right where he happened to be looking."

The goldfish seemed to have grown since it first joined the family. Its stomach had filled out; the faint patches of red were now a deeper hue; and with each passing day it looked more and more like an adult fish. Everyone enjoyed watching it dart briskly around its bowl on the sunny windowsill.

"I don't think I've ever seen such a peppy goldfish before," the mother said.

"Yes, we should count ourselves lucky," the father replied. "Let's hope he stays that way."

Every other day the mother changed about half of the water and sprinkled in a pinch of salt, and every third day she gave the fish some bread crumbs or pieces of crackers or cookies. When the children wanted to feed it, she made them take turns, and she kept track of the days to ensure they didn't feed it too much or too often.

The father did not help with the fish, but from time to time he would go into the children's study and watch it move about in its bowl. Such poise! he marveled. With the slightest flick of its fins and an occasional twitch of its tail, the fish could hold itself perfectly still, going neither forward nor backward, for as long as it wished.

He and the children had recently made a second trip to the fishing pond. This time, however, the little tin bucket proved useless, for they failed to catch even a single fish. Nor were they the only ones to come up empty-handed; nobody else's luck appeared any better, at either of the ponds.

As evening approached, the air over the pond grew heavier and heavier. "This time it looks pretty hopeless," the father sighed. "No one's getting anything." Even changing the bait seemed a waste of effort. Still, he stuck it out at the same spot until the hour they had paid for was up.

The fish he had caught the last time now became more precious than ever. There was a big difference between catching one fish and catching none at all. To have hooked that one fish almost began to seem like a special meeting of fates.

An old man wearing a hunter's cap started to put his gear away. "I should've known better than to come today," he muttered grumpily as he left. "Fishing's never any good when the wind's out of the east."

A few minutes later they were all given a start. Over at the other pond, a boy who had been watching his father fish fell into the water with a loud splash. Everyone turned to see the fisherman pulling his son out. The child, soaked from the neck down, looked about ten years old.

A gentle wave of laughter spread among the few people remaining at the pond. The incident dispelled the oppressive mood that had descended over the place, and everyone relaxed again.

Frustrated and tired from an afternoon spent in vain, the man had apparently started to doze off. When he leaned over against his son, the boy had lost his balance and tumbled into the water.

Having retrieved his son—instead of a fish—from the pond, the man could hardly go on fishing. The sun was low in the sky as the two left for home, the hapless boy sloshing awkwardly along behind his father.

"I wonder what's wrong with this thing," the father mumbled to himself. "It manages to flower all right, but it always looks so straggly."

On Sunday morning he had stepped out into the yard to take a closer look at the lilac bush. His eyes moved from the long, spindly branches, to the clusters of tiny, purple flowers, and to the ground underneath the bush.

The bush had been planted in the spring five years before, the year after they had moved to this house. But once it had reached a height slightly taller than he was, it had stopped growing. It never developed a main trunk; instead, it had split at the base into a mass of skinny branches that fanned out toward the sky.

He had originally hoped it would grow large and full enough for the children to hide behind when they played games of hide-and-seek. This no longer seemed likely.

He was still contemplating the lilac when he saw a band of street musicians come into view down the road. The man at the head of the troupe pranced about nimbly in time with the music, turning first one way, then the other.

He keeps people's attention that way, thought the father. If he walked along normally, there wouldn't be anything to watch.

From where he stood inside the fence, the father continued to follow the dancer's movements as the band moved closer. Suddenly he saw that the dancer was not a man at all, but a woman, a rather skinny woman dressed in men's clothes and made up with white greasepaint.

Behind her came a second dancer in a similar outfit, only this one actually was a man. Third in line was a woman in a black beret playing the clarinet. Next came the drummer, beating with exaggerated flourish on the rack of gongs and tom-toms strapped to his chest. A trumpet player wearing a radioman's cap brought up the rear.

The procession came to a halt. The three musicians continued playing while the two dancers went from house to house passing out handbills.

The older boy had come out of the house to watch from the side of the road. Now the drummer approached him and said something. The boy stared back, but his lips did not move.

Why didn't he answer? the father wondered. What could the man have said?

The group slowly moved away again, and the boy came back into the yard.

"Did the drummer say something to you?" the father asked.

"Un-hunh."

"What did he say?"

"I had my fingers in my ears," the boy said, "and I was pushing them in and out to make the music sound real loud and then real quiet." He demonstrated as he explained, putting his fingers to his ears again. "So the man said if I had to plug my ears like that, I shouldn't come close, I should go somewhere else."

"I see," the father nodded.

"I guess he thought I didn't like their music," the boy grinned.

On Sunday evening the father took out his sketchbook and began to draw a picture of his daughter. She had gotten ready for bed after an early bath, then settled down on the tatami in the front room to read. She saw what her father was doing and tried her best to sit perfectly still for him.

"Are you getting stiff?" he asked her after a while.

"No, not particularly." She sat with her legs flopped to one side and the book open in her lap. The big toe of one foot peeked out from behind the other knee. Her father started sketching the toe.

"No, that's too big, I guess," he said, mostly to himself.

"What's too big?" the girl asked.

"Your toe."

"It better not be," she giggled.

"Do you remember your grandpa?" her father asked as he rubbed the toe out.

"A little," she nodded.

"I was just thinking of the time he told me to make a drawing of your feet."

"My feet?"

"Un-hunh."

"What for?"

"It was a day or two after you were born."

"Why my feet?"

"He said it'd be fun to have later on." He started outlining the toe again. "All I had with me was my address book, so I drew a little sketch in that. Just the bottoms of your feet. I suppose it got thrown out somewhere along the way."

"Too bad."

"Yes, I wish we still had it. You'd get a kick out of it. With my knack of losing things, I wonder if Grandpa really thought I'd keep it all this time. . . Hmm, I guess this hand isn't quite right either." He started to reshape the hand holding the book. "I remember how impressed Grandpa was with the hospital room. He kept saying it would make a great apartment, and that they should rent it out to us."

"Can I move my legs a little now?" the girl asked.

"Sure, go ahead. It really was a nice room. A quiet room, perfect for reading. The window faced the nurses' dormitory, and every once in a while we'd see one of them dash across the street through the rain. I remember there was a big paulownia by the front entrance. . . Why can't I get these fingers right? The more I work on them the worse they get."

The girl looked up and glanced at her father's sketchbook.

"That day," he went on, "as I was leaving the hospital, I ran into your grandpa coming through the rain, wearing a hat but without an umbrella. He was on his way to see your mother. We stepped under the eaves to talk for a couple of minutes, and do you know what he said? He had never been to a maternity ward before; he had never visited anyone who'd just had a baby. So I decided to go back to the hospital with him. Later, when we were leaving, he told me not to worry—for every day a baby lives it builds up that much more strength to survive. You see, we were having a terrible time getting you to drink your mother's milk. You kept falling asleep as soon as you got the nipple in your mouth, even when the nurse tried pulling on your ear. We didn't know what to do with you."

The girl giggled sheepishly.

"Guess what we found at school today," the girl said at the dinner table. "A mole cricket. We were digging in the flower bed, and—"

"Another mole cricket!" exclaimed her mother. "Yesterday it was your brother who found one. He comes in the door after school, and, before

I even have a chance to ask him how his day was, he dangles this ugly creature in front of my face and says 'Look, I brought you a present.'"

"You should've seen her jump," the boy said gleefully.

"Of course I jumped. How many times do I have to tell you? You can bring home anything you like as far as the front door, but I won't have you bringing bugs into the house."

"So-o-rry."

"So what did you do with the mole cricket in the flower bed?" the father asked.

"Mine was in the sandbox," the boy said.

"The sandbox? You mean you brought it home all the way from school?"

"Yep."

"When we caught the one in the flower bed," the girl said, "we held it like this and asked it, 'How bi-i-ig is so-and-so's brain?' and it would sort of wiggle in surprise and spread its front legs."

"Whoever thought *that* up?" the father wanted to know.

"We all thought it up together. When you say your own name, you say 'BI-I-IG' real loud," she said, putting extra stress on the B. "Then it spreads its legs way far apart, like this. But when you say someone else's name, you say the words real soft: 'How big.'" This time she lowered her voice to a whisper. "Then it only moves its legs a tiny bit." She demonstrated with her arms as she spoke.

"You've got to be making this up," her mother said.

"No, it's true, it was like the mole cricket really heard. So we started doing the same thing as the cricket, and spread our arms real wide, too, when we said our own names."

"As if the poor thing wasn't startled enough already," her father said.

The girl seemed endlessly amused by the way the mole cricket squirmed in surprise. She went through her "How bi-i-ig" antics several more times, transforming herself from little girl into mole cricket and back again, then collapsing in a fit of laughter.

"How bi-i-ig?" the older boy said, moving his arms like his sister.

"How bi-i-g?" the younger boy imitated.

"So-o big."

"So-o big."

"All right, all right," the father said when they all started doing it together. "That's enough. Let's have some quiet for a change. Please."

Even now, in the deserted schoolyard where the children had played that day, the mole crickets would be quietly burrowing their way through the sandboxes and flower beds.

Two stuffed toys, a tiger and a rabbit, shared the wide windowsill where the goldfish swam in its bowl. The tiger lay on its stomach, its legs thrust forward. Its head was tilted to one side so that its nose almost touched the ground, and it looked as if it were scrutinizing the movements of some industrious ant. The rabbit, wearing polka-dotted pants, faced the opposite direction. It lay on its back and stared up at the sky.

During the daytime, the two animals sat like this on the sill. Then, when night came, they were taken off to bed by the children. The younger boy always got the rabbit—there were never any quarrels about that. But the older boy and the girl had to take turns with the tiger, and many an argument broke out when one or the other of them would miss a day.

One night, the father was getting ready for bed in his room at the end of the hall when he heard the children's voices rise to a fighting pitch. A moment later his wife intervened: "All right, now, who had it the day before yesterday? And yesterday? No, no, you both know the rule— forgetting doesn't count."

It was their own fault if they missed a turn, she explained, as she had so many times before. They could not demand their turn the next day. If that were allowed, neither of them would be able to count on their regular turn any more, and there'd be no end to the fighting. If they forgot, it was just too bad. They would have to wait for their next turn.

How had this all started? the father wondered. How long had they been having these squabbles?

Sometimes several days went by without either of the children re-membering to take the tiger to bed. Since neither of them could recall who had had it last or how long it had been, even their mother couldn't settle whose turn it should be. Eventually, to make sure this didn't hap-pen again, she had begun keeping track by marking the calendar with the children's initials.

The father shook his head as he got under the covers. It was beyond him why they would want to take something like that to bed with them. *He* had slept alone when *he* was a child. And he had taken it for granted that everyone else did, too.

The children's dispute finally came to an end. That night, the tiger would sleep with the girl.

"Lucky stiff!" the boy grumbled loudly.

As the father picked up one of the books lying at the head of the bed, his thoughts drifted off to another stuffed toy they had once had—a puppy, neither so small nor so soft as the tiger the children had just been fighting over. He recalled the Christmas morning, more than ten years before, when he had found the puppy standing beside his baby daughter's bed. The tall, husky puppy had seemed so enormous next to the tiny figure of the baby.

Now what did she go and buy something like that for? he remembered thinking to himself.

Only a few minutes earlier, he had been equally surprised when he first awoke to find a box, neatly tied with ribbon, sitting beside his pillow. The box had contained a fedora.

Had he said he wanted one of these? He couldn't remember, but perhaps he had, sometime or other, and his wife had taken him seriously. Or perhaps he had only commented on how nice someone else's looked.

How much did hats like this cost? He really couldn't imagine. He had never considered buying one for himself, or envisioned himself wearing one to the office, so he'd never had cause to explore the hat section of the department store. His knowledge of hats was pretty much limited to the corduroy cap he got out in the summertime. But that was one of those things you could roll up and stuff in your pocket—it hardly counted as a real hat. The only other hat he had ever worn was a boater, in his student days. He remembered having to hold it with one hand on top to keep it from flying off as he raced to get on the train before the doors closed.

He knew he hadn't paid very much for that boater. But fedoras were in a different class altogether. It must have cost a small fortune. Why had his wife made such an extravagant purchase without consulting him?

She knew they didn't have that kind of money to spend.

Sitting up in bed, he tried on the new hat. He liked it, the way it gently pressed against his head. But he wasn't sure what position he should wear it in. If he pulled it down too far, his head would push out the crease on top and make it look like a bowler instead of a fedora. How did other people wear them? He would have to pay more attention from now on.

He returned the hat to its box and closed the lid.

Since it was a holiday, he could sleep later than usual if he wanted. But the surprise of the hat had left him wide awake. He decided to go ahead and get up.

The quiet of morning filled the house. Outside, clouds hung heavily in the sky.

It was then, when he poked his head into the next room to see if his wife and daughter were awake, that he had had his first glimpse of the toy puppy.

For several moments, all he could do was marvel at its magnificent size and beauty. In any display of stuffed toys, this puppy was bound to reign as king of beasts. Once you had seen it, all the other toys would look like mere knickknacks by comparison.

Clearly it had been made to last. It could probably hold a child on its back without collapsing.

But once again he wondered about the cost. Although he knew even less about stuffed toys than about hats, he could guess it had been expensive. What could his wife have been thinking, spending so much money on a toy like that? With all the daily expenses they had to worry about, she should show a little more sense.

He would have to give her a little scolding, he decided. In fact, he would do it right then and there. So what if it was a holiday? It was already later than usual and time she got started on breakfast.

He called her name, but she slept on without so much as stirring. His wife was one of those people who always looked as though they hadn't had enough sleep, and at night she was lost to the world the moment her head touched the pillow. She seldom dreamed, and was never wakeful. But when the alarm went off the next morning, or when he called her, she would be up in an instant. In all the time they had been married, he couldn't remember having had to call her twice.

"Hey, wake up," he said again, reaching over to shake her shoulder. All of a sudden he noticed that what she had on was not what she normally wore to bed.

As the father lay reflecting on that morning, he thought again of the puppy. It had proved to be just as sturdy as his first impression had suggested. The girl had played with it for a long time, riding on its back, hanging on with her baby fists clutched tightly around its soft, fluffy ears. She had started doing this even before she learned to walk. When their first son came along, he had played with it, too, bouncing up and down on its back no less gleefully than his sister. But it had still held up as good as new.

Later, when they moved to their new house, the puppy had come with them. The father remembered packing it to be shipped with the other baggage.

"The fedora was a different story, though," he sighed. *That* he had lost almost right away. At a movie theater. He had put it on his lap during the show, only to forget about it when he stood up to leave. He was all the way outside before he noticed, and by then it was too late. One of the ushers had kindly gone to retrieve it for him, but came back saying the theater was too crowded. He had had to give it up for lost.

When the boys asked for an "S" again one evening, the father told them another story about the old hunter.

"Next to hunting," he began, "the old man's favorite pastime is fishing. He became a hunter first, and he's been making regular trips into the mountains for more than forty years, since he was a young man. Then about thirty years ago, when he moved to the town where he lives now, he took up fishing. He liked the town so much, he's lived there ever since, and he's spent a lot of time at the nearby river ever since, too. He got started fishing, he says, because he found a good river-teacher there."

"A river-teacher?" the older boy laughed.

"That's right. Maybe you've only heard of schoolteachers, but there are river-teachers, too—and mountain-teachers, and even ocean-teachers. A long time ago, this river-teacher had worked as a raftsman for a lumber company. You see, when a lumber company cuts down trees up in the mountains, the logs are tied together into rafts so they can be floated down the river to the lumber mill. The raftsman is the person who steers the raft down the river, through the rapids and between all the rocks and things sticking up out of the water. It's a really dangerous job. Anyway, after this river-teacher had worked as a raftsman for a while, he decided to settle down in one of the towns along the river and become a fisherman instead. He knew that river like the back of his hand. No one could match him. He could tell you exactly how many fish there were and what they were doing or which way they were swimming anywhere along the river, even in the roughest and deepest places. If you were fishing with him and he said, 'One more,' that meant there was only one fish left in that spot. And he'd be right!"

"Wow!" the older boy exclaimed.

"Wow!" the younger boy mimicked.

"That's incredible," the first added.

"The old hunter couldn't get over it either. He said he'd never heard of anyone who knew so much about rivers and fish. The river-teacher's name was Katsujirō, but since his father's name had been Katsuzō, everyone called him Little Katsu. People still called him that when the hunter met him, even though he was an old man by then."

The older boy laughed when his father said "Little Katsu."

"The problem was that since Little Katsu depended on catching fish for his living, you could never believe what he told you. If you asked him where was a good spot, he would lie and send you off someplace he knew was lousy. The hunter got to be his best friend, and they would drink together almost every night, but he still couldn't get a straight answer out of him. For instance, he might ask if today was a good day, and Little Katsu would say, 'No.' Well, that would turn out to be a lie— the days he said 'No' were in fact the best days. So pretty soon the hunter tried doing the opposite of whatever Little Katsu said. If he said 'No,' the hunter would set out for the river. And sure enough, Little Katsu would be there."

"So he had to listen to him backward," the older boy said.

"That's right. With a teacher like Little Katsu, that was how you learned. Even then the hunter got tricked a lot, so he tried something new. Instead of asking Little Katsu directly, he would sneak up to his house and peek in to see if he was at home. If he found him puttering

186

around the house or just taking a nap or something, he knew there was no sense in going to the river."

"'Cause he knew he wouldn't catch anything even if he did," the boy said.

"Un-hunh. Now, I said Little Katsu lied a lot, but actually there were some things he didn't lie about. Like how to cast a net so it would spread out the way you wanted it to. Or what's the best way to tie the hook to the line. Or how when you're fishing for dace and get a nibble you have to give some slack instead of pulling it in right away as most people do.

"It was lucky for the hunter that Little Katsu told the truth about these things. Otherwise he might never have learned how to cast the special sweetfish net that's used only on that river and nowhere else. It's about fifteen feet long, like a huge ribbon, and getting it to spread out just right is pretty tricky. If it goes into the water in a straight line, like this," he drew a line with his finger, "the fish will get away. They can swim right around it. To keep them from doing that, you have to make the net hit the water curved like a bow. Like this." He indicated the curve with a sweep of his arms.

"Like this?" the older boy said, making a similar arc.

"Like this?" his brother imitated.

"The reason it makes a difference, you see, is that sweetfish can't turn around very well. When they bump into the net, they just wriggle a little to one side or the other and keep trying to push ahead. That means if both ends of the net are curved back like this, then the fish are forced to swim toward the middle." The father cupped his left hand and poked at it with his right index finger to show how the fish bumped against the net and kept swimming forward until they wound up trapped in the center. The boys paid close attention.

"But if you just leave them there," he went on, "the fish eventually get turned around and find their way out. So, to make sure that doesn't happen, the old hunter swims down underwater to where the net is and breaks their spines."

"What's 'spines'?" the older boy asked.

"Right about here." The father patted the back of his neck. "Then later, after he's got quite a few, he brings them in all at once. He says

187

he used to catch thirty, even forty, in a single night back when he first started fishing. On nights like that he wouldn't even notice how cold the water was. Until he got home, that is. Then he would start shivering like crazy. He'd take a good hot bath and jump into bed with the covers pulled all the way up over his head, and he still wouldn't be able to keep from shaking. Even in the middle of summer. But you know what? No matter how bad the shivering was, he'd be right back at the river again the very next night. It's hardly a wonder he developed so many aches and pains as he got older, but he just shrugs and says, 'That's the way it goes.'"

"Tell us about the fox," the older boy broke in again.

"Okay. That happened when he was snagging, which is another way to catch sweetfish. Instead of a net, you use a line with a lot of hooks spaced three or four inches apart, and you snag the fish by their gills. Sometimes you can catch five or six all at once. With this method, too, the best fishing is at night, especially when the river is swollen and muddy after some rain. You can haul in dozens.

"Anyway, one night when the old hunter was snagging out in the middle of the river, a fox came along the bank and stopped to watch him. For a long time it just stood there like a little statue, not moving a muscle." The father got on all fours and made a fox's face, then continued. "Now, the hunter wouldn't have minded about the fox except that his basket of fish was sitting on the bank. You see, he had two baskets for the fish he caught—a small one that he tied around his waist, and a larger one that he left on the riverbank. Whenever the small one filled up, he would go back to shore and empty it into the larger one. The problem was the fox had stopped only a few steps away from this larger basket."

"Chase him away!" the older boy cried.

"Chase him away!" the younger boy echoed.

"You can imagine the hunter got pretty nervous about the basket. He picked up a rock from the riverbed and threw it hard at the fox, thinking that would surely send it scampering. But no, the fox just ambled a few steps to one side, stopped, and turned to eye him again. Then after a few moments it sauntered back toward the basket."

"Throw some more rocks!" the older boy said.

"Right. He picked up another rock and yelled 'Beat it!' as he hurled it off. But the fox wasn't any more impressed than the first time. The old hunter said he had never seen such a lackadaisical fox. Then, just as he was trying to decide what to do next, the fox grabbed the basket in its snout and trotted away."

"Too-o ba-a-ad," the older boy said sympathetically.

"Too-o ba-a-ad," the younger boy repeated.

"Hey Mom, Ikuko and I are going to make doughnuts this afternoon, okay?" the girl asked one Sunday, a little before noon.

"It's fine with me," her mother nodded.

"She said she'd bring the ingredients."

"She doesn't have to do that."

"That's what *I* said."

"I'm sure we have everything you need."

"I know, I told her that, but she insisted."

Ikuko arrived around two, bringing with her a bag of flour and an egg. She was a cute, cheerful girl, who never seemed to stop smiling.

"Can I help?" the older boy asked.

"There you go again," his father admonished. "Always getting into other people's projects. For girls, making doughnuts is like doing homework. You'd be in the way."

"But I want to do some homework too."

"Look, there's not enough room in the kitchen for all three of you to work in there at the same time."

"Yes there is," the boy whined. He stuck out his lips in a pout. His eyes filled and a tear or two trickled down his cheek.

"All right, you can help," his mother agreed. "But don't get carried away now. Understand?"

"Oka-a-a-y," he promised. A smile had already spread across his face. The switch from sad to happy was just that quick.

The father looked on as his wife got the children started. Then, having nothing better to do, he decided to go and lie down for a while. "Make them small," he said as he stood up to leave. "They're better that way."

189

In the back room he folded a cushion in half to use as a pillow and stretched out on the tatami. Even from there he could hear the voices in the kitchen.

"Stop taking so much," the girl scolded the boy. It seemed he had gotten carried away after all.

Then his wife was saying something. That was the voice of the woman he had married, he thought to himself as he listened. That was how she sounded when she did things with the kids.

For some reason he was reminded of the muffled sobs he had once heard, a long time ago. When had it been? Oh yes, it was in their old house. He was taking a nap upstairs late one Sunday afternoon—he even remembered using a folded cushion for a pillow, just like now—when all of a sudden he began to hear what sounded like a woman crying. He lifted his head to listen more closely, but the sound stopped. Then, while he was still puzzling over what to make of it, it started up again.

Was something wrong? Who could it be? Why should anyone be weeping?

Going downstairs, he found their second child fast asleep on the baby bed and his wife rinsing some spinach at the kitchen sink. Their daughter had gone out to play.

"Did you hear anything?" he asked his wife.

"No, not that I noticed," she replied, turning around with a bright face.

"That's strange. I could have sworn I heard something. That's what I came down for—to see what it was."

What could it have been, then, that sound of short, broken sobs? Something being jostled by the wind, perhaps, rubbing against something else. But why had it sounded to him so much like his wife's voice?

He went back upstairs, but the sound did not return.

The father now lay on the tatami in the back room staring into space as he thought over the incident that had puzzled him so. His wife had had no cause for weeping then. And in fact she *hadn't* been weeping.

"This one's mine," the boy's voice broke through the father's thoughts. "I put a mark on it so I could tell."

A few moments later someone began to laugh. Then they all laughed.

Footsteps came running down the hall and the door slid open. It was the younger boy. "They're done. It's time to eat," he said, and went dashing back toward the kitchen.

The father got up and followed. He found the others at the low, round table in the front room, the doughnuts divided up onto several small plates. There was an extra plate for him.

"Ummm, perfect!" he said between bites. "Just as I said, the small ones are best." He finished the doughnut and sat back to watch as the others ate theirs.

"Have some more," his wife urged.

"No thanks. One's enough for me." He pushed his plate toward the children.

"That was fun," the girl said as she took her last bite.

"And delicious," Ikuko added, finishing hers.

The boy, too, was down to his final bite, when his sister suddenly cried out, "Wait! Save a little piece!" But it was too late. The last bit had vanished into her brother's mouth. "Ohhh well," she said, disappointed.

"What's the matter?" her mother asked.

"We forgot to save any for the goldfish."

The boy tapped his cheeks as if to prove that the doughnut was completely gone. Neither on the plates nor on the table did a single crumb remain.

"We listened to the *New World* Symphony in music class today," the girl said one evening near the end of dinner.

"How nice!" her mother said. "Did you like it?"

"It was beautiful."

"Yes, it really is a beautiful piece."

"But you know what? When the teacher told us he was going to play it, the boys all groaned and didn't want to listen. Only the girls wanted to hear it."

"Why? What did the boys have against it?" the father asked.

"I don't know. All they said was 'Bo-o-oring. Bo-o-oring.' I guess they didn't think it would be much fun. They must have liked it more than they expected, though, because once it started they all listened quietly."

"Do you get to choose the music you listen to?" her mother asked.

"Un-hunh. Every once in a while the teacher asks us what we'd like to hear and makes a list on the board. One time, not too long ago, a lot of people wanted the *New World* Symphony. But he didn't have it taped yet."

"Oh, so you listen to a tape," the father broke in.

"Un-hunh. He's got lots of different music on tapes."

"I see."

"Anyway, today he came in and said he'd finally had a chance to record the *New World* Symphony the other night, so let's all listen to it. But first he explained that the beginning wasn't recorded very well—he hadn't had time to adjust all the knobs before the symphony started because he forgot until the last minute that it was going to be on the radio that night; he only barely got the tape recorder set up in time. And he said there was a place in the middle where we would hear his son's voice."

"Did you?" her brother asked.

"Un-hunh."

"What did he say?"

"I couldn't tell. Something like 'Ahhh-yooo.'"

"Ahhh-yooo?"

"I couldn't really tell, it went by so fast."

Several evenings later the girl had another story.

"In Ikuko's class," she began, "they listened to *Invitation to the Dance* today. The teacher told them beforehand that the composer—I think his name was Weber—had dedicated it to his wife, and that it was a flowery sort of piece."

"So that's what you call it," her father said.

"Then after he started the tape, he explained what was supposed to be happening at each place in the music." She had begun to speak a little faster, as she always did when she neared the best part of a story. "Well, evidently there's a place in the middle where the music stays kind of low for a while and then gets high, and the teacher explained that the low part was where the men go up to the ladies and ask, 'May I have this dance?' Then when it came to the high part, he started to tell them that that was where the ladies turn all red and say, 'Ohhh, something-

or-other.' But just as he said 'Ohhh,' his false teeth came loose, and they almost fell right out of his mouth!" Unable to hold back any longer, she burst out laughing.

Her parents stared at her in disbelief.

"His false teeth?" her father asked.

"It's really true! They almost fell out!" She laughed so hard that tears came to her eyes and she had to hold her stomach. Before long her father began to laugh, too, and then her mother and the boys. They laughed and laughed, unable to stop.

Finally the older boy asked, "So what did the teacher do?"

"Ikuko said he turned the other way and fixed them in a real hurry," the girl answered.

A bagworm the older boy had been keeping in a small cardboard box disappeared.

At the time, the father did not yet know about the bagworm. No one had thought to mention it to him. It was not until afterward that he heard the story.

The boy had originally found the bagworm on a tree in their neighbor's yard when he and a friend were gathering nuts to use as pellets in their toy guns. His friend told him that if he stripped the cocoon off and put the worm in a box with some leaves and bits of paper, it would make itself a new cocoon in about three hours.

The boy brought it home and did as his friend had said. But when he peeked into the box that night, the bagworm had not moved. The next morning it still hadn't moved.

He then forgot about the worm, and three days went by before he thought to check its box again. This time it had crept into a corner and begun building a little tentlike shelter on its back. The boy poked at the half-finished canopy with his finger. To his surprise, it flipped right off.

A day or two later he found the tiny creature crawling across the floor of the study. This time, too, it had a tent on its back, about the same size as the one before. The boy carefully returned it to its box.

After that, once again, he neglected to check on the bagworm for several days. When he finally remembered, it was no longer in the box.

With his mother to help him, he scoured the floor of the study from under the sewing machine to behind the toy basket, but to no avail.

Then one evening about two weeks later, the mother went into the study and found the bagworm in a cocoon on the wall, a little way below the picture of the star children.

"Here it is!" she exclaimed in surprise.

The lost bagworm had made itself a new cocoon out of the persimmon twigs and newsprint scraps the boy had given it, plus bits of lint it had gathered on its own. Patchwork though it looked, it was a perfectly good cocoon.

Where could it have been hiding all that time? the father later wondered. Someplace no one would find it, that much was clear. Perhaps behind the bookshelf, where there was plenty of lint it could use to make a cocoon. Then, when it had finished weaving its new quarters, the worm had crawled out to a bright, sunny spot near the southern windows.

The boy was in the bath shooting his water pistol at the walls and ceiling. Caught up in his game, he had stayed in much longer than he should have.

"Dry yourself off and come on out here. We've got a surprise for you," his mother and sister called to him.

Little imagining that the "surprise" would be his bagworm, the boy jumped out of the bath and dried himself as fast as he could.

The last one to see the cocoon was the father. He had gone out that evening and did not get home until late, long after the others had gone to bed; it was the next morning before he finally heard about the bagworm from his wife.

Out of doors, he had never given bagworms a second thought. But there was something rather curious about a worm that built itself a cocoon when it was inside a house with a solid roof and ceiling overhead.

"I wonder what it has in mind," he said to his wife. "Does it intend to set up house there, do you think?"

"It certainly looks that way."

He noticed a tiny piece of bright red paper stuck to one side of the cocoon. Had his son put some bits of construction paper in the box too? Or was this something the worm had picked up in its travels around the room?

At the other end of the bay window from where the two stood inspecting the cocoon, the goldfish swam quietly in its bowl. It nibbled for a moment at some moss that had formed along the edge of the water, then lost interest and turned away.

WITH MAYA

Shimao Toshio
Translated by Van C. Gessel

Once in a great while a reader stumbles across what the Japanese refer to as a "crane in a dunghill," a true gem of a writer whose work has not been widely recognized, but who obviously deserves our attention. Such a writer is Shimao Toshio, a profoundly moving author whose name was virtually unknown to the reading public in Japan until 1977, when the publication of his novel Shi no toge *(The Sting of Death) earned him every literary award that could be offered. Since that time a wealth of critical studies have appeared, some of them suggesting that Shimao may well be the finest novelist at work in Japan today.*

Born in Yokohama in 1917, Shimao graduated in Asian history from Kyushu University in 1943 and at once volunteered for service in the Japanese Navy. Given a year of training, he was then appointed commander of a suicide squad that was sent to defend the Amami Islands between Okinawa and the mainland. After nearly ten months of daily preparation for death, the orders to ready for launching finally came—on August 14, 1945. The bizarre experience of living daily life for the sake of death, and of a reprieve that was no real release from anxiety, has formed the core of Shimao's fiction. Many of his short stories deal with his war experience, such as "Shuppatsu wa tsui ni otozurezu" (The Departure Never Came, 1962), which was shaped by his suicide corps experience.

Shimao has also written a string of surrealistic, nightmarish stories in which mundane everyday life easily slides into the horrors of chaos and uncertainty; the finest of these stories is "Yume no naka de no nichijō"

(Daily Life in the Midst of Dreams, 1948). But the decisive incident of his life, which reinforced his apprehensions during wartime, came in 1954, when his wife Miho suffered a severe nervous breakdown. In response, Shimao had to terminate his teaching and writing careers for a time, joined Miho for treatment in a mental hospital, moved his family back to her native home on the Amami Islands, and converted to Roman Catholicism. Removed from the center of literary activity in Tokyo, Shimao published "Ware fukaki fuchi yori" (Out of the Depths I Cry, 1955), the first of many stories dealing with his tormented relationship with his wife. Over the ensuing twenty years, Shimao published several volumes of stories on the same theme. These were eventually brought together as Shi no toge, one of the finest modern novels written in Japan.

"Maya to issho ni" (With Maya, 1961) is a touching, self-conscious story set on the fringes of Shimao's personal anguish. In it Shimao writes gently of an emotionally disturbed little girl, one of the victims of family battles described in his other works. Maya is a symbol very much like the deformed baby in the writings of Ōe Kenzaburō: a portrait of modern man, ravaged and anguished by life but unable to express in words the source of all that pain.

*   *   *

The patients, who leaned against the corridor walls or sat on sofas waiting for their doctors, resembled fish that dwell at the bottom of the ocean. They wore expressions like fish that know their bodies will shatter if they come too close to the bright surface of the sea, and suffer from the sharp difference they can see between their own faces and those of fish that move in shallower waters. I felt an affinity with that look, realizing that it mirrored my own nature perfectly.

I wrapped my raincoat around my legs and folded them under me on the sofa, hoping to ward off the chill that was creeping from the soles of my feet up through my entire body. Doctors and nurses in white coats streamed down the hallway and in and out of rooms, but I had no idea what connection they might have with our appointments.

In an attempt to assert control over this oppressive waiting, I took a book out of my coat pocket and began reading. The book was made up of fragments taken from an unusual life by a novelist who was no longer living. I wanted to let those episodes pass through my mind once again, and then forget them completely.

Maya walked up and down the long hallway as though battling the winds across a vast plain. She wore the slacks we bought her after our arrival here in K City; her oversized jacket was in fact one of my wife's old coats, which had hurriedly been retailored for our trip. With half-hearted, aimless steps she would wander to the far end of the corridor, then return. On her way back, she would thrust out her chin a bit and stare with open mouth at the faces of the people standing in the hallway or walking past her. Each time she came up to me, I stroked her hair, moved over, and sat her down beside me. But she was on her feet again immediately, to continue her restless wandering. As she walked she swung the long string of her little handbag, which was decorated with clusters of colored glass beads. She was tall for her age, but gave an impression of frailty and slenderness that was exaggerated by the thread-bare coat.

The nearest exit was a glass door down the corridor; through it, the row of square windows in the white building across the street was distorted in the rain. One could see only a small portion of the building even through the large windows here in the clinic. Maya flattened her nose and cheeks against the glass door and stood there for what seemed an eternity. I finally got up from the sofa and went over to her.

"What can you see?" I put my hand on her shoulder and peered through the glass, but she looked up at me without responding. The pupils of her eyes were immobile, and her face revealed no emotion. Still, I recognized this as a look of trust.

I could see the two-dimensional shapes of cars and people moving in various designs along the broad, rain-soaked asphalt far below.

"Is it interesting?" I tried to inject some enthusiasm and makeshift cheer into my voice, but her answer was a simple "Nope," the negative phrase that all the children in our island village used with their peers.

"Are you cold?"

"Nope."

"Do you hurt anywhere?"

"Nope."

I changed my tactics. Touching her abdomen, I asked, "Is your tummy all right?"

Finally she laughed, as though I had tickled her.

"What are you up to? You really worried Daddy. You were wandering around with a really funny face, and then all of a sudden I find you standing over here staring out the window. You tell me right away if you start hurting anywhere. Don't try to keep it a secret."

I had no way of knowing whether she could understand what I was saying. Once she had told me her stomach hurt, when she was actually trying to let me know that she was hungry.

My examination was over quickly, and I was sent to a different room to have some gastric juices drawn. I put my arm around Maya's shoulders, hugging her tightly to me, and we walked down the hallway in step. My spirits were high, and I felt like whistling.

"After they take some of Daddy's stomach juices, it'll be your turn to see the doctor. We have so much to do! What do you think Mommy and your brother are doing now? I bet they're thinking about Maya. Are you worried about Mommy? You don't need to be. You're with Daddy now. Do you wish we were back on the island right this minute?"

"Nope." She gave the pat answer, but after a moment's thought she revised it to, "A little."

"You wish we were back home a little? Well, Daddy wishes we could go back now, too. Daddy likes it best when Mommy and your brother are with him."

"Maya too?"

"Of course Maya too. Mommy and your brother and Maya and everybody all together. Do you like this city?"

"Yep."

"Why?"

"Lots of everything," she answered in a soft, hesitant voice. It was easy to miss much of what she said unless you were used to that voice.

The room I was shown into was merely a cubicle with a bed, a desk, and some diagnostic equipment crammed into it. The steam-heated air carried the odor of an unfamiliar medication.

A young woman was helping a feeble old man out of the room just as I started in. Following the nurse's instructions, I lay down on the bed. It still retained a faint warmth from the old man's body.

A doctor in a white coat was in the room, and I nodded to him, but he offered no reply, and merely looked me over the way one would study an inanimate object. Without altering his expression he said something to the nurse, but the words meant nothing to me.

"It must have just slipped your mind, Doctor, that. . ."

I understood the words in the first part of her remark, but the rest seemed to involve some private matter. The two halves of the phrase came together, skittered across my body, and were gone.

The doctor spoke only a word or two and then left the room. All they were going to do here was extract some of my gastric juices, so he probably didn't need to be present. The nurse had removed her white cap. She looked like an office girl who didn't care much about anyone but herself. I didn't like the idea of having this young woman work on me, perhaps because the image of gastric juices was unpleasant. Thanks to her makeup and the steam that filled the room, her cheeks were dyed an unnatural red. She rolled a cart up beside my bed. On it were several test tubes and some rubber tubing. Maybe it was just my imagination, but she seemed to dislike this particular procedure.

"Please turn this way." She helped me turn over, held out the rubber tube to me and said perfunctorily, "Swallow this down to the white line."

I sat up and looked over at Maya. Seated on a round chair in the corner of the room, she had taken a tiny doll out of her bag and, with lowered head and pursed lips, was avidly dressing and undressing it.

"You keep playing over there, Maya. Don't touch any of the machines." I swallowed the rubber tube.

The odor of rubber was like the smell of entrails seeping from somewhere deep underground. When the cold metallic tip of the tube poked the walls of my throat, I gagged and coughed it back up.

"Can't you get it down?" the nurse asked reproachfully.

I moved my jaw in a chewing motion as I reflected that she had probably never tried to choke down a rubber tube. Though it threatened to come up again several times, the tip eventually worked its way down toward my stomach. It left me feeling trapped and anxious; it was like wondering what would happen if you were in the middle of surgery when an earthquake struck. The tears that spilled out and moistened the corners of my eyes did nothing to settle my nerves. I took a handkerchief from my pocket and dabbed at my eyes.

"Are you in pain?" the nurse asked. I tried to say a word in reply, but again I felt like retching and kept silent. She ought to have known, having done this so many times, that it was difficult to speak. Yet she seemed disappointed when there was no answer. The faintest ripple of cruelty stirred within me, and the comfort of knowing I had shut myself off from an outsider flickered through my mind. I thought of the doctor's apathy and the nurse's hard, businesslike manner, and felt I understood them to some extent.

When the wave of nausea subsided, I lay back and rolled onto my side, where I remained motionless. The end of the rubber tube poking out of my mouth was pinched off with a clip and hung over the edge of my pillow. I stared at the procession of alien substances from my own stomach that was passing before my eyes.

Maya, apparently absorbed in her doll, was not making a sound. I supposed that when she finished changing its clothing, she would comb its hair, styling and restyling it.

Another doctor came in, but unlike his predecessor he spoke in a loud, confident voice, using a dialect I had difficulty understanding. He babbled on to the nurse about some sort of party for a colleague, then went out again. Neither doctor had even seemed to notice Maya. I couldn't imagine how they could miss seeing a little girl playing with dolls right next to the person they were treating.

The nurse moved all around the room, busy with what seemed to be a variety of chores. At intervals she removed the clip from the end of the tube, guided the tip into a test tube, and carefully examined the fluid that poured out.

Though it was a part of me, I was disgusted at the sight of this heavy, viscous liquid that came from deep within my body. It tickled the walls of my esophagus as it made its lukewarm way to the outer world. Yet the nurse did not seem disturbed. I marveled that she didn't seem to react even when some of the fluid spilled onto her fingers as she fiddled with the tube. If it had been me, though the juices were my own, the nerve ends in my fingertips would have recoiled. But the tips of her fingers casually came in contact with this gastric fluid. I had difficulty reconciling her initial distant manner with the movements of her fingertips. I avoided her face and instead concentrated on her hands. As she worked, the tepid air inside my abdomen was displaced repeatedly by the cool outer atmosphere.

"If you're bored, you're welcome to read your book."

I doubted my ears. But I pulled out the book I had stuck under my pillow and began reading where I had left off. Unlike the hallway, where the cold had worked its way up from the bottom of my feet, reading here on the bed in a room softened by warm steam, I had no desire to skim over the words. Instead I was able to relax as I read, allowing my mind to formulate whatever associations it wished between the lines. As a result I experienced a story I had read before in a totally new light, and when I occasionally came across familiar passages, I felt as though I were reaffirming my own past in the pages of the book.

Maya quietly slipped around the foot of the bed and tugged on my sleeve until I looked in her direction.

When I shifted my eyes from the book to Maya, she held out a piece of candy nestled in the palm of her hand.

"She gave me," Maya said, glancing toward the nurse.

I was gratified that the nurse had acknowledged our situation. From the time that Maya's speech became garbled and she stopped talking loudly enough for most people to hear, she had, in fact, spoken less frequently; instead she resorted more and more to attempts to communicate with her body. If she walked up to you, it meant that she wanted something. If she could not get her message across, though, she would leave without a word. Even after she was gone, her ungratified desires seemed to drift in the vacuum she left behind. Gradually I would come to realize what it was she wanted, and the more brittle layers of my heart would crumble. But Maya seemed to have no inclination to press her requests and thereby expand her sphere of influence.

Once an array of light and dark fluids had been gathered in the test tubes, Maya and I left the room.

Time ticked by relentlessly; already it was near noon. Although an entire morning had been peeled away from my life, I felt I had attended to something that needed doing. The morning was done. Now there was only an afternoon to get through, as swiftly as possible.

We went to the neurology clinic for Maya. There I stiffly set forth the circumstances of her affliction, as I had done so many times in the past. I was drained by a fear that I would leave out something significant and by the weariness of repeating the familiar story. Sometimes I volunteered every detail, sometimes not, depending on the responsiveness of the doctors and my own state of mind. There were times when I was unable to muster any enthusiasm at all, knowing that this first encounter could well be our last. I could not shake off the suspicion that once something went wrong with a person mentally or physically, that malfunction could never be corrected. The fact that any number of doctors who had examined Maya had been unable to diagnose the cause of her speech impediment only etched that doubt more blackly on my brain. It was reassuring, all the same, to meet specialists who would listen to my pleas and undertake some form of treatment for Maya's symptoms. They would try to get her to say a word or two, but she would tilt her head, look up at me imploringly, and make no attempt to respond to the doctors' requests. That was the inevitable outcome; not once in the course of an examination had a doctor persuaded her to speak or even move her tongue. When they tapped her knees with a rubber mallet, had her pull one leg up to her chest, thumped on her legs, or made her walk around, she would turn a coquettish look on them and then intentionally move her arms and legs in an awkward way. It seemed as though Maya had planned out a perfect mime of the behavior they expected her to display.

As we waited in the empty, drafty room, a young woman staffer dressed in a white lab coat came in.

"Why don't you and I have a little talk?" she said to Maya, taking her and sitting her down by the desk in a corner of the room. "Has she ever had an IQ test?" she asked me.

"I think they probably did one at her school. But I'm afraid I don't keep track of things like that, so I can't say for sure."

"Her name is Maya, isn't it?"

"That's right. Maya."

"Well, Maya," she said, turning back toward my daughter, "there's nothing to be afraid of. I'm not going to give you a shot or anything like that. You and I are going to study together, okay? You answer the questions I ask you. If you don't know an answer, it's all right to say so."

She set something out on the desk and showed it to Maya.

"What's this? I bet you know, don't you? Tell me—what is it?"

As usual Maya turned around and glanced at me bashfully.

"This is an easy one. Please tell me. Don't you want to say it? Well then, take this pencil and write it down on the paper. You can do that, can't you? What is it? That's right! It's a little mouse. See, I knew you could tell me what it was. That was terrific! Now, how about this?"

The crude, businesslike desk and couch took up the greater part of the room. From my perspective in the corner, the two of them seemed to be inside a compartment partitioned off by diagonally arranged screens. The desk was near the window, and looking at them against the light and at an angle from behind, their forms seemed to shimmer. It was oddly moving. The woman leaned forward to ask Maya questions, and Maya, unwilling to default on an answer, seemed almost in pain as she cocked her head and twisted her body in the effort to respond. Eventually she began to utter a phrase or two in that small, hesitant voice. She's let down her guard! I thought, and inwardly I mumbled encouragement to her: "Loosen up! Loosen up!" Maya seemed even younger than ten years old as she darted her eyes about, thrust out her chin, and opened her mouth vacantly. It was a shock to consider how profoundly different she was from other girls her age—shrewd, robust, competent girls who were beginning to display a touch of worldly wisdom. Like a fragile piece of machinery, Maya in all her workings was delicate, and seemed unable to tolerate even the most imperceptible exchange of emotions.

Still, I could sense in her a ready sympathy and tenderness that spoke directly to my heart. Which of her physical or mental processes had ceased to function normally? She was virtually unable to do any sort of mathematical calculation, but her memory for everyday matters was the most vivid in our household. We were amazed by her precise recollection of appointments her parents had forgotten, or of places where we had tucked away coin purses and the like. When we lost something, Maya would nonchalantly announce its whereabouts in sparing phrases, then silently lead us to the spot.

Bathed in the light from the window, the features of the two grew indistinct, but their profiles stood out in bright relief, evoking a quiet, harmonious excitement in me. Even though Maya was tongue-tied and taciturn, my head was filled with images of an incorrigible chatterbox. I imagined that her face sparkled, something that almost never happened during an examination. Tense with anxiety and fear and bewilderment, Maya was focusing all her energies on trying to accommodate herself to the unpredictable new situations that were presenting themselves one after the other. Grief invariably followed on the heels of resignation each time she abandoned the effort to communicate, but Maya was content to bear the consequences, and made no unreasonable demands on herself.

The rain continued, and as we stood at the door of the hospital, for the briefest moment a white emptiness overcame me. My mind tends to be in disarray when I'm on a trip, and though there were several places I needed to go to, I didn't feel like going to any. A number of destinations flickered through my brain—places too distant to walk to and too close to ride to. Only the knowledge that we had hotel reservations saved me from giving up entirely. The ricocheting drops of rain left pockmarks inside my head and stomach and combined with the chill air to enshroud us both in misery.

I had come to K City primarily to take care of some business. With that completed, my next objective was to have Maya examined. Getting my stomach looked at was a lesser priority. Over the last year or two Maya's speech impediment had become obvious. In the beginning it had been so subtle we wondered if she were feigning the disorder, but soon there was no room for doubt. At the country clinic on our tiny island, the doctors could detect no cause of her problem. For some time we had wanted to have her examined at the well-equipped general hospital in K City, a city many times larger than our island village, but somehow the opportunity had never arisen. Now our hopes had been realized. But we could hardly expect them to come up with a precise diagnosis during the brief time I was here on business. I was told they would not be able to arrive at any conclusions until they had observed Maya for a fixed period of time and had conducted certain tests. But circumstances and my own lack of resolve would not permit us to remain here very long. We had already had the doctors do everything within their power at the island clinic. Other new tests had been administered here, but the results were no more illuminating. They could suggest no better treatment than continuing the pills she was already taking.

I raised my hand and hailed a passing taxi, hoping to dispel the numbness that had come over me.

I had not made up my mind where I wanted to go, but as I sank into the cushions in the back of the cab, the name of a destination pushed its way between my lips.

It was a place where I still had work to complete. Basically I had finished my business here, but there are always those extra tasks to perform, so I was never without something to occupy my time. Maya waited motionless in a chair beside me, while the adults engaged in their dull conversations. As a child, I occasionally accompanied my father on business visits and despaired of the grown-up chatter, never knowing when it might come to an end. Bored beyond endurance, I would tug on my father's sleeve, only to be stabbed by a sharp glare from his eyes. Though Maya squirmed in her chair, gnawed by tedium, the hard crust I had acquired as a façade kept her from pulling at my sleeve.

Maya and I finally left after five, past the end of working hours. The rain was now a misty drizzle, not heavy enough to soak us. The sun had already set, and the city was preparing itself for the labors of the night.

Whenever I travel away from home, I am tormented by a concern that what I'm doing may prove, at any given moment, to have been a mistake. That feeling intensifies abruptly in the evenings, when I've been released from my duties at work. Inevitably I end up thinking that I've made an inexcusable blunder simply by being somewhere far away from my family. I know I have left them to look after a home in a place quite surrounded by water and separated from me by overwhelming distances. If some frightening, unforeseen calamity should occur in my absence, I could not rush to their aid. Before word of the mishap could reach me, a legion of futile hours would have slipped away. No one would know where to contact me from the time I left my hotel in the morning until I returned at night. Even if news reached me quickly, the ocean stretching between K City and our island was a daunting barrier. Were I lucky enough to make the ferry connection just as it sailed from the dock, I would still have the crossing to contend with: fourteen or fifteen hours of slow, eddying time. The simple effort it took to imagine such things all but tore my emotions out of the realm of reality.

My anxiety was alleviated somewhat on this trip by having Maya with me. She observed my every action, giving me the reassurance that my entire day's activities were being recorded on film within her dense, enclosed world, where feelings were not shared with anyone outside. From now on I would probably take Maya with me no matter where I went. The moment I imagined myself beyond the range of her gaze, I felt darkness close in with its morbid black shadows.

At such times a nightmare appeared before my eyes: I saw my wife and son suddenly plunged into a lunatic frenzy, while the villagers all walked quickly along, their bodies bent slightly forward, their mouths tightly clenched. I had no idea where they were going, but they continued to walk, half stumbling, crossing each other's paths from the left and right, with no sign that they intended to stop. There was no escaping these visions, even with Maya at my side. I was gripped by an urge to abandon my work and the doctors' examinations and race home on the first available ship. None of my business in town seemed so pressing any more. If there was one responsibility I had, it was to keep the four members of my family together, and never leave our island.

As I waited in the long hospital corridor for someone to call my name, I realized that this period of waiting was full of possibilities.

I had no notion when I would be called, or what sort of schedules the doctors kept. Since the time until my summons (no matter how long or short) was left to their whims, I had to remain where I was. But I was free to pursue some simple, fulfilling projects while I waited. I had my reading, and Maya had her strolls up and down the hallway. The best use of my time was to find a story I had already read in one of my books. Since I had nothing else to do, I could read it again without distraction, trapping and holding whatever power and resilience it had.

Eventually the door of the room in front of us would open and the doctor would call my name.

On one side of the hallway was a glass door that looked down onto a square courtyard. In one corner of that shadowy, unused space, scraps of paper tossed from the hospital windows lay dirty and stained, exposed to the elements.

Maya was desperately tired. I wanted to let her rest at the hotel, but I couldn't bear leaving her there alone. We had to do everything together. I had dragged her along with me to the city office, to the homes of acquaintances, and to dinner parties. Perhaps that was why her eyes swam unsteadily, like those of a sleepwalker. More frequently now she would drop off to sleep with her mouth gaping open.

"Maya, do you hurt anywhere?"

As always, her answer was "Nope."

"Be sure to tell me if you do hurt. You must tell Daddy."

"Um-hmm."

"I wonder why you're so jittery?"

"Don't know."

"You're tired, aren't you? Oh dear. When we get through here, we'll go right back to the hotel, okay? Now, let's see a smile for your dad."

Maya curled her lips into a little grin, which quickly gave way to a look of exhaustion.

"I'm sleepy," she sighed.

"Sleepy? Well of course you are. You were up late again last night. We shouldn't have gone to that party. Your daddy hates parties too. But I had to go to that one. Everybody there really thought you were cute, though. That made it fun, didn't it? Come over here and lie down. You can put your head on Daddy's lap and go to sleep."

I placed her head on my lap. She stretched out on the couch while I stroked her hair.

She lay with her mouth propped weakly open, but her eyes did not shut, so I stroked her eyelids closed with my fingers, repeating softly: "Go to sleep, go to sleep."

My wife had often put our young children to sleep that way. "Close you eyes, and go to sleep."

But Maya could not sit still. Before long she lifted her head. "Go to sleep, go to sleep," I insisted, pushing her head back down, my hands stroking her soft, red-tinged hair. Her eyelashes and the hair at her temples were long. There was a full-blown femininity in her face, the look of a grown woman in miniature. We had lived in Tokyo until she entered elementary school. There she had been a vigorous child and spoke a crisp Tokyo dialect. She would go everywhere by herself, and even tried to retaliate on her brother's behalf when he lost a fight with another child. There was no trace of that nimble spirit in Maya now.

I held her down lightly to get her to sleep. She closed her eyes, apparently giving in, but her eyelids continued to flutter. Finally she seemed to abandon the attempt and tried to sit up again.

"Are you okay, Maya? Do you hurt anywhere?"

"Go pee-pee," she answered.

"Pee-pee? Oh dear. Can't you wait? I suppose you can't hold it, can you? Daddy has to stay here. . . I have an idea. Can you try to go by yourself?"

"Uh-hmm."

"You'll be okay, won't you?"

"Uh-hmm. Okay."

"Daddy doesn't know where the bathroom is. Can you find it by yourself?"

"Can find."

"Well, you go ahead then. Come right back. Remember now."

Maya took a few steps, then returned and asked, "Can I buy chew gum or something?"

"Of course. You can buy chew gum or anything you like. Do you know where the snack bar is?"

"Uh-hmm. Know," she said lightly.

Maya was surprisingly good at remembering routes she had taken, the faces of people she met, and where things had been put. She may have seemed flighty and unobservant, but it was as if she had been blessed with a special talent for accurately recalling circumstances involving herself. Before I knew what was happening, I had let her go off alone. But she was scarcely out of sight before I began to squirm with the anxious fear that I had made a bad mistake.

The door in front of me remained closed. I still had no idea when it would open and my name would be called. I was nervous about missing my turn, so I couldn't bring myself to leave my seat. I shifted my eyes to the words in the book I was reading, but my gaze merely stroked the surface of the written symbols and left me with no sense of their meaning.

I realized at some point that my eyes were dreamily chasing after the characters printed on the page, an indication that I was nodding off to sleep. I lifted my head instinctively and looked around. Maya was nowhere to be found. The shock that she had not returned increased my fear. It seemed as if a long time had passed since Maya had left me, but having no watch I could not be sure. During that time my eyes had skated over a succession of words. Though I could not grasp their overall meaning, I had a clear sense of the gist of each individual phrase. Perhaps Maya had been confused by the layout of this large hospital, where all the wards looked alike. In my imagination a vision of Maya's face quickly took shape—the face of a girl falling into a black despair because she could not find her father. There was little chance that Maya could even find the words to explain her dilemma to someone else. And even if she made a decisive effort to express herself verbally, there was no guarantee she would be understood. Perhaps fear would make her lose her mind.

I had piled blunder on blunder. In trying to impose some sort of order on the petty details that swam about in my head, I had paid too little attention to more important matters. I could not rid myself of the image of a member of my family being driven to distraction as a result.

Aimlessly I stood up from my chair and thrust the book into my pocket. My hand brushed against something. I pulled it out to find the wrapper from some chocolate I had bought for Maya. When had it got stuffed in there? I was as startled as if I had suddenly seen Maya's ghost. My heart began to pound, and in distress I hurried to the end of the corridor. But all I could see was the familiar figures of hospital employees and patients scattered at various points along the hallway. My eyes could not find what they were looking for.

A feeling of irretrievable loss swept over me. I did a quick about-face and retraced my steps, but the odds of finding Maya there were very slim.

Inexplicably, I had a vision of Maya collapsed and bleeding beside a white porcelain toilet. That image overlapped with one of my distraught wife. I decided it was unwise to torment myself needlessly, and abandoning the course on which an impulse had led me, I turned back to check once more in the direction Maya had disappeared. As I turned the corner, I saw her coming toward me in a crowd of people.

How haggard she looked!

Surrounded by other people, her bewildered expression was grotesquely conspicuous, and darkness pressed in on me. I searched her face in vain for a trace of her usual blunt inquisitiveness. Instead she seemed resigned to being under constant surveillance herself.

She wore the same top and slacks I put on her every morning. Her clothes were rumpled, badly in need of starch and a good pressing. The elastic waistband on her pants had stretched out of shape and dangled limply. When she saw me she did not react; it was as though she were looking at a stranger. Wandering was second nature to her now; in need of none of my feeble protection, she was setting off alone for a destination far beyond my reach.

"You were gone a long time, weren't you, Maya? Where did you go? I thought maybe you didn't know the way back. Did you find the bathroom? Did you go pee-pee?"

Maya nodded.

"It took you a long time, didn't it? Daddy was really worried. Did something happen?"

"Nothing. Got my underpants a little dirty. Okay? You mad?"

"Of course not. Don't worry. Nobody came in, did they? You didn't fall down in the bathroom, did you?"

"Nope. Nobody came. Didn't fall."

211

"That's good. I guess you didn't get your underpants off far enough and so you got them wet. Well, nobody's going to get mad at you. Daddy was afraid you'd fallen down in the bathroom and couldn't get up. Your underpants aren't very wet, are they? If they are, you'll have to take them off."

"Not very wet."

"Will you be all right until we get back to the hotel? You will, won't you? We'll change them as soon as we get back there."

I stared intently at Maya. Something bothered me—a fear that she would go off somewhere beyond my power to do anything for her. Apparently she had gone to the snack bar: melted chocolate rimmed her mouth like whiskers.

"Here, turn your head this way. You've got chocolate on your mouth. Hold still and I'll wipe it off. Maya. You mustn't stare at other people like that, with your mouth open all the time. You've got to control your feelings. If you don't, people will think you're an idiot."

Since Maya could not give a detailed account of her actions and feelings, I had to rely on the fragments I gleaned to get even a rough idea of how she felt. As the days passed here in K City she had obviously grown more and more exhausted. I should have kept a careful watch on her, but being away from home I ended up pushing myself until personal concerns were forced into the background and dealt with only in half measures. And Maya was forced to take part in it all with me. I could not imagine leaving her alone in the hotel room.

It was nearly noon when my name was called and I entered the black-curtained room. We had spent much of that day in the hospital corridor. In the darkened room I swallowed some barium, and afterward the doctor rubbed, patted, and poked my abdomen with supple hands. The entire procedure did not take long. Strangely, when I climbed onto the X-ray platform, the dull ache in my stomach disappeared. I felt as though I had hoodwinked the doctor, but the palms of his hands had transmitted his concern for my afflicted area, and that stirred a pleasant rhythm within me.

Maya was very tired, so we took a taxi, and I put her to bed as soon as we got back to the hotel. She went to sleep without dinner that night.

Since she was still asleep the next morning, I let her rest. Her soft hair looked like seaweed at the bottom of the ocean.

Near noon she opened her eyes and said she was hungry. I gave her an apple. She seemed to have revived, so I suggested, "Why don't we go and have something to eat at a department store?"

She smiled her approval.

That put me in high spirits, and I said, "What would you like to eat? Name anything you want."

"Sushi."

"Great. We'll have sushi. What else?"

"Ice creams."

"Daddy'll have some ice creams too."

"Wanna buy a present."

"That's right, we do have to get some presents. Should we go home if there's a boat tomorrow? I really want to see Mommy and your brother again."

"Teacher too."

"What should we get for your teacher?"

"Pencil is nice. Wanna look at lots of things."

"Well then, we'll make today our present-buying day. How do you like that?"

"Great!" she grinned. Exhaustion must have led to yesterday's incident. A good sleep, and she was back to normal now. I called the shipping line to confirm the sailing schedule for the following day, and then we set off cheerfully for the department store. We had our sushi and "ice creams" at the restaurant and went looking for presents. I didn't venture any opinions as we walked around, letting Maya choose what she wanted to get. It was not long before I felt as though I were out shopping with my wife.

There was still a little time before sunset when we came out of the department store, so I finally gave in to Maya's entreaties and took her to a movie theater. She insisted that she wasn't tired and wanted to see the film, so I had no reason to refuse.

The film involved several lively exchanges between two cheerful sisters in an American family, and each time something funny happened, Maya laughed out loud.

213

I breathed a sigh of relief, and the waves of anxiety that still surged faintly within me had nearly subsided when I felt Maya leaning against me. At first I thought it was because she could not control her laughter. But it seemed a little peculiar for her to be laughing, since the scene had changed to a conflict between the sisters over some man. I really hadn't been paying much attention to her, until I realized that her laughter had nothing to do with the images on the screen. I looked at her in surprise, to discover that she was staring at the floor with a handkerchief crammed tightly in her mouth.

"Maya. Maya!" I shook her, but she would not take the handkerchief from her mouth. She had been crying, not laughing, but I had no idea why. I hurriedly got up from my seat and took her out of the theater, with my arm around her shoulders.

The handkerchief was soaked with saliva, and her flushed face and even her hair were wet with tears. Her eyelids were puffy and swollen. Remorse hit me like a sudden blow to the pit of the stomach, destroying my lively mood. We grabbed the nearest taxi.

Maya buried herself in the seat cushions and continued to sob. She looked like a tiny wife burdened with grief.

"Maya, why did you start crying? You were laughing so hard at first. What was sad?" I knew what her answer would be.

"Don't know."

"Was it because you felt sorry for them?"

"Don't know."

"Was it because it was sad?"

"Don't know."

"Was there something scary? Or did you remember something scary?"

"Don't know."

In resignation I stopped interrogating her. As I wiped her face and hair with my own handkerchief, I was aware that some incomprehensible fate hovered over her.

When we got out of the taxi, Maya tugged at my elbow and said, "Always." I had no idea what she was talking about, and asked her two or three times to repeat it.

She thought about it for some time, and after groping for a way to express her feelings, she finally spoke in tones meant to convey the enormous weight of the words she had hit upon: "I always cry when I see movies."

I had not made Maya take a single bath since our arrival in K City. Mounting exhaustion had drained her of the inclination to bathe. Once the agitation that overcame her in the movie theater subsided, my anxiety dissipated, and I began to treat Maya in the usual manner. I decided it would be nice to have a bath before we went back to our island, so I took Maya with me to the public bathhouse.

When I had finished washing her, conscious of the willowy form that was growing taller without seeming to add a pound of weight, I shifted my attention to my own body. A short time later I glanced around, to find Maya with her head totally submerged in the soaking tub, while she vigorously pretended to wash her hair.

Horror surged through me like a flash of light, and I called out in an unexpectedly sharp voice, "Maya!"

Slowly she lifted her head, peered up at me from an angle, and smiled a tentative smile.

"What are you doing, Maya? Are you trying to tease me?"

I softened my tone, reminding myself that I mustn't get excited, and waited for a response. I had to remain calm and consider things carefully.

Hesitantly she answered, "Maya felt funny. All confused."

"And did it make you feel better to wash your hair?"

"Don't know."

"Maya, look Daddy in the face. Are you dizzy? Why did you wash your hair there in the tub?"

"Don't know. Got confused."

"Maya, where are we?"

"The bath."

"Do you know who I am?"

"I know."

"Let's get out, okay?"

I cut my bath short and took Maya straight back to our hotel room. I put her in a nightgown that I had finally bought her here in the city after many requests. As I dressed her, changing the several layers of underpants that my wife had told me to have her wear, I found they were soiled. I could hear her at the hospital again saying, "Got my underpants a little dirty. Okay?" I had wanted to keep a close watch on Maya during this trip, to make sure that I never deserted her. Yet at every turn something like this happened, bringing the inadequacy of my supervision into stark focus. I was now confronted with direct evidence of a time when my gaze had wandered. As I struggled to deny my negligence, I noticed that some clotted blood was mingled with the stain.

"Maya, do you remember going to the bathroom by yourself at the hospital? Did you just go pee-pee then? Or did something else come out?"

"Don't know."

"You said you got your underpants dirty. How did you get them dirty?"

"Thought I just needed to pee-pee. But my stomach hurt and went b.m. too."

"And you put your underpants back on dirty?"

"I wiped!"

Inscribed at the back of my brain was a vivid picture of Maya walking down the hospital corridor in a state of near collapse. I had not been sensitive to the feeling of abhorrence that must have enveloped her when she was left all alone to take care of the clothing she had soiled in the bathroom. Somehow I could not bring myself to imagine Maya coping with the predicament herself. I found myself wondering if Maya didn't in fact know everything that was going on, and when she was away from us and around other people, if didn't speak quite clearly and bustle about like a hardworking housewife.

Her torso swayed precariously as she stood there in her nightgown, so I quickly made up her bed and laid her down.

"Do you hurt anywhere?"

"Nowhere."

"Does your tummy hurt?"

"Not hurt."

But I continued to inquire, refusing to take her at her word.

"Does your head hurt?"

"Hurts a little."

"Which part?"

"Hurts right here."

"How does it hurt?"

216

"Hurts a little."

"Does it always hurt there?"

"Um-hmm."

"When did it start?"

"Lots of people together. Daddy's friends. One was nice to Maya. Maya tried to go bathroom, fell down. Hit head."

I had been busy talking with some acquaintances and had no recollection of Maya, who nearly always stayed right beside me, leaving the second-floor meeting hall and going downstairs to the bathroom. Here was yet another piece of evidence that my supervision was inadequate. I had difficulty visualizing just how Maya was able to recover in that moment of despair. In places unknown to me, Maya had been falling down or soiling her underpants, but my head was filled with images of her that were strangely unreal. Even so, I had to conclude that what I had found was bloodstains. But I hadn't the slightest notion whether that sort of thing could possibly happen to a girl not yet in the fifth grade. Perhaps it was some presentiment of its onset. I looked down at Maya. I wanted to hurry back to the island and report this to my wife, and discuss it with her.

"Go to sleep now, Maya. There's nothing to worry about. Go fast asleep."

Notes on the Translators

MICHAEL C. BROWNSTEIN is an Assistant Professor of Japanese at the University of Notre Dame. He received his Ph.D. in Japanese from Columbia University in 1981 and is currently researching the evolution of Japanese literary thought during the eighteenth and nineteenth centuries.

ANTHONY H. CHAMBERS, a native of California, received his Ph.D. in Japanese language and literature from the University of Michigan in 1974. He is the author of several studies of the works of Tanizaki Jun'ichirō; his translations include *The Secret History of the Lord of Musashi and Arrowroot* and *Naomi*, by Tanizaki. He is Associate Professor in the Department of Asian Languages and Literatures at Wesleyan University.

BRETT DE BARY is an Associate Professor of Japanese Literature at Cornell University, where she teaches modern Japanese literature and film. She has translated works by postwar authors such as Hara Tamiki, Miyamoto Yuriko, and Ōe Kenzaburō, and also published articles on them. Her *Three Works by Nakano Shigeharu* was published by Cornell University East Asia Papers Series in 1979. She is now preparing for publication a manuscript on Japanese literature at the end of the Pacific War.

VAN C. GESSEL received his Ph.D. in Japanese from Columbia University. He has translated two novels and a short story collection by Endō Shūsaku—*When I Whistle, The Samurai*, and *Stained Glass Elegies*—and written critical articles on modern Japanese theater and Japanese Christian writers. He recently completed a monograph on postwar literature titled *Japan's Lost Generation*. He is Assistant Professor of Japanese at the University of California, Berkeley.

MARK HARBISON, a Ph.D. candidate at Stanford University, is presently studying in Tokyo and writing a dissertation on "Inter-textuality as Method in the *Shinkokinshū*." He has done a wide variety of translations from Japanese texts, including several volumes of Konishi Jin'ichi's *History of Japanese Literature*, and short stories by Nagai Kafū, Furui Yoshikichi, and Abe Akira. He is preparing a translation of Ōe Kenzaburō's *Atarashii hito yo mezameyo*.

GERALDINE HARCOURT, a science graduate, has been studying Japanese since high school. A native of New Zealand, she now lives in Tokyo. Among her published translations are Tsushima Yūko's *Child of Fortune*, Yamamoto Michiko's *Betty-san*, and Gō Shizuko's *Requiem*. Currently she is at work on a collection of stories by Tsushima Yūko.

CAROLYN HAYNES is a Ph.D. candidate in Japanese literature at Cornell University. Her article "Parody in Kyōgen: *Makura Monogatari* and *Tako*" appeared in *Monumenta Nipponica*.

AMY VLADECK HEINRICH received her doctorate in Japanese literature in 1980 at Columbia University, and has taught at Columbia, New York University, and Princeton. Her book, *Fragments of Rainbows: The Life and Poetry of Saitō Mokichi, 1882–1953*, was published in 1983. She is currently working on a comparative study of modern women writers and their place in the Japanese and English literary traditions.

ADAM KABAT did his undergraduate work at Wesleyan University. He has recently completed a master's degree at the University of Tokyo with a comparative study of the works of Izumi Kyōka and Mishima Yukio, and is now on a doctoral course there. He is also preparing a translation of a novel by Yoshiyuki Junnosuke.

STEPHEN W. KOHL is currently Associate Professor of Japanese and Chairman of the Department of East Asian Languages and Literatures at the University of Oregon. His primary field of interest is the interpretation and translation of modern Japanese literature. He is the author of over a dozen articles and translations, including *Cliff's Edge and Other Stories* by Tachihara Masaaki. He has also made a study of early relations between Japan and the Pacific Northwest.

WAYNE P. LAMMERS received his Ph.D. at the University of Michigan and is presently Assistant Professor at the University of Wisconsin. He has published a translation from *Utsubo monogatari* in *Monumenta Nipponica* and is preparing a collection of translations of stories by Shōno Junzō. He has also been an instructor of English language and literature at Iwate University.

KÄREN WIGEN LEWIS did her undergraduate work in Japanese at the University of Michigan, and is now pursuing graduate work in Japanese geography at the University of California, Berkeley. Her translation of Yasuoka Shōtarō's *Kaihen no kōkei* received the 1981 Translation Prize from the U.S.-Japan Friendship Commission, and was published as *A View by the Sea* in 1984 by Columbia University Press.

VIRGINIA MARCUS is a graduate student at the University of Michigan. Her annotated translation of selected stories from *Yorozu no fumihōgu*, a collection of epistolary tales by Ihara Saikaku, was published together with an introductory essay in *Monumenta Nipponica* in 1985.

TOMONE MATSUMOTO received her doctoral degree in 1979 from the University of Arizona. Her dissertation was a study of modern Japanese intellectual history, focusing on the career of Kamei Katsuichirō. She is currently teaching modern Japanese language and literature at Griffith University in Brisbane, Australia.

JACK RUCINSKI is a Senior Lecturer in the Department of Asian Languages at the University of Canterbury in Christchurch, New Zealand. His previous translations from Hori Tatsuo have appeared in *Poetry* and *Translation*. He has also published articles on Japanese literature and art in *Monumenta Nipponica* and *Orientations*. At Harvard University, he is presently researching illustrated books from the early Tokugawa period. He received his Ph.D. in 1978 from the University of Hawaii.

EDWARD SEIDENSTICKER is Professor in the Department of East Asian Languages and Cultures at Columbia University. His numerous translations of modern and classical literary works have placed him among the foremost interpreters of Japanese fiction and poetry.

CECILIA SEGAWA SEIGLE, a native Japanese, has taught classical and modern literature and language at the University of Pennsylvania, where she received her Ph.D. Her published translations include Shimazaki Tōson's *The Family*, Mishima Yukio's *The Temple of Dawn*, and Kaikō Takeshi's *Into a Black Sun* and *Darkness in Summer*. For the 1985–86 academic year, she is a Japan Foundation Fellow, and is writing her second book on Yoshiwara.

YUKIKO TANAKA was co-translator and co-editor of *This Kind of Woman: Ten Stories by Japanese Women Writers, 1960–1976*. Her Ph.D. dissertation at UCLA focused on narrative technique in the works of Kojima Nobuo. She has translated Kojima's novel *Hōyō kazoku* and short story "Happiness," and is now at work on a book on Japanese women writers.

JOHN WHITTIER TREAT received his doctoral degree from Yale University in 1982 with a dissertation on the literature of Ibuse Masuji. At present he is an Assistant Professor at the University of Washington.

WILLIAM J. TYLER, Assistant Professor of Japanese Studies and Director of the Japanese Language Program at the University of Pennsylvania, did his undergraduate work at International Christian University in Japan, and his graduate study at Harvard. His Ph.D. dissertation was on Ishikawa Jun, and he has published a translation of Doi Takeo's *The Psychological World of Natsume Soseki*. He is currently translating Ishikawa's stories and novellas, and preparing a study of Tōkai Sanshi.

ROBERT ULMER first left his native Toronto in 1973 to study in Japan. He received his Ph.D. in Japanese literature from Yale University in 1982. He is now working for the Japan Trade Centre (JETRO) in Toronto.

Selected Bibliography of English Translations

A number of the authors represented in the present anthology are appearing in English translation for the first time. Through the efforts of qualified and dedicated translators, however, a wide range of modern Japanese literary works has been made available for the interested reader. For translations published before 1978, the reader is referred to *Modern Japanese Literature in Translation: A Bibliography*, compiled by the International House of Japan Library and published in 1979 by Kodansha International. The selected list that follows is a compilation of translations in English which have appeared since the date of that original bibliography.

ABE AKIRA

"A Napping Cove" (Madoromu irie). Tr. by Mark Harbison. *Japanese Literature Today*, vol. 9 (1984), pp. 11–23.

ABE KŌBŌ

Secret Rendezvous (Mikkai). Tr. by Juliet Winters Carpenter (New York: Knopf, 1979). 190 pp.

"You, Too, Are Guilty" (Omae ni mo tsumi ga aru). Tr. by Ted T. Takaya. *Modern Japanese Drama: An Anthology*, ed. by Ted T. Takaya (New York: Columbia University Press, 1979), pp. 1–40.

DAZAI OSAMU

Selected Stories and Sketches. Tr. by James O'Brien (Ithaca: Cornell University Press, 1983). 248 pp. Includes: "Memories," "Transformation," "The Island of Monkeys," "Toys," "Das Gemeine," "Putting Granny Out to Die," "My Older Brothers," "Eight Views of Tokyo," "On the Question of Apparel," "Homecoming," "A Poor Man's Got His Pride," "The Mound of the Monkey's Grave," "Taking the Wen Away," "Currency," "The Sound of Hammering," and "Osan."

Return to Tsugaru (Tsugaru). Tr. by James Westerhoven (Tokyo: Kodansha International, 1985). 220 pp.

Tsugaru (Tsugaru). Tr. by Phyllis Lyons. *The Saga of Dazai Osamu* (Stanford:

Stanford University Press, 1985), pp. 271–385.

ENDŌ SHŪSAKU

A *Life of Jesus* (Iesu no shōgai). Tr. by Richard A. Schuchert (New York: Paulist Press, 1978). 179 pp.

The Samurai (Samurai). Tr. by Van C. Gessel (London: Peter Owen, 1982; New York: Harper and Row/Kodansha International, 1982; and New York: Vintage, 1984). 272 pp.

"The Shadow Figure" (Kagebōshi). Tr. by Thomas Lally, Ōka Yumiko, and Dennis J. Doolin. *Japan Quarterly*, vol. 31, no. 2 (April–June 1984), pp. 164–73, and vol. 31, no. 3 (July–Sept. 1984), pp. 294–301.

"Shadow of a Man" (Kagebōshi). Tr. by Shoichi Ono and Sanford Goldstein. *Bulletin of the College of Biomedical Technology, Niigata University*, vol. 1, no. 1 (1983), pp. 80–94.

"Something of My Own" (Watakushi no mono). Tr. by John Bester. *Japan Echo*, vol. 12 (1985), pp. 23–29.

Stained Glass Elegies: Stories by Shusaku Endo. Tr. by Van C. Gessel (London: Peter Owen, 1984). 165 pp. Includes: "A Forty-Year-Old Man," "The Day Before," "Fuda-no-Tsuji," "Unzen," "My Belongings," "Despicable Bastard," "Mothers," "Retreating Figures," "Old Friends," "The War Generation," and "Incredible Voyage."

Volcano (Kazan). Tr. by Richard A. Schuchert (London: Peter Owen, 1978; New York: Taplinger, 1980). 175 pp.

When I Whistle (Kuchibue o fuku toki). Tr. by Van C. Gessel (London: Peter Owen, 1979; New York: Taplinger,1980). 277 pp.

IBUSE MASUJI

Salamander and Other Stories. Tr. by John Bester (Tokyo: Kodansha International, 1981). 134 pp. Includes: "Pilgrims' Inn," "Yosaku the Settler," "Carp," "Salamander," "Life at Mr. Tange's," "Old Ushitora," "Savan on the Roof," "Plum Blossom by Night," and "Lieutenant Lookeast."

INOUE YASUSHI

Chronicle of My Mother (Waga haha no ki). Tr. by Jean Oda Moy (Tokyo: Kodansha International, 1982). 164 pp.

Lou-lan and Other Stories. Tr. by James T. Araki and Edward Seidensticker (Tokyo: Kodansha International, 1981). 160 pp. Includes: "Lou-lan," "The Sage,"

"Princess Yung-t'ai's Necklace," "The Opaline Cup," "The Rhododendrons," and "Passage to Fudaṛaku."

KAIKŌ TAKESHI

Into a Black Sun (Kagayakeru yami). Tr. by Cecilia Segawa Seigle (Tokyo: Kodansha International, 1980). 220 pp.

KANAI MIEKO

"Rabbits" (Usagi). Tr. by Phyllis Birnbaum. *Rabbits, Crabs, Etc.: Stories by Japanese Women*, tr. by Phyllis Birnbaum (Honolulu: University of Hawaii Press, 1982), pp. 1–16.

KOJIMA NOBUO

"Happiness" (Happinesu). Tr. by Yukiko Tanaka, with Elizabeth Hanson Warren. *Japan Quarterly*, vol. 28, no. 4 (Oct.–Dec. 1981), pp. 533–48.

"Shōjū" (Shōjū). Tr. by Elizabeth Baldwin. *Faith and Fiction: The Modern Short Story*, ed. by Robert Detweiler and Glenn Meeter (Grand Rapids, MI: William B. Eerdmans, 1979), pp. 213–26.

KŌNO TAEKO

"Ants Swarm" (Ari takaru). Tr. by Noriko Mizuta Lippit. *Stories by Contemporary Japanese Women Writers*, ed. and tr. by Noriko Mizuta Lippit and Kyoko Iriye Selden (Armonk, N.Y.: M. E. Sharpe, 1982), pp. 105–19.

"Crabs" (Kani). Tr. by Phyllis Birnbaum. *Rabbits, Crabs, Etc.: Stories by Japanese Women*, pp. 99–131.

"The Last Time" (Saigo no toki). Tr. by Yukiko Tanaka and Elizabeth Hanson. *This Kind of Woman: Ten Stories by Japanese Women Writers, 1960–1976*, ed. and tr. by Yukiko Tanaka and Elizabeth Hanson (Stanford: Stanford University Press, 1982), pp. 43–67.

KURAHASHI YUMIKO

The Adventures of Sumiyakist Q (Sumiyakisuto Q no bōken). Tr. by Dennis Keene (Queensland: University of Queensland Press, 1979). 369 pp.

"Partei" (Parutai). Tr. by Yukiko Tanaka and Elizabeth Hanson. *This Kind of Woman: Ten Stories by Japanese Women Writers, 1960–1976*, pp. 1–16.

ŌBA MINAKO

"Fireweed" (Higusa). Tr. by Marian Chambers. *Japan Quarterly*, vol. 28, no. 3

(July–Sept. 1981), pp. 403–27.

"Sea-change" (Tankō). Tr. by John Bester. *Japanese Literature Today*, no. 5 (March 1980), pp. 12–19.

"The Smile of a Mountain Witch" (Yamauba no bishō). Tr. by Noriko Mizuta Lippit and Mariko Ochi. *Stories by Contemporary Japanese Women Writers*, pp. 182–96.

"The Three Crabs" (Sambiki no kani). Tr. by Yukiko Tanaka and Elizabeth Hanson. *This Kind of Woman: Ten Stories by Japanese Women Writers, 1960–1976*, pp. 87–113.

ŌE KENZABURŌ

Hiroshima Notes (Hiroshima nōto). Tr. by Toshi Yonezawa; ed. by David L. Swain (Tokyo: YMCA Press, 1981). 181 pp.

SHIMAO TOSHIO

"The Sting of Death" and Other Stories by Shimao Toshio. Tr. by Kathryn Sparling. *Michigan Papers in Japanese Studies*, no. 12.

TSUSHIMA YŪKO

Child of Fortune (Chōji). Tr. by Geraldine Harcourt (Tokyo: Kodansha International, 1983). 186 pp.

"Island of Joy" (Yorokobi no shima) and "To Scatter Flower Petals" (Hana o maku). Tr. by Lora Sharnoff. *Japan Quarterly*, vol. 27, no. 2 (April–June 1980), pp. 249–69.

YASUOKA SHŌTARŌ

A *View by the Sea* (Kaihen no kōkei). Tr. by Kären Wigen Lewis (New York: Columbia University Press, 1984). Includes: "A View by the Sea," "Bad Company," "Gloomy Pleasures," "The Moth," "Rain," and "Thick the New Leaves."

YOSHIYUKI JUNNOSUKE

"Birds, Beasts, Insects and Fish" (Kinjū chūgyo). Tr. by M. T. Mori. *Japan Quarterly*, vol. 28, no. 1 (Jan.–March 1981), pp. 91–102.

"Scene at Table" (Shokutaku no kōkei). Tr. by Geraldine Harcourt. *Japan Echo*, vol. 12 (1985), pp. 42–45.